REBELS
by Accident

REBELS by Accident

PATRICIA DUNN

sourcebooks
fire

Published by Sourcebooks Fire, an imprint of Sourcebooks, Inc.
P.O. Box 4410, Naperville, Illinois 60567-4410
(630) 961-3900
Fax: (630) 961-2168
www.sourcebooks.com

Library of Congress Cataloging-in-Publication data is on file with the publisher.

Printed and bound in the United States of America.
VP 10 9 8 7 6 5 4 3 2 1

For my son, Ali—and the people of Egypt.

chapter ONE

This isn't my first visit to the Mayflower Police Station. The last time I was here, Mom brought me with her to register a complaint about a pothole. It was the size of a quarter, but Mom insisted it was dangerous to drive over when she had a child in her car. I was thirteen.

This time, I'm at the Mayflower Police Station as a criminal. Sixteen (well, almost sixteen), and I'm behind bars. Okay, maybe I'm being a bit dramatic. It's not as if I'm locked up with serial killers or slashers, but I'm in a cell. Deanna's with me, along with about thirty other underage girls who were also at the party and didn't run away in time or convince the police to let them go.

As we piled into squad cars, I watched these girls (and even a few guys) put on all the moves—crying, flirting, screaming, fainting, even begging—to get out of the arrest, but none of it worked.

I have to say Deanna gave it her best. Not being able to crack a smile really worked to her advantage when the officer in charge said to her that he was glad someone was taking the situation seriously. She wasn't kidding when she said she was a great litigator like her mom. When the cop found me hiding in the bathtub with the shower curtain drawn (could I have picked a more obvious place?) and dragged me downstairs with the rest of the crowd, there was Deanna, telling the police we shouldn't be responsible for the actions of some stupid guys who brought beer to the party. She almost had one cop convinced to let us go when Karen, the bane of my existence, stepped forward and threw up on his shoes.

All through elementary school and middle school, Karen and her drone Beth talked trash about me and my family. Their favorite insults were that my dad was in Al-Qaeda and my mom was only one of his many wives.

At least she's not in our cell. They put her, and all the other vomiting kids, in a separate cell—with buckets.

Still, it stinks in here. I stick my nose between the bars, trying to breathe air that doesn't smell like puke, beer, or raw fish. Who has an open sushi bar at a high school party? Then again, what would I know about parties? This is the only party I've been to since first grade.

"Come on, Mar. It's not that bad." Deanna pushes against my shoulder. I don't budge. I don't say anything.

"Funny how we started the night trying to break into the party, and now we just want to get out." Deanna stands closer to me, but I can't even look at her. If I do, I'll start to cry. And I'm already the biggest freak at school.

"Look, I know you're flipping out here, but everything will be okay."

"Are you kidding me?" I turn to her and lower my voice. "I'm in jail. Do you know how happy this is going to make my parents?"

"Happy?"

"Now they can feel totally justified when they never let me leave our apartment again."

"Relax."

Relax? We've just been arrested! We are in a holding cell with girls who have picked on me—or, worse yet, ignored me—since kindergarten. On top of that, my parents are going to kill me! Why did I let Deanna talk me into going to this party?

Okay, the truth: she didn't have to talk me into anything. I wanted to go. I would've done anything, even lie to my parents, to crash a party. I knew I wasn't invited and that I'd probably be kicked out as soon as someone saw me. But forcibly removed—by the police? That I didn't expect.

Still, I shouldn't blame Deanna for helping me get what I wanted. But I do. It was an amazing night of music and dancing. Yes, I danced with three guys! And nobody made jokes about my dad being a towel-head or my uncle being Bin Laden.

Ever since those people tried to build their mosque near Ground Zero and there was all that controversy, my life has been worse than ever. The kids at school treat me like I'm one of those people. But I'm not. My family may be Muslim, but I don't think they should put a mosque so close to Ground Zero either. I mean, I believe in freedom of religion and all, and I know Muslims died at Ground Zero too, but why would they want to be where they're not wanted? I don't get it. If it's causing so much trouble, why not just build their mosque somewhere else? It's selfish to cause so many problems.

But tonight I was dancing and laughing. I wasn't a freak or a weirdo; I was just another girl having fun.

"Actually," I say, turning to Deanna, "thanks."

"You're thanking me?" she asks.

"Hey, I know I'm in big trouble but tonight was an adventure— probably the last one I'll have until I'm thirty."

"Don't mention it," she says. Most people would say she has no expression on her face, but I can tell she's smiling.

When I met Deanna last summer, she'd just moved to Mayflower from San Francisco with her mom. I was the first person she told about her face. I Googled it to try to better understand why her face doesn't make expressions like most people's, but after reading pages and pages of medical blah, blah, blah, it really just boils down to what Deanna told me about it: "The muscles in my face don't work."

"Does my hair look okay?" some voice behind me asks. "Do I have anything in my teeth?"

Another voice says, "No, but do I have anything in my teeth? Is my mascara smeared?"

"Are they kidding?" Deanna asks me. "We're in a jail cell, and they're worried about their makeup. It's like we go to Airhead High."

"Shush," I tell her.

"Mar, no one is listening to us. They're all too busy hearing themselves not think."

The only reason Deanna even wanted to crash the party was so she could show me what I wasn't missing. But look at these girls: not one seems the least bit freaked out. Are their parents that laid-back? Maybe that's the secret to their coolness—cool parents. If that's true, I don't stand a chance.

"Well, it could be worse," she says.

"How?"

"Oh crap," she says. An officer unlocks the large cell door. There stand Beth and Karen—the Mayflower Mean Girls.

"In you go," the officer says.

Deanna looks at me. "We're going to be locked in here with them."

Karen stares at me. "Who're you supposed to be? Cleopatra?"

I rub my eyes. Black eyeliner wipes off on my fingers. I'd forgotten Deanna had done my makeup before we went to the party. "You look like an Egyptian queen," Deanna had said. But not just any Egyptian queen. She insisted I was Hatshepsut, the queen who ruled Egypt for more than twenty years. Deanna says Hatshepsut was the queen who was king. Deanna loves anything Egyptian, which is probably why she's friends with me. But I don't want to look like an Egyptian queen, even if she was incredibly powerful. I don't want to look like an Egyptian anything. I rub my eyes some more.

"Back off," Deanna says, moving between Karen and me. Karen is a half-foot taller than Deanna, but my bet is on Deanna.

Karen steps back, then smirks. "Hey, Beth. I just realized why these two are best friends."

"They come from the same place," Beth says, like the two of them had rehearsed this scene. Now everyone is listening. "Cleopatra and the Sphinx."

"You mean Sphinx Face." Karen laughs.

"She did *not* just say that," someone whispers loudly from the other side of our cell.

"Yes, she did," someone else says.

Beth lifts her hand to high-five Karen, but Deanna grabs both their wrists and, like a professional wrestler, pulls their arms behind their backs.

"Fight, fight!" people shout around us.

"Get off me," Beth shrieks, struggling. Karen winces.

"Apologize." Deanna pulls their arms harder.

"You're hurting me!" Beth stops struggling.

"Apologize," Deanna demands.

"Fine. Fine. I apologize."

Deanna lets them both go. "Get out of my face."

Beth scrambles to the other side of the cell. "You're crazy," she says, but it's obvious she's trying to save face with everyone watching. I know Deanna hears this, but she doesn't take her eyes off Karen. Karen opens her mouth, but before anything comes out, she closes it and walks over to Beth.

"You okay?" Deanna asks me.

I nod, but I have never felt lamer. She stood up to both of them, and I just stood there. They called her Sphinx Face, and I didn't do or say anything. And she wants to know if I'm okay?

"Deanna…"

"You'll get it next time," she says, like she's just treated me to a mocha cappuccino.

I force a smile. I can't imagine being as courageous as Deanna.

chapter TWO

An officer with the largest nose I've ever seen unlocks the cell door. "When I call your name, I want you front and center," he says as he flips through the pages on his clipboard. He starts reading off names, but I don't even bother to look up again until I hear "Deanna Roberts and…Mariam… How do you pronounce this one? Is it Indian?"

"Egyptian." Deanna rolls her eyes.

He slides the cell door open, and Deanna and I file out with the other kids whose names he called, following him to the station's front desk. I hear Mom before I see her.

"Mariam! Thank God you're okay!" She has her arms wrapped around me so fast and so tight I feel like an octopus's prey. Any minute, the life will be squeezed out of me—which may be the best I can hope for right now.

"You're going to suffocate the poor girl," Baba says, but then he hugs me almost as tight.

I look around the room. Parents shout at, then hug their kids, while the kids beg for forgiveness, all with the same look of fear and regret on their faces. I guess their parents aren't as cool as I thought.

Karen stands with some woman who looks like her, only gray haired. The woman's yelling so loudly that one of the officers tells her to quiet down. Karen doesn't look upset though. She actually doesn't look like she's feeling much of anything. I turn away. I don't want her to catch me staring.

Then I hear Deanna's voice. I turn back to my parents. Deanna is standing nearby with her mother, nodding and repeating, "Yes, yes, yes."

Baba pulls me in for a squeeze, then lets go of me, steps back, and says, "What are you wearing?" I'd forgotten I had on Deanna's clothes. Baba hates it when I wear black. He says black is for mourning and for people trying to hide their hips. Baba likes me to wear what he calls "bubbly" colors, like sunshine yellow. If it were up to my father, I'd walk around looking like a lemon.

"And your face…" Mom pulls a tissue from her pocket, spits on it, and starts to scrub my cheeks. "Do you know how worried we were?" Mom's mascara is smeared, and her eyes are red. Mom never cries—ever. Baba cries, but not Mom. Actually, Baba looks like he's been crying too.

"I'm so sorry—"

"You were supposed to be home by ten thirty!" Mom screams at me. "Why didn't you call?"

"I forgot my cell at Deanna's—"

"None of these kids had a phone you could borrow?" Mom asks.

"Yes, but—"

Baba places his fingers over his lips. "It's best that you stay quiet now."

Mom shakes her head. "Just be grateful that Ms. Roberts has convinced the police to let you go home without any further action."

"I want you to thank her," Baba says. We walk over to Ms. Roberts and Deanna.

"Ms. Roberts," I say, "thank you for all of your help."

"Deanna wants to say something to your parents as well," Deanna's mom shares. I can tell from her face that Deanna is in as much trouble as I am. Deanna looks down at the floor.

"Go ahead, Deanna." Ms. Roberts nudges her.

"Mar didn't want to go to the party, but I begged her to. I am so, so sorry. Hate me all you want, but please don't be mad at Mariam. She was just being a good friend." The way Deanna looks at Baba and Mom, she doesn't have to be able to move her face for them to see she's not lying. She really is sorry.

"Thank you for your honesty, Deanna," Baba says.

"But Mariam is old enough to take responsibility for herself," Mom adds. Mom turns to Ms. Roberts. "Thank you so much."

"We are indebted to you." Baba puts his hand over his heart to show how grateful he is. I appreciate Deanna's mom helping me out, but my parents are acting like she just got me off a first-degree murder charge. The police probably took us all into the station just to scare us.

"I'm just glad I could help." Ms. Roberts smiles, and she looks just like I imagine Deanna would if she could smile.

Baba nudges my arm. "Thank her again."

"I am very grateful for your help. Thank you, Ms. Roberts."

"Feel free to call me Carole," she says.

I look at Mom, expecting her disapproval (encouraging a child to call an adult by her first name—how disrespectful!), but all I see is admiration in my mother's eyes.

As my parents usher me to the door, I turn to catch Deanna's gaze. I'm sure I won't be seeing her for a very long time, at least not until winter break is over and we're back in school. I'm going to miss her. A lot. Even her craziness. Actually, I'll miss that the most.

On the ride home, Mom adjusts the rearview mirror so she can't see my face in it. She keeps the radio off. Baba looks out the passenger window the whole time. It's not until we walk into the kitchen that Mom speaks.

"We'll talk in the morning," she says. Then she goes to her room and slams the door.

Baba stands there, shaking his head at me.

"I'm so sorry," I say.

"As your *sittu* always says, '*Sorry* can't make some things better.'"

"I know I should've called to tell you I was going to be late, but we weren't drinking or anything."

"Drinking? That's the least of it."

Oh no. Did Baba find out I was dancing with those guys? But how?

"Do you know how blessed you are that Ms. Roberts was there to help us? You could have had a serious drug charge to deal with."

"Drugs? Baba, I didn't use any drugs."

"All I know is that you were at someone's home without adult supervision and the police found enough marijuana to get all of you kids in a great deal of trouble."

"Pot? I didn't know people were smoking…" I remember the place smelling weird, but I thought it was some kind of incense, like patchouli. "But Deanna's mom, she made it all okay, right?"

"You destroyed my trust. Your mother's trust. And you think it is all okay?" Baba starts to leave but quickly turns back to me. "It's going to be a long time before it is okay."

*　　*　　*

From my room, I hear my parents arguing. I almost go into my closet to press my ear against the wall—that's how I always find out what my parents are really thinking. But tonight I don't want to know what their plans are for me.

I slip out of Deanna's skirt and into a pair of pajama pants, but I leave on her shirt. I'm not ready to take it off; it still smells like my first night of being a true teenager. I climb into bed, and as I fall asleep, I think about how I can't go back to living the cloistered life of a Muslim nun. Somehow, I have to convince my parents to trust me again.

When I wake up a little while later, my whole body is on fire. I'd been dreaming about some guy I don't know, but in the dream, I liked him a lot and he liked me, and then… I can't remember the details. All I know is there's no way my parents can stop me from living my life. They can lock me up in this apartment, but I'll figure out a way to escape, even if I have to climb out the window.

Oh my God, that's what they're going to do: ground me for life. I can't let that happen. I have to talk to them.

I jump out of bed and rush to their room, hoping they're still up. I listen at the door. I don't hear anything. I quietly push it open and look through a crack. My mother is sleeping so far on the right side of the bed and my father so far on the left that they leave a huge space in the middle—a space big enough for me.

For a moment, I want to crawl into bed with them, the way I did after I'd had a nightmare when I was little. Sleeping between them always made me feel like life was exactly as they wanted me to believe it was: beautiful and safe, as if nothing was ever going to hurt me. But I'm too old to crawl into that space, and this time I'm the one who did the hurting.

I close the door and go back to my room. It's a struggle to fall asleep. All I can think about is how I've let my parents down.

chapter THREE

When the phone wakes me up, I don't run to answer it like I usually do. I know Deanna won't call this morning. She's crazy, but she's not that crazy.

I pee and wash my hands and face. As I look down at the mascara and other gunk left on the towel, I'm reminded of how much trouble I'm in. I walk down the hallway to the kitchen like I'm going to the dentist to get my teeth drilled—without anesthesia.

"Morning, Baba." I watch him take his coffee from the freezer.

He doesn't answer, but he never does before he's had his morning coffee. And it can't be just any coffee. It has to be this special Arab coffee that he drives an hour and a half to Brooklyn to buy.

"Mariam, my coffeepot—have you seen it?" Baba asks, like he does every morning.

"In the cabinet over the sink," I say, like I always do. Instead of feeling annoyed, today I'm grateful for our routine.

"Mariam, it's not here." Baba's pulling out the old coffeepots, none of which he'll use, because, as he's said more times than I can count, the Turkish copper coffeepot makes the best coffee he's had since he left Cairo. But Mom won't let Baba throw away the old ones, just like she won't let me throw away the baby shoes in my closet. She says she's going to give them to charity. But unless a shoeless kid with a caffeine addiction shows up at the door, my closet and the kitchen cabinet will remain stuffed with things none of us can use.

"Did you check the dishwasher?" I ask.

"The dishwasher?! Who put it in the dishwasher?" Baba grabs his copper coffeepot from the top rack. He turns to me. "Why are you still wearing that black shirt?"

I look down at Deanna's shirt, all wrinkled now. "Oh—I'll go change."

"Eat your breakfast first."

I'm not hungry, but this isn't the time to argue—not that I ever do. I get the plastic stool I've used since I was five and reach for the Healthy O's on top of the refrigerator. I told Mom I wanted to try this brand because it's the one Deanna eats. I wasn't expecting it to taste exactly like the Cheerios I love so much, but the organic cardboard flavor was a surprise. Because we don't waste food in this family, I have to finish the box, even though I hate it.

I go to the dishwasher, which Baba left open, and pick out a spoon and my ceramic bowl with the faded bunny in the center, the one I've also used since I was five. Then I sit down at the kitchen table.

"I forgot the milk," I announce, hoping Baba will get it for me. His eyes are glued to the coffeepot. If you don't take it off the heat as soon as it comes to a boil, the pot will spill over. And Baba never lets his coffee spill over.

I get up and open the refrigerator, and when I lift the milk carton, it's light. It's light because it's empty. This is so not going to be my day. Mom enters right on cue. She's dressed already.

"Good morning," she says, walking past me, skipping the kiss on my cheek she's given me every morning as far back as I can remember.

I drop the empty milk carton in the recycling bin. On any other morning, I'd ask her if she was the one who left it empty in the fridge.

Mom turns on the gas under her teakettle. "The coffee!" she shouts.

Baba pulls the pot off the heat but not before most of it has overflowed onto the stove.

Baba grumbles something in Arabic, grabbing a sponge.

Mom takes the sponge out of his hand. "Go take your shower. I'll clean up the mess and make you another pot, okay?"

Baba nods, and as he leaves the room, he says, "If I get a call, come and get me, even if I'm in the shower."

I sit down with my cardboard cereal, take one bite, and almost choke because it's so dry.

"Are you okay?" Mom asks, handing me a glass of water. "Why are you eating dry cereal?"

I gulp down the water. "No milk."

Mom walks back to the sink and rinses out the sponge. Now I know she's furious with me. If things were even just a little okay, my mother would've offered to make me something else to eat—an omelet, toast, anything.

"I'm really sorry, Mom."

"Mariam." She turns to me. "Your father and I have decided—"

The phone rings. I can't take this. The punishment can't be as bad as the waiting for it.

Before either one of us can answer, Baba comes running into the kitchen, wearing only a towel around his waist. He grabs for the phone.

There's a short pause as Baba listens; then he begins to speak in Arabic. He doesn't look upset anymore; he's almost smiling.

Mom's staring so hard at him she's not even blinking. I know she doesn't understand much Arabic, so she must know what's going on.

"*Alaikum salaam*, Mama," Baba says in closing. Baba's talking to Sittu. After Baba hangs up, Mom moves closer to him. "She's very happy," he says. Baba looks over at me and back at Mom. They exchange that not-in-front-of-the-child look I know all too well.

"Mariam, make the coffee," Mom says.

"Sure," I say, as if I could say anything else. But they have never, ever let me make the coffee. I have to beg to boil water. Whatever is going to happen to me must be bad. Really bad.

"Make sure you bring it to a boil three times," Baba reminds me as he and Mom head to their bedroom.

Like I don't know this already. Eventually, the coffee boils. I lift. I count out loud like Baba does. "One…two…three…four…five…" As I put the pot back on the stove and wait for the second boil, the phone rings again. Baba left the phone on the counter beside me, and I can see that the call is from ROBERTS, CAROLE.

For a second, I think it might be Deanna's mom, but when I answer, it's Deanna. She is crazy.

"I don't think we should talk right now," I say.

"Did your parents tell you?"

"Oh no, the coffee!" I drop the phone and run to the stove. Too late. The coffee has overflowed onto the stove again. "Crap!"

"Mariam! Your language!" Baba says as he walks into the kitchen. He says language is too beautiful to corrupt, so we shouldn't swear. "What has gotten into you these days?" he asks me.

"We already know what. There are too many bad influences around here," Mom says, standing behind him.

"Sorry," I say. "The phone." I point to it lying on the table where I dropped it.

Mom picks it up. "Hello? Deanna? She can't talk to you right now." She clicks off the phone and says, "Mariam, please sit down."

"But the stove," I say.

"Don't worry about that now," Baba says. The three of us sit before he starts talking again.

"Mariam, I think you know how disappointed we are in your behavior." He pauses, but I don't dare say a word. I know anything I say, now and forever, will be held against me for life. "You lied about going to this party. Drugs, Mariam. Drugs."

"I didn't know there was—"

"You didn't know," Baba says. "This I believe. And I blame myself for you not having better sense about such things."

"Do you know that you and Deanna could have been facing a prison sentence?" Mom looks at me like she's expecting an answer, but I just nod. I don't even want to breathe too loudly.

"Thank God Deanna's mother is an attorney; otherwise, you would be facing a judge in court right now." He shakes his head.

"We're at a loss. But we don't blame you." He's trying not to sound upset, but it looks like his head may explode. "Your mother and I have just not been strict enough with you…"

Not strict enough? It already feels like I'm living a life sentence. My only fun is watching reruns and reality TV. And that's if my parents aren't around to tell me to turn it off and do something more productive. They never let me do anything. Before Deanna moved here, all I did was go to school and come home and study.

Oh my God, Deanna. She's the only thing they have to take away from me. They're going to tell me I can't see her anymore. I hold my breath, but I really want to stick my fingers in my ears so I don't have to hear what's coming next.

"We're sending you to Egypt," Mom says.

What? In the middle of the school year? My parents never let me miss school unless my temperature is above 101.

"We think some time spent—"

"You're not serious. Are you?"

"This is not an easy decision, but—"

"What about school?" I interrupt. "This is the end of my junior year. Colleges are going to look at my grades—"

"I've already talked to your principal this morning," Baba says.

"You talked to the principal?"

"She thinks this would be an enriching experience for you," Mom adds. "You just have to keep up with the assignments, which your teachers post online anyway, and do a research paper on the experience, which you will present to the school at a special assembly."

"Special assembly?" They expect me to stand up in front of the whole school and talk about Egypt? Like I don't take enough crap because everyone sees me as some freak from pyramid-land.

"Honey," Mom says, her voice softer, "I know this is a lot to take in—"

"How long?" I ask.

"We don't know yet," Mom says.

"Maybe the rest of the school year," Baba says.

"That's five months!"

"We think that some time spent with your *sittu* will help you gain perspective," Baba explains. The calm in his voice makes me want to scream.

"Sittu? You're kidding me, right?"

"You think your grandmother is a joke?" Baba's voice starts to rise.

Mom gives the arm he still has wrapped around her a squeeze. "You don't know your grandmother very well…"

I haven't seen my grandmother since I was two years old, but from the stories my baba has told me over the years, I feel like I know her. I would probably have more freedom in jail. Every story Baba tells about my grandmother always start with, "If you think I'm strict, you should live with your grandmother." It sounds like Baba spent his entire childhood chained to his desk, not allowed to do anything but go to school and study. Like father, like daughter.

"You're getting on a plane?" I ask my mother. Since the attack on the Twin Towers, my mom won't get on a plane—not even when we took a family trip to Disney World, and that's only a three-hour flight. We drove for two days. There's no driving to Egypt.

"Your father and I aren't going. We can't take the time off work."

"Wait a minute. You won't let me go to the mall alone, but you're going to let me fly to the other side of—"

"Mariam, you've given us no choice." Baba's voice is getting louder again.

"This will be good for you," Mom says.

"Good for me? I used to beg for you to take me to Egypt when I was little, to go and see the pyramids and ride the camels. Both of you would always say, 'Maybe next year.'" I'm surprised to hear myself talking back like this.

"After your behavior last night," Mom says, "and lying to us like that, some time in Egypt with your grandmother will teach you about honesty and respect."

"Like some sort of international scared-straight camp?"

"Mariam!" Baba bangs the table. "You CAN'T talk to us this way."

"I'm sorry I lied. I'm sorry about the whole mess, but you can't send me to that awful place."

"Awful?" Baba asks.

"You hated that backward country so much you ran away."

"Mariam!" my mother shouts.

"No, Mom. For years, I've heard Baba talk about how everything sucks in Egypt and how everything is so much better here." I stand up. "I make one mistake, I do one thing wrong, and you're going to punish me like I'm some criminal! And you know what? Jail would be better than spending *any* time with that horrible woman!"

Baba reaches out and slaps me across the face. Mom doesn't say a word. I'm too shocked to do anything but hold my cheek. My father has never hit me before—not once in my entire life.

"Don't you ever show such disrespect for your *sittu*!"

"You're the one who says she rules with an iron fist and was hard on you. So now you want me to suffer the way you did? For one mistake?"

"Go to your room, right now!" Baba stands up.

I've never heard him yell like this either, but I don't care. I look my father straight in the eyes. "You want me to live in a country where women are second-class citizens who take orders from men and have to cover their hair because the men are so perverted they can't be trusted!"

"This is why I don't want her watching television!" Baba slams his fist on the table.

Mom stands up and moves between Baba and me. "Go to your room now, Mariam," she says quietly.

"The lies, Rose! Look at the lies she believes about her own people!"

"My own people?" I move around my mother so I can see Baba. "You may be my father, but I'm not like you. I'm American. I'm a real American. Not some wannabe—"

"MARIAM! YOUR ROOM! NOW!" Baba yells.

This time, I listen.

I drop down on my bed. I know I'm crying, but I'm too numb to feel the tears running down my cheeks. Mom's right behind me.

She sits down at my side and sighs. "I know you're very upset, but the way you just talked to your father—"

"Can I at least say good-bye to Deanna?" I say into my pillow.

"That won't be necessary."

I flip over and sit up. I pull Deanna's T-shirt to my face and wipe my tears. "Mom, please. Just one call."

She wipes the hair from my face. "Deanna's going with you."

"What? Why would she be going with me?"

She must see the look of horror on my face, because she says, "You don't want her to go with you?"

Sure I do. But I can't let them do this to her.

"She'll never survive, Mom. I'm used to having no freedom, but Deanna comes and goes when she wants. Sittu will crush her."

"Your grandmother is a little tough, I'll admit, but she isn't a female Attila the Hun."

No, she's just Darth Vader's evil sister.

"Deanna's mother is very worried about her. With her job keeping her so busy right now, Carole needs Deanna to have supervision. The poor girl has no father. And on top of everything, there's her deformity…"

"I told you, Mom. It's a facial difference. Don't call it a deformity."

"You know what I mean." Her tone tells me I'm not winning any points.

"I'm sorry. But look, I have an idea. She can stay here, at home with you. We both can!"

"Sweetie, I'm sorry, but after last night and the way you just spoke to your father, there'll be no talking him out of this."

"Please, Mama." I wrap my arms around her neck.

"You haven't called me *mama* since you were a little girl," she says as she strokes the back of my head.

"So, I can stay, and you'll call Deanna's mother and tell her we're not going?" I ask quietly.

She pushes me off her and stands. "Mariam, I don't know what has gotten into you, but if anyone can straighten you girls out, it's your *sittu*."

chapter FOUR

"T *ehebb asir?*"

I pull off my cheap airline headphones. "Excuse me?" I rub my ear as I look up at the flight attendant.

She hands me a small container of orange juice.

"Thank you." I take the juice.

The attendant reaches over me and hands a juice to Deanna.

"*Shukran,*" Deanna says.

"*Afwan.*" The flight attendant flashes a wide smile at Deanna before she moves on.

"*Shukran* means 'thank you,'" Deanna says. "*Afwan* is how you say 'you're welcome.'"

"Deanna, I was there too, remember?"

Baba spent the last several days before our trip cramming Arabic down our throats, like he was trying to make up for the years when the only Arabic words I ever heard him speak were the ones muttered under his breath when he was angry or those I overheard when he talked to Sittu on the phone. Except for these endless Arabic lessons and his crash course in "How to be a proper Egyptian when in Egypt," Baba hardly spoke to me at all since our blowup.

Deanna shrugs. "Well, you didn't seem to be listening."

After everything that had happened, I was not going to just suck it up, be happy, and learn Arabic.

"You know, Mariam, you should at least try." Deanna digs around in the pouch in the seat back in front of her. She pulls out a Sky Mall magazine, a safety instruction card, a barf bag, a half-empty potato chip bag, and finally our vision book.

This is one of Deanna's California things. We started it at the beginning of December to be sure we got what we wanted out of the upcoming year. She believes that if you write down what you want, it will happen. I wrote that I wanted to be accepted at school and not treated like a freak. Now I don't want to have anything to do with the book. The only vision I have for this year is one of a natural disaster: Hurricane Sittu. The only hope I have is that the saying "time flies" also applies when you're not having fun—like when you're having the worst time of your life.

"When my mom and I traveled to Mexico," Deanna says, all excited, "people really appreciated it when we tried to speak their language."

"English works just fine for me," I say, taking a sip of juice. Awful. Tastes like something you'd pour on Healthy O's—plastic-tasting juice to go with cardboard-tasting cereal.

Deanna puts the barf bag back in the pouch and takes out the tourist guide she bought when her mother told her she was going to Egypt. It's called *Let's Go Egypt*. I'd told her she should have bought one called *Let's Go Nowhere* because, aside from the airport, the only traveling we'd do was to the dining room for supervised work on our school assignments, and the only sights we'd be taking in would be Sittu's bathroom, kitchen, and bedrooms. Deanna just said, "Don't be ridiculous," so I dropped it.

Deanna pulls down her tray table and starts taking notes in our vision book, flipping through the tourist book at the same time. She fills half a page before she asks, "Want to know what I'm writing?"

I'm staring, but I'm not trying to read what she's writing. I just have no interest in watching the in-flight movie, even though it's *17 Again* and I never saw the end because Baba made us leave in the middle because it showed a guy's naked butt. A bunch of kids from school were in the theater too, and they all watched Baba, muttering Arabic under his breath, drag me out of the exit, right at the front of the theater. I couldn't have been more embarrassed. Why were they showing an old movie on the plane, anyway? Obviously, we were flying on Backward Airlines. "Come on, don't you want to know?"

"Let me guess. You're writing down all the awesome things you want to happen on this trip."

She puts the notebook up to my face.

In big letters, it says, "Fall in love for the first time and help Mariam get her first kiss."

"The look on your face," Deanna says, laughing for both of us. "Mar, we're best friends. You don't have to turn tomato red every time I bring up guys. It's cool that you haven't had any experience. But this trip will change all that."

"You're a little late with your vision for me," I lie.

"*What?!*" Deanna shouts so loud that a man with salt-and-pepper hair sitting in front of her turns and looks at us over his seat.

"Something wrong?" he asks.

"Nothing," she snaps.

"Why are you so rude?" I whisper to her.

"American tourists are always so obnoxious. Why can't he mind his own business?" she whispers back.

"What makes you think he's American?"

"Duh—his accent."

I think about that for a second. I didn't think he had an accent at all.

"Don't change the subject," Deanna says. "Who did you kiss? When did it happen? And why didn't you tell me?" Deanna sounds like she's been slapped in the face.

"Some guy at the party," I say, totally lying. But the idea of Deanna trying to get me kissed by some sleazy Egyptian guy makes me sick to my stomach.

"How could you not tell me?"

"When could I? My parents didn't let me out of their sight until this plane took off."

"You could have texted me!"

"My parents read all my texts, remember?"

"Well, you should have found a way, somehow."

"Next time, I'll use Morse code," I joke. But Deanna's not finding any of this funny.

"What was it like?"

"It was okay."

"Just okay?"

"All right, it was amazing!" I grin—the big, goofy grin I always use when I'm lying. I'm sure Deanna knows this, but she plays along with me.

"I'm so happy for you," she says.

Deanna crosses out "first" on her list and writes "second" in its place.

"We kissed three times, actually." Why stop lying now?

"Three times?" I've never seen her eyes so wide. She definitely knows I'm lying. "Well, that's great, but I'm talking about kissing another guy."

"I don't want another guy."

"Look, Mariam, we're going to Egypt. Have you seen how cute Egyptian guys are? You can always hook up with that guy when we get back to New York. I just can't let you give up the chance to have the most romantic time of your life."

"Look, Deanna, I know you don't get this, but I'm not interested in Egyptian guys, okay?"

"We'll see about that."

I open my mouth to tell her we won't see about anything, but then remember Sittu and how locked down we're going to be, so arguing about meeting some Egyptian hottie is a total waste of time. Because unless he comes walking through Sittu's living room, it's just not happening. This goes for Deanna meeting her first love too. But why crush her dreams now? We will be landing in Cairo soon enough.

* * *

A new attendant stands over me. She's wearing one of those little hats I've only seen flight attendants wear in movies from the sixties, back when they were called "stewardesses."

"I only speak English," I say before she has a chance to speak.

"Please pull down your tray table. Fish or beef?" she asks with a British accent.

"I'm not hungry, thank you."

"I speak a little Arabic...*shway shway*," Deanna says. "Fish. *Shukran.*"

The flight attendant flashes Deanna one of those phony, it's-my-job-to-smile smiles. "Good accent," she says, and passes Deanna her fish.

"You don't speak any Arabic?" the flight attendant asks, looking down at me.

I shake my head.

"Well, you are a good pair. You look Egyptian, and your friend here sounds Egyptian."

"Did you hear that?" Deanna says. "I sound Egyptian. How awesome?" Deanna raises her hand to high-five me, but I let her hand hang. I've looked Egyptian all my life, and all it's ever gotten me is trouble.

"*Ahlan wa sahlan,*" the flight attendant says with a smile, then continues down the aisle.

I look at Deanna for translation.

She shrugs. "I don't know what that means."

"Welcome," says the man sitting in the seat in front of Deanna. This time, he doesn't even turn around.

"Excuse me?" Deanna leans closer to the back of his seat.

"*Ahlan wa sahlan*," he says louder, but still doesn't turn toward us. "She's welcoming you to Egypt."

"*Shukran!*" Deanna shouts back at flight attendant.

"You're welcome," replies the man.

"He speaks Arabic," Deanna says, sounding impressed. "*Ahlan wa sahlan*," Deanna repeats to herself. "Welcome to Egypt."

For the rest of the flight, I close my eyes and try to sleep, but all I think about is how I'd rather be flying over the Bermuda Triangle. Disappearing forever would be better than what's ahead of us.

When the wheels of the plane hit the runway, all the passengers applaud. I tap Deanna, who has just finished reading *The Rough Guide to Egypt*, the other guidebook she brought with her. It was a gift from my mother, who wanted me to have it, but I told her the only travel book I needed was *The Rough Guide to Sittu's Apartment*. "What's that all about?"

"People are just thanking the pilot for getting us here safely," Deanna says. "They did that when I went to Paris last summer."

"I didn't know you went to Paris."

"I've been to lots of places in Europe. Before my mom took the job in New York, she had lots more time to travel."

"Welcome to Cairo. Please remain seated until the seat belt sign is turned off," says an unseen voice in a heavy British accent. "We are waiting for clearance to taxi to the gate." The Arabic that follows starts with *Ahlan wa sahlan*, so I assume it's the same announcement.

"You okay?" Deanna asks, staring at my hand.

I'm pressing the volume buttons on the armrest, up and down, up and down. "Fine."

"You know what F-I-N-E stands for: Freaked out, Insecure, Neurotic, and Emotional."

All of the above. But I say, "It's nothing."

"I know you don't want to be here, but give it a chance. You might be surprised."

"I hate surprises."

The man sitting in front of Deanna bangs his armrest and stands up. "This is ridiculous. Like our time means nothing to these Egyptians." He climbs over the person sitting in the aisle seat with an, "excuse me," but he doesn't sound as if he cares if he's excused or not.

Once he's in the aisle, he pulls down his carry-on luggage from the overhead compartment. The flight attendant who gave me the juice comes running over to him.

"Sir, please stay in your seat until the seat belt sign is turned off. It's for your own safety." He responds in Arabic and doesn't sit down.

The flight attendant looks at him like she's trying to figure out her next move, but before there's a showdown, the seat belt sign turns off. The cabin door opens, and the man strides up the aisle away from us.

"Come on," Deanna says, grabbing her backpack and making her way up the aisle too.

"What's the hurry?" I shout after her. But she doesn't turn around.

Now everyone seems to be in a rush to exit the plane, so I have to wait, standing in front of my seat until a woman with a baby in her arms motions for me to step out of my row. I gesture for her to go on, but she refuses. I take my backpack down from the overhead compartment, then turn to her and say, "*Shukran.*"

"*Afwan,*" she says, and smiles.

I smile back and run off to find Deanna.

chapter FIVE

When I exit the plane, Deanna is waving like she hasn't seen me in years.

The airport looks normal so far. I mean, nothing seems strange or old, like I expected. It doesn't look all that different from the terminal at JFK in New York.

"Why did you run off like that?"

"I was trying to catch up with that guy. He was just so rude."

"So what were you planning to do? Give him a lesson in manners?"

"You'd better believe it."

"You're kidding me, right?"

"Doesn't it bother you how American tourists can be so obnoxious? I mean, they give us all a bad name. When my mom and I travel anywhere, if we hear someone complain or act like a total jerk to a waitress or a hotel person, we know they're American. My mom says it's like Americans think they're so much better than everyone else."

"Let's not exaggerate."

"I'm not. You'll see. Next time we hear some pushy person

yelling at someone who is just trying to help, I'll bet you anything he's American."

"Deanna, we're Americans too," I point out.

"Exactly. And that's why people like that man make us all look bad. He's probably some business guy or government person who learned Arabic to come here and cheat people out of their money. Worse than a tourist."

"You know all that from just looking at the guy. What's that smell?" I cup my hand over my face.

"I like it. I think it's him," Deanna says, nodding to a tall man a few feet from us. He's wearing a fancy suit and tie, talking on his cell phone.

"His cologne, my God—"

"I love it when guys wear cologne."

"It smells like he took a bath in it." I prefer a guy to smell clean, like he just bathed with hypoallergenic and environmentally friendly soap. "Let's just get our luggage and get out of here," I say.

It takes us a while to find the baggage area because Deanna insists on asking for directions in Arabic. It's not until I finally ask someone in good old American English that we're directed to the right place.

When we get there, instead of conveyor belts helping you easily find your bags, the luggage is just scattered all over the ground. What a mess.

Deanna and I walk around, like, hundreds of suitcases and boxes, trying to find the red suitcase Mom bought when we went to

Disney World. It's a blinding red, so it should be easy to spot, along with Deanna's banana-yellow bags. But I don't see it anywhere.

"Listen," Deanna says. "Do you hear that?"

"All I hear are lots of people speaking Arabic." I step around an overstuffed suitcase with rope holding it together. "Here's a question. Where's our luggage? I bet they lost it."

"But, Mariam, doesn't it sound cool? All the—"

"There!" We point at the exact same time.

Deanna chatters on, but I'm not listening. A man in gray overalls follows us to our bags. He says something in Arabic, and then takes Deanna's bag. She pulls it away from him.

"Help!" I scream. A few people turn to look at me, but when the man yells something else to us in Arabic, they turn away.

"*Shukran. Yalla*," Deanna says.

"*Yalla*," the man says, pulling harder on Deanna's suitcase.

"*Yal-la*," Deanna says slower. This time she yanks her suitcase free. "Mar, get your luggage. Hurry!"

I try pulling out the extendable handle to roll my suitcase, but it's stuck, so I just grab the regular handle. Deanna picks up her other suitcase, and we run.

We don't stop until we reach customs, which looks like a total mob. Deanna wheels her suitcases behind her. I try my handle again—still stuck. *Of course*, I think.

"Wow, I can't believe that guy tried to steal your luggage," I say, as we pass a family going in the direction we just came from. The mother is holding two babies in her arms; both are crying, but she seems too determined to get where she's going to notice.

"He probably thought it was his."

"Deanna, come on. How many people have banana-yellow suitcases?"

"Well, it was strange—I kept saying '*yalla*' to him, and instead of letting it go, he just kept saying '*yalla*' back to me."

"What does *yalla* mean?"

"You should have paid more attention to your Arabic lessons. *Yalla* means 'I go.'"

"See? I told you. He was trying to take your suitcase. He was saying 'I go' back to you."

"Maybe," Deanna says, "but right there in front of all those people?"

"Mom says sometimes the worst crimes happen in front of a whole lot of witnesses who do nothing. Hey, do you think we're in the right place?"

"The signs say 'Customs.'" Sarcasm oozes out of her. "And see those guys up front, sitting behind the brown tables, checking passports? Well, I bet they're customs officials."

"I know this is customs, but how do we know when it's our turn?"

"Let's wait here a few minutes and see what happens."

I agree, not knowing what else to do.

"The *galabeya* looks so much more comfortable than a suit." Deanna nods her head toward the man standing next to us.

"You mean the man dress," I say.

"It's traditional clothing for Arab men."

"How do you know these things?"

"Internet. I did a lot of research. And your dad answered a lot of questions for me."

"At least he's talking to you."

"He was talking to you too."

"No, he was talking at me." I look at the *galabeya* again. "They do look comfortable," I say.

"A lot more than those do." Deanna points to a man wearing Bermuda shorts. "And those look so tight they just have to hurt." This time she points to a policeman who's carrying a machine gun. This would freak me out—the machine gun, not the pants—had Baba not warned me the police here carry guns, like soldiers. The machine gun does seem like overkill though. And where was this guy when we were almost robbed?

"At least with the *galabeya*," she says, "guys don't have to worry about getting caught in their zippers."

"Deanna!"

"What?"

"Watch what you say. We're not in New York, where people are used to—"

"Obnoxious Americans?" she says, like she just proved her point. "Speaking of obnoxious," Deanna says, staring at a woman who is walking our way in a tight shirt and a skirt so short it can hardly be called a mini.

I laugh.

"Uh, Mar?"

"What?"

"I have to go to the bathroom." Deanna bounces from her left to her right foot.

"You're kidding me."

"I don't think I can hold it too much longer."

"Okay. There has to be one around here."

We pick up our luggage and walk around until Deanna says, "Here."

"WC?"

"It stands for water closet," Deanna says, looking up at the woman's silhouette under the two letters. "It was the same in France."

Of course, as soon as we go inside, I have to pee too. I wait until Deanna comes out of her stall, so she can watch our luggage. I try to cover the seat with toilet paper like Mom always tells me to do, but the toilet paper comes out in small pieces, so I take my chances and sit down. There's a knob right next to the toilet. Maybe that's how you flush? I turn it to see what happens, and—whoa!—cold water shoots up the crack of my butt. I turn the knob back to the off position and get out of there.

"Hey, Deanna," I say, coming out of the stall, "did you notice—?" But there is another woman in the bathroom now, so I stop talking and wash my hands. Deanna is watching the woman spray her hair with something in a silver plastic bottle. "I use the same product," Deanna says. "It's from France. Hard to get in New York." The woman doesn't respond; she probably doesn't speak English.

The woman's eyes meet mine in the mirror though. I smile. She smiles back.

"I like the color," Deanna says, pointing to the woman's lips, which are a light shade of pink.

I turn the water off. Reflected in the mirror, I see a woman wearing a blue-and-white uniform come up behind me. I turn to her. She gives me a paper towel.

"You have a dollar?" Deanna asks. "You're supposed to tip her."

I reach into my pocket and pull out a very crumpled bill. I'm almost embarrassed to give it to the attendant, but I hand it over anyway.

"*Shukran*," she says. I just nod because right then, I can't remember the word for "you're welcome." When I turn back, the woman with the pink lipstick is gone. Another woman is standing in her spot, but I can't see her lips or her hair or anything. She's covered head to toe in her black cloak—what Baba calls the cockroach suit. It makes him mad when he sees women dressed like this, especially on the news, because he says it makes Muslims look bad. He says it has nothing to do with Islam and it's just about the oppression of women. Then he goes on and on about the history of Islam and how it's about equality and justice and blah, blah, blah. If Mom's around, she joins in. Usually all I want to do is to change the channel and watch *Dancing with the Stars*. Still, it always makes me laugh when Baba says the cockroach thing…but right now, it feels like a mean thing to say, even if he doesn't support it.

"Cotton Candy," the woman in the cloak says to Deanna.

"Excuse me?" Deanna says.

"The color of my lipstick is 'Cotton Candy.'"

"Oh," Deanna says. "It matches your shoes." Deanna points to the bit of pink sneaking out from under the cloak.

"Exactly." The woman adjusts herself so her shoe is no longer showing. "Have a wonderful holiday," she tells us as she leaves the bathroom.

"How cool is that?" Deanna says to me.

"How cool is what?"

"That's the same woman I was just talking to; now you see her, now you don't. She slips the black cloak over her head and presto, change-o, she's gone."

I glance at myself in the mirror and think it would be nice to be able to just disappear when I want to.

chapter
SIX

When we get back to customs, Deanna's rude friend from the airplane is there in his wrinkled blue suit, with a pushcart full of suitcases. I'm hoping to God she doesn't see him.

Deanna walks right over to him. "Hi," she says.

"Deanna, please don't start," I mutter under my breath.

The man turns to us. "Hello, girls from the plane," he says. "Would you look at this?" Now his accent sounds less New York and more Upset Baba. "Ridiculous. It's like we're moving backward. Look at all these people just pushing ahead; no respect for order at all. I guess this is Egypt. What can I expect?"

"Where are you from?" Deanna asks.

"Excuse me?"

"Where are you from?" she repeats.

"I'm an American citizen. I live in Detroit."

"You have a Brooklyn accent."

"That's where I lived when I first got to the States."

"So you're not American?" Deanna asks, surprised.

"I just told you, I'm an American citizen."

"I don't mean your citizenship. Where were you born?"

"Why? Do you work for the Egyptian security forces or Homeland Security?"

"Deanna, let's go." I pull on her arm. It's clear this man doesn't want us bothering him.

"I just think when American citizens travel to other countries where we are guests, we should be respectful and not act like jerks."

"Deanna!" I say. "Sir, please excuse my friend. She's just—"

"No." He puts the palm of his hand in front of my face. "Don't make excuses for her." He squints at Deanna, and she looks back at him like they're in a staring contest.

"Giza," he finally says.

"Giza?"

"That's where I'm from."

"You're from where the pyramids are?" It's like Deanna just met King Tut himself.

"That's the place."

"So why are you complaining?"

The man doesn't respond, but he looks at Deanna like he's thinking over her question. Finally, he says, "Well, it's hard to get used to a place when you've been away for a while."

"How long have you been away?" I ask, thinking about Baba.

"Haven't been back since 9/11." He looks into Deanna's eyes like he knows she's going to ask why. "It's a long story, but mostly life has a way of stealing time."

"Didn't you miss your family here?" Deanna asks.

"The questions. All the questions," the man says. "What's your name?"

"Deanna." She extends her hand.

"Ahmed," he says as he shakes her hand. "My pleasure. I like a person who speaks her mind—usually." He smiles.

Obviously, Deanna doesn't smile back, but I can see in her eyes she's starting to like him.

"This is Mariam," Deanna offers. "We're visiting her *sittu*."

Ahmed speaks to me in Arabic, but I just stare at him.

"Oh, you're the girl who thinks English is good enough." He looks past me a moment, then says, "What stupidity!"

"Excuse me?" I ask.

"No, not you. Them." Ahmed lifts his chin toward the row of customs officers in front of us.

"Why are you coming into this country?" he imitates. "Do you hear the stupidity of that question? Why? Who cares why? And if it were a bad reason, would the person tell them?" Ahmed sounds even more irritated than he did on the plane. Isn't this guy just doing his job? "And look, see that man?"

"The one whose suitcase they've opened?" Deanna asks.

"Watch the trouble they give him." A customs officer takes everything out of the man's luggage. "There goes his underwear."

"I don't want some stranger looking at my underwear," Deanna says.

"They might?" I ask him.

"No worries. They don't stop everyone." Ahmed's smile looks so forced, if I wasn't worried before, I am now.

We stand there for what seems like forever, inching our way forward, not saying a word, watching men, women, and children move through customs and out a set of sliding glass doors.

"What's happening there?" Ahmed stares at the far end of the customs tables. Deanna and I look. A man in a brown suit, more wrinkled than Ahmed's, is carrying a little boy no older than two. Standing next to him is a woman with dark hair like mine. A customs officer moves his head back and forth between his computer screen and some document, probably a passport. The man in the wrinkled suit is speaking rapidly in Arabic. He sounds scared.

The officer is now motioning to one of the security guys in tight pants. He walks toward the table, carrying a machine gun.

The man in the wrinkled suit hands the little boy over to his wife and begins shouting.

"Ahmed, what is he saying?" Deanna asks quietly.

"Shush."

With the butt of his gun, the soldier pushes against the man's back. The man refuses to move. Another police officer rushes over, yelling in Arabic, then the man starts to walk. His wife tries to follow, but the first soldier's gun blocks her. She shouts in Arabic, and her little boy begins to cry. The soldier doesn't say a word.

The man is escorted to a green metal door. The police officer bangs the butt of his gun against the door, and it opens. The officer pushes the man inside. The wife begins to cry louder than her child. She reaches after him. The soldier still won't let her by.

Then, out of the mob in front of us, a woman in a black cloak marches around the barrier and right up to the soldier, stepping in between him and the wife. She shouts at the guard, gesturing with her black-cloaked arm, and the mother slips around her and runs to the green door. She bangs and bangs until it opens to let her inside. The door slams shut behind her.

The guard looks at the door, then the woman in the black cloak. He shouts at her, gesturing toward all of us on the other side of the customs barrier. Without saying another word, she goes back to her place in the crowd.

"Wow, that took guts," I say. What I don't say is how shocked I am that someone who would cover herself up like that could have the courage to stand up to a soldier with a machine gun. She's the invisible hero.

"Look." Deanna nudges me. "Pink shoes."

Oh my God. It's the cotton candy lipstick lady.

"What's on the other side of that door?" Deanna asks Ahmed.

"Always wanting answers. You know, you should be careful what you ask."

Deanna glares at Ahmed. She's not going to let it go.

"An interrogation room," Ahmed says.

"What did he do wrong?" I ask.

"Maybe he's one of those bloggers who criticized Mubarak," Ahmed says.

"It's illegal to blog here?" I say. This country is worse than I imagined.

"Only if you say something the government doesn't like."

"I read about this," Deanna says. "Most of the bloggers are older, like in their early twenties—"

"That's young to some of us," Ahmed says, and smiles.

"Whatever you say." Deanna flips her hand at Ahmed. To me, she says, "All they did was write about the rich people who live so well while others are starving in bread lines in this country. It was so depressing."

"Yes, it's very depressing," Ahmed says. "But starvation is not the problem in this country. We are not respected by this government. Mubarak—over thirty years he's been in power, and he kicks us like dogs."

"Why do people keep voting for him?" I ask.

"Mar." Deanna rolls her eyes. "You can't be that naïve. It's all fixed. The elections here aren't real."

"But that man they arrested looks too old to be a blogger," I comment, just to say something. I'm embarrassed that I really don't know anything about Egypt's government.

"Older people can't blog?" Ahmed says.

"I just mean…" I stop myself. I don't know what I mean. I guess I just can't believe someone would be arrested or stopped from visiting a country or returning to his country because of a blog post. Ahmed glances at another soldier. "That man may not have written anything, but maybe his cousin who he hasn't spoken to in years did. Or maybe he doesn't know why they are giving him this hard time, and maybe he will never know. All I do know is that man will be in that room a lot longer than we will be in this line, unless he's able to put more than a few dollars in those soldiers' pockets or throw around a few big-shot names of people he knows. But if he could do that, he probably wouldn't have been pulled aside in the first place. This is what it's like here. Harassment. Always harassment."

"But the woman and the boy—are they going to be sent to jail too? They didn't do anything."

"The officials probably thought it would be easier to let her in than to have her scream out here. You don't want to upset the tourists. They probably would've arrested her and the woman in the *burka* if they were men."

"*Burka?*" I say.

"The one all covered up."

"Weren't there women bloggers who were arrested too?" Deanna asks.

"True," Ahmed says.

"Deanna, we have to call your mother. She's a lawyer. She'll know how to help these people," I say.

"My dear girl, that is very sweet, but American lawyers are not what those people need right now. Prayers are what they need," Ahmed tells me. I know if my face is showing how I feel, he can see how freaked out I am. "Look, don't worry. In a few hours, *insh'allah*, they will probably let them go. Like I said, it's just harassment. People are used to that sort of thing here."

"How can they take it?" Deanna asks.

"Some protest—mostly on campuses—but security in Egypt is very good at containing dissent."

A soldier—the same guy Ahmed was just looking at—walks over to us. He stares at Deanna and me for what feels like forever, then says something to Ahmed. A question, maybe, it's hard to tell. Ahmed shows him his passport, waves toward us, and nods a lot. The soldier looks at the passport, glances at us again, then clicks his tongue and says something else in Arabic. What is he saying? Is Ahmed in trouble? Deanna grabs my hand. Her palm is sweaty but so is mine. If they take Ahmed into that room, I don't know what we'll do. What can we do? I want to go home.

"*Shukran*," Ahmed says as the soldier gives him back his passport and walks away.

"What was that about? Are you in trouble?" Deanna asks Ahmed, letting go of my hand.

"We are all—"

"In trouble?" I shout.

"We're in the wrong line. We need to be over there." Ahmed lifts his chin to the sign that says "Foreign Visitors." "We're in the line for the Egyptians. Come on." He starts off without looking back, his long legs taking him quickly away from us.

"I thought you and Mariam were Egyptians," Deanna says as she drags her two rolling suitcases behind her.

"I'm American. I was born there, and I'm proud to be one," I correct her, scurrying to keep up with her and Ahmed.

The "Foreign Visitors" line is straight and orderly, like the cafeteria lines at school.

Ahmed whispers to us as we fall in behind him, "This is good he noticed you. They treat you better if you're American."

"That doesn't make any sense," Deanna says.

"It doesn't seem fair," I add.

"Welcome to Egypt." Ahmed pulls out a handkerchief that's the same blue as his tie and wipes his forehead.

"Are you feeling okay?" I ask, now noticing how much sweat is dripping off his face.

"The air conditioner is not working too well in here. No surprise."

. "I guess," I say, though I'm actually feeling a little cold.

"Hey, is that your *sittu*?" Deanna asks, pointing toward the glass doors behind the customs officers. Standing next to a man holding a cardboard sign with Arabic letters written on it is a thin woman with white hair. "Maybe. How do you know what Sittu looks like?" I ask.

"There are pictures of her in your living room."

I had forgotten about them. But in the pictures, Sittu's hair has very little gray in it.

"Wave, Mar. Wave," Deanna says, swaying her arms back and forth. "Mariam's *sittu*! Mariam's *sittu*!" she yells until the doors slide closed. "Maybe that's not her. She didn't wave back or anything."

Now I'm sure it's her. Sittu doesn't seem like she'd be the waving type.

"What am I thinking? Of course she didn't wave back," Deanna says. "She doesn't even know me. Mar, when the doors open again, you wave."

"I don't want to," I tell her, but as soon as the doors slide open again, Deanna lifts my arm in the air, shouting, "This is Mariam!"

The woman shakes her head like we're embarrassing her or something, and I'm sure the expression on my face matches the one on hers, which tells the world, "I'm only here because I have no choice."

"Your *sittu* is a very attractive woman," Ahmed says, looking better than he did a moment ago.

"Aren't you married?" Deanna asks, looking down at his gold wedding band.

"Please excuse me. My comment was not meant to be in any way, uh, sleazy." His accent sounds like Baba's again. "I was only commenting like one comments on a work of art."

"Oh brother," Deanna mutters.

"In this case"—Ahmed smiles before he gives us the punch line—"it would be more appropriate to say, 'oh sister.'"

"You're a funny guy," Deanna says.

I shake my head and look toward the doors again, but Sittu is no longer standing there.

"Next."

It's our turn to meet the customs officer. "It was nice meeting you." Deanna extends her hand. She and Ahmed shake, and Deanna dashes to the officer.

"Very nice," I say, extending my hand too.

But when Ahmed takes my hand in his, he doesn't shake it. He holds on to it with both his hands and says, "Have a good time in Egypt. And, Mariam, I bet your *sittu* isn't as tough as you fear."

I stare at him for a moment, trying to remember if I'd said anything about Sittu on the plane. I know he was eavesdropping on our conversation, but I'm almost positive I never said a word out loud about Sittu. Maybe he's a mind reader. I pull my hand from his and rejoin Deanna.

The officer takes our passports. He examines them for a moment, then taps Deanna's passport. Deanna turns to me. "You don't remember how you say hello, do you?"

"Hello," I say.

"I mean in Arabic."

"*Ahlan*," the customs officer says dully. It doesn't sound like he appreciates that Deanna is trying to speak his language.

"That's it! *Ahlan!*"

The customs officer starts looking back and forth between his computer and Deanna's passport, exactly like the other officer did before the guards took the man away.

"*Asalaam alaikum*," I say, just like Baba taught me.

"*Wa-Alaikum-Salaam.*"

He can smile. I smile back.

"My favorite color." He points to my red suitcase.

"Mine too," I say as I smile wider.

"You are sad?" he asks Deanna as he points to her mouth.

"Just tired," she says, skirting the question.

"What is the reason for your trip?"

"We're here to see my grandmother."

"Her *sittu*," Deanna adds.

This makes him smile again.

"Before I let you both through, you have to promise me one thing." The officer pauses, waiting for our answer.

"Yes," we say in unison.

"You must learn to speak Arabic." He laughs this time.

"That's the plan," Deanna says.

I nod.

"*Ahlan wa sahlan*," he says. "Welcome to Egypt."

As we head for the sliding glass doors, Deanna and I glance at the green metal door. We don't say a word, but I know we're both hoping the family is okay.

"You told your *sittu* about my smile thing, right?" Deanna asks. "I don't want her to think I'm not happy to see her when we first meet. First impressions are important, you know."

Deanna always acts like she doesn't care what people think of her. I envy that. So why does she have to pick now to care about what someone thinks? Especially someone who is as uptight as Sittu?

"She's going to love you," I say, wanting to believe it, but I can't imagine Sittu loving a rebel.

chapter SEVEN

Sittu kisses me on both cheeks so hard I feel like she's leaving bruises. I'm glad the kisses she gives Deanna seem a lot softer. Sittu looked taller from a distance. Standing next to her, I see she's short like me. Still, Ahmed's right. She really is beautiful.

"Wasn't there someone to help you with your bags?" Sittu asks, looking down at our luggage. "Didn't you see the men wearing the gray uniforms? They're usually there to help, grabbing the tourists' bags."

Deanna and I look at each other. I guess that guy wasn't trying to rob us after all.

Sittu says something in Arabic to me.

"Sorry." I shrug.

"You don't speak Arabic?" she asks, shaking her head, but I know she knows I don't speak Arabic. "All those books I've sent you! Your father should be ashamed of himself. I suppose that's what happens when people move to the big U.S. of A. They forget where they came from."

I want to tell her Baba hasn't forgotten, that he talks about Egypt all the time. But somehow, I think she'd be able to tell I was lying.

"Deanna, you are very beautiful," Sittu says. "Are you sure you are not Egyptian?" I'm relieved she's being nice to Deanna.

"I wish," Deanna says. "My mother's a little bit of a lot of things: English, Italian, Swedish, German, Portuguese, and some Irish. There's some Native American mixed in there too. And my father…"

Deanna pauses, but before she continues, Sittu says, "My son told me about how much your mother wanted you."

"That's me—a spermie," Deanna laughs.

Sittu looks confused.

"It's what Deanna calls herself, because her mom used a sperm bank."

"Very funny. My son did mention what a good sense of humor you have."

"Your son's pretty cool," Deanna says.

"Well, he can be a bit of a hothead," Sittu says—almost the exact same thing Baba said about her. Baba actually said "heated head."

"Mariam's *sittu*—"

"What is this 'Mariam's *sittu*'? Just call me Sittu."

"Okay, Sittu. I don't know if your son also told you about… Well, I just want you to know it may not look like I'm happy to be here, but I am. I'm so happy."

"What are you talking about? I have never seen happier eyes in all my life, and I have been alive a very long time." Sittu touches Deanna's face where her smile should be. "When you walk into the room, the sun enters with you."

Deanna looks like she's actually turning red. I've never seen her get embarrassed before.

I nudge Deanna. "Now you're supposed to say something nice to her."

"Like?"

"The flowers only grow when you arrive," I say. Baba and I did this all the time when I was younger. I used to think it was a game Baba made up.

"At least your *baba* taught you a few things," Sittu notes, as if I'm not a complete disappointment to her.

"You keep going back and forth, trying to top each other with compliments," I explain to Deanna, trying to avoid Sittu's gaze.

There's something in the way Sittu stares at me that reminds me of when I was interviewed for private high school. My parents thought it would be a safer environment for me. Both Baba and Mom were going to have to work two jobs just to pay the tuition, yet they really wanted me to go. I did really well on all the tests, but the woman who interviewed me shook her head throughout my interview, as if everything I said was wrong. She even shook her head when she asked me my name, and I know I got that answer right.

"So it's like a contest?" Deanna says.

"Something like that," Sittu says. "Mariam's father was always good at contests." She kisses me on both of my cheeks again but not as hard as before. "*Yalla.*"

"So you want us to wait here for you?" I ask. "Or is there a better place to wait?"

"Wait?" Sittu looks confused. "Why would you wait here?"

"You said *yalla*, 'I go,' right?"

Sittu shakes her head. "Mariam." She sighs like I just failed some big test I didn't even know I was taking. "*Yalla* means 'let's go,' as in 'we go.' Even the little Arabic you know is wrong." She shakes her head again.

I glare at Deanna, but she's too busy looking at everything around her to notice. Now it makes even more sense why the guy kept pulling harder on Deanna's suitcase every time she said *yalla*. The poor guy thought she was telling him we were all going with him.

"*Yalla*," Sittu repeats as she goes for my suitcase.

"I can carry it," I say.

"Why carry it? It has wheels." In one easy motion, she pulls the handle up and it's ready to roll. Of course.

I grab one of Deanna's suitcases, and together, the three of us *yalla*.

*　　*　　*

When we exit the airport, the sun is so bright Deanna pulls a pair of sunglasses from her backpack. Sittu pulls a pair from her handbag. With their sunglasses on, they look like they're related and I'm the friend.

"You didn't bring glasses to protect your eyes?" Sittu again shakes her head at me. I'm starting to feel like I have a bobblehead doll for a grandmother.

"I forgot them." I squint at the men calling us to their cabs. Sittu waves them off.

"Well, try not to squint. You'll make wrinkles."

"Hey, I got it!" Deanna shouts. Several people walking toward the cabs stop and look at us. Sittu and I turn to Deanna. "With your beauty the world needs no flowers," she says.

Sittu lets go of my suitcase and kisses Deanna on the forehead. "Deanna, you are Egyptian!" Deanna must be beaming inside.

Maybe Egypt won't be so bad for Deanna after all.

I'm another story.

"There's our driver," Sittu says, walking toward a man about Baba's age wearing a blue polo shirt and beige khaki pants.

Without a word, he takes a couple of our suitcases and slides them into his trunk.

"*Shukran*," I say, thrilled I said *thank you* in Arabic so naturally.

"*Afwan*," he replies. That's how you say "you're welcome." I have to remember that.

"This is Salam," Sittu says.

"Your name means *peace*," I say.

Sittu peers at me over her sunglasses. "Very good."

I feel like I just answered the $100,000 question on *Are You Smarter Than a 5th Grader?*

"Welcome to Misr," Salam says in an accent a lot heavier than Sittu's. He starts loading the rest of our bags into the trunk.

"Misr?" Deanna looks at me.

"That's the real name for Egypt," I explain.

Sittu nods.

"Why don't we say Misr too?"

"Too hard to pronounce, I guess."

"Misr," Deanna says. "That's not so hard."

"Americans can be lazy." Sittu lifts her cheeks like she's trying to smile, but she looks more like she's snarling at me.

Is she calling me lazy? I want to tell her Americans work all the time, but I don't want to be rude.

Salam holds the passenger door of the backseat open for us. Sittu insists Deanna and I each take a window seat while she sits in the middle. I feel around for my seat belt, but there doesn't seem to be one.

"Are you missing something?" Salam asks.

"No, nothing," I say.

Salam closes the door. He walks around to the driver's side and gets in. He takes a drag off a cigarette burning in an ashtray on the dashboard.

"Salam," Sittu says, pointing at the ashtray.

"Sorry," he says in English, and flicks his cigarette out the window.

"I don't mind if he smokes," I say.

"I do," Sittu says.

And we're off.

I start to rub my arms. It's colder than I ever imagined it would be. Baba said January is one of the cold months in Egypt, but I thought he meant sweater-weather cold. This feels like winter-jacket cold.

"Salam." Sittu taps the back of his seat. "Please put on some heat."

"Madam?" He looks at us through his rearview mirror.

"My granddaughter seems to be cold."

"I'm fine." I stop rubbing my arms. I don't want to cause trouble. Salam turns on the air, and it smells like something died.

"Awful, Salam." Sittu holds her nose. "Just awful."

"Excuse me, Salam"—Deanna leans into the front seat—"but do you have the vent open or closed?"

Salam plays with a button on his climate control panel, and instantly, the air smells much better. "*Shukran*," he says.

"Don't mention it," Deanna says.

"She's a smart one," Sittu says to me. I smile, but I have to admit there's a part of me that wishes I were the smart one.

Sittu leans over Deanna and points out her window to a large steel gate. "That's Kiddie Land."

I bend my head, and I can see the lights of a Ferris wheel in the background. "Is it a place for little kids?"

"It has stuff for older kids too. The Rainforest Cafe is there," Sittu says.

"I love the Rainforest Cafe," Deanna says. "I've been to two of them in the States."

"I've always wanted to go there," I say.

"We shall go then," Sittu says.

"Really?"

"Why so surprised?"

"I'm not surprised." I'm shocked. Maybe Sittu is just acting nice in front of Salam, and when we get back to her place, she'll be all lock-us-up-and-throw-away-the-key.

"Your eyes are the size of dinner plates," Sittu says.

"See, I told you," Deanna says.

"Told her what?" Sittu asks, turning to Deanna.

"She just thought—"

"Nothing," I say through gritted teeth.

"If it's nothing"—Sittu turns her head to me—"then it has to be something."

Great. Now she's correcting my English too.

"Well," I say. "I just thought—well, Baba said…"

"That I ruled with an iron fist?"

"Actually, a metal fist."

"Your baba always did have trouble with American idioms."

"Did you live in the States? Your English is awesome," Deanna says.

"When I was a child, the British still occupied Egypt. My father, Mariam's great-*giddu*, made us all learn how to speak 'the language of the enemy,' as he called it. This way, they can't put you down to your face."

"But how do you know American?" Deanna says.

"American?" Sittu asks. "Is this a new language?"

"I mean you say things like an American…with an English accent."

"Satellite." Sittu smiles. "I love those American sitcoms."

"You have a television?" I say.

"Again, the dinner-plate eyes. What did Baba say about me now?"

"That you thought television destroyed the brain."

"The young brain. But at my age, I say there's not too much damage left to be done. Salam, some music."

Salam doesn't respond. He's looking down at his phone.

"Salam?!" She taps him on the back. "What did I tell you about texting while you drive?"

"Is that an iPhone?" Deanna bends her head into the front seat. "I really want one, but my mom doesn't want to change phone companies."

"Sorry, madam. But I was just looking at my Twitter feed. My cousin says there is a call for demonstrations—"

"Like what's happening in Tunisia?" Deanna slides forward even more. "That would be so cool."

"What's happening in Tunisia?" I ask, regretting the words as soon as they leave my mouth.

"You don't know what's happening in Tunisia?" Sittu sounds as if I'd just told her I didn't know who the president of the United States was.

"My parents don't watch the news," I tell her.

"Because your parents choose to be ignorant about the world, does that mean you have to be ignorant too?"

I don't know how to answer this, so I just look out my window.

Sittu makes the same sucking sound with her tongue and teeth that Baba makes when he's disappointed in me. Until the other night at the jail, I hadn't heard that sound in a very long time. "There's a revolution happening in Tunisia, Mariam. People have taken to the streets. They have had enough of the corruption."

"A lot of people were killed," Deanna adds, turning to us.

"Is that going to happen here?" I ask, trying to hide the panic in my voice. What were my parents thinking? Sending me to Cairo when people are dying in Tunisia? Actually, I have no idea where Tunisia is or how close it is to Egypt. I don't dare ask.

"Salam, please," Sittu says.

"Music, of course," Salam replies.

"Is that a cassette player?" Deanna leans forward, pointing to a slot in the dashboard. "How old is this car?"

"If something works, why replace it?" Sittu says.

Salam pops a cassette into the player.

"Classic," Sittu says. "My favorite singer in the whole world."

"Great sound," I say, hoping to score some points. "Who is it?"

"Umm Kulthum," Sittu says. "She died in the seventies. I sent you some of her music. Didn't you listen to it?"

"Oh, of course," I say. "I just didn't recognize—"

"How could you not recognize Umm Kulthum? No one sounds like her."

"The cassette is of poor quality," Salam interjects.

"Yes, this isn't a very good copy," Sittu says.

Salam and I make eye contact in the rearview mirror. He nods as if he understands I am thanking him for saving my butt. I never listened to any of the music Sittu sent me for more than a few seconds. Once I heard the Arabic, I turned it off. Not to mention the music was on cassettes and we no longer have a cassette player.

"She's no Lady Gaga, but she has a great voice," Deanna says.

"Lady Gaga? This is her name?"

"She's popular," Deanna says.

"You like her?" Sittu asks.

"Very much," Deanna says. "She's awesome."

"Maybe I'll like her too, then. You seem like a girl of good taste."

"*Shukran*," Deanna says, bringing a huge smile to Sittu's face.

We're barely moving now because of heavy traffic. Under her breath, Sittu says, "This is a country of crazy drivers."

I really can't make out any rules or lanes, and the traffic lights are pretty much ignored. Still, somehow, no one is crashing into anyone else. It's as if everyone knows what the other driver is going to do next. I wish I had those instincts. I look over at Deanna, who's fighting sleep. Every few minutes, her head falls back; then she jerks awake and holds her eyes open very wide.

Suddenly, Salam hits the brakes. Deanna manages to grab the back of Sittu's blouse, stopping her from flying into the front seat and banging her head against the dashboard.

A dirty-faced boy, maybe eight or nine years old, with a soccer ball in his hand stares back at us through the windshield. He doesn't look freaked out, as I would be if a car almost hit me. Like coming this close to dying happens all the time.

Salam rolls down his window, and the stink makes Deanna and me cough.

"The window, please," Sittu says, covering her nose and mouth. "There's so much corruption they won't spend the money to take the garbage away."

Salam rolls his window halfway up, then yells at the boy in Arabic. I'm assuming he says something like, "Are you crazy? Watch out!" Then Salam rolls the window up the rest of the way.

The boy just looks away, kicking his ball to another boy, who is wearing dollar-store flip-flops that look like they are at least two sizes too big.

"These kids have nowhere to play. Maybe if the military gave up some of its country club space… We all know the garbage is always cleaned from there," Sittu says. Turning to Deanna, she continues, "*Shukran.* You saved me from a very ugly lump on my forehead."

How does Deanna do it? Even half-asleep, she makes all the right moves.

We're all quiet for a long while after. From the corner of my eye, I catch Sittu smiling at Deanna. Maybe Sittu's not mean; maybe she just doesn't like me.

chapter EIGHT

We pull up in front of Sittu's apartment building, and Salam unloads our luggage from the trunk. Sittu and Salam talk in Arabic for a few minutes. They talk like someone has died, but then, anyone speaking Arabic sounds ultraserious to me. He nods at her and offers to take our bags upstairs, but Sittu tells him to get home to his family.

"Nice meeting you," Deanna and I say.

"The pleasure is mine." Salam puts his hand to his heart the way Ahmed did at the airport.

I press the elevator button in the lobby.

"We take the stairs," Sittu says.

"Is it broken?" Deanna asks.

"The landlord charges you more if you want to use the elevator. It's not a lot of money, but it's the principle of the thing."

"That's crazy to have to pay to use an elevator," I say.

"Not when the rents on these apartments are controlled," Sittu says. "The rent's so low the landlord tries to squeeze money out of his tenants in other ways." Sittu shakes her head. "At least this landlord isn't stupid. Some build on extra floors without making sure the structure can handle the weight, and entire buildings have collapsed as a result. Too many people have died this way."

"Still, you won't pay the extra money for the elevator?" I ask.

Sittu gives me the same look Baba gives me when I've asked a question he feels he's already answered.

"*Yalla*," Sittu says.

"*Yalla*," Deanna and I say, and we follow Sittu up five very long flights of stairs.

Deanna and I are breathing heavily when we get to Sittu's door. Sittu's breathing like she just got out of a long, hot bath. There's nothing old about this woman.

"America makes you soft!" Sittu slaps both Deanna and me on our butts.

"*Ahlan wa sahlan*." She opens the door, and I'm hit in the face with cold air.

"It's cold in here," Sittu says. "Did I leave the balcony open?" She walks over to the balcony and pulls the doors shut.

"I never think of Egypt as being cold," I say.

"Well, it seems like Americans don't think about Egypt much, except for pyramids, Nile cruises, and our relations with Israel."

I turn my face away from her. I don't want her to see that her comment hurts my feelings. Yes, I'm American, but she talks as if I'm a know-nothing American.

"There's a space heater in your room if you need it at night. As you can see, it can get chilly this time of year, and these buildings are built to keep things cool."

"*Shukran*," Deanna and I say.

"You're welcome," Sittu says. "Leave your bags here, and we will have the tour."

We follow Sittu through her long entranceway and dining room. Photos of me cover the walls. I see a lot of "first" photos: the first time I was on a swing, first day of kindergarten, and every other first day of school until high school, when I told Baba if he didn't put the camera away, I wasn't getting out of his car. Posing for my dad like I was a kindergartener, with the entire school population there as witnesses, would have sealed my fate as the freshman freak. That's when I still had hope that I could reinvent myself. That was before I realized a new school building didn't mean a new school population. At least now, as a junior, I no longer hold the title of Mayflower High's Number One Weirdo. Thanks to Deanna moving to town, I'm now weirdo number two, though I'm sure once word gets out that it was my parents who sent us to Cairo for the rest of the semester, I will be back in first place.

"Hey, is that you?" Deanna points to a black-and-white photo of a young Sittu smiling at a very handsome man in a suit. The man is smiling back at her like she's the most beautiful woman in the world.

"Yes, that was me before the snow settled." Sittu touches her white hair.

"Is that your husband? He's hot," Deanna says.

"Deanna!" Calling my grandfather hot—*what is she thinking?*

"I didn't mean any disrespect."

"That's quite all right," Sittu says, looking at his picture. "He was hot. Very hot." Sittu kisses her middle and index finger and places them over my grandfather's face.

"Mar, is this you with your grandfather?" Deanna looks sideways at me, questioningly.

Sittu smiles. "That's Mariam and her *giddu*."

"That ice cream cone is bigger than I am."

"Your *giddu* loved to take you for ice cream. He always bought you three scoops, knowing he'd have to finish it for you."

I smile like I remember, but I don't. Not until this moment do I realize that we don't have any photos, anywhere, of my grandfather. And the only picture in our apartment of Sittu is of her holding Baba when he was an infant. Now I wonder if it was my grandfather who took that picture.

Sittu puts her hand on my shoulder. "He loved you very much."

It's nice to hear this. I want to ask her what happened between my dad and his father, why Baba never talks about him. It's like Baba doesn't want me to remember my grandfather at all.

"Come on, let me show you your room." Sittu drops her hand from my shoulder and walks out of the living room. When we get to the hugest bedroom I've ever seen—bigger than my living room and kitchen put together—Sittu says, "This is your room. I hope you don't mind sharing."

"Of course not," I say. The last thing I want is to be alone in this place.

"This is great," Deanna says, bouncing on one of the two twin beds. "You have a beautiful home."

"It's more beautiful now you are both here."

"Thank you," Deanna and I say in unison.

"You don't need to thank family," Sittu says.

"Was this Baba's?" I ask, sitting down at a huge wooden desk and touching the surface around the computer. Baba talks about his desk all the time. Every time he sees me doing homework anywhere but at mine, he says, "When I was a child, I did all of my homework at my desk. There was no doing homework at the dining room table. My mother wouldn't have it any other way." When he talks like this, I picture him chained to the leg of his desk. I look down. No chains.

"This was his room." Sittu picks up a framed photo of a class of children in school uniforms. "This is your *baba* right here." She points to a small boy with big ears, sitting in the first row.

"Can I see?" Deanna looks over my shoulder.

"That's him." I tap the child Sittu just pointed to.

"He's so cute," Deanna says.

"Yes, but those ears!" Sittu laughs and kisses the photo before putting it back down. I like her laugh.

"These look like Catholic school uniforms," Deanna says.

"Lycée Français was a Catholic school."

"Catholic? Really?" Deanna says.

"Yes. Muslims often go to Catholic schools here, especially when they are of such quality." Sittu sounds a lot like Baba. Baba is only a snob when it comes to education. "You've had a long journey, so rest a bit, and then we'll have you both call home."

"My mom says I need to buy a cell here because mine won't work," Deanna says.

"Cell?" Sittu asks.

"Mobile," I say, which is what Baba calls it.

"We can get that at the mall."

"The mall?! There's a mall?" I'm more excited than if she'd handed us a box of puppies.

"We have a few. Rest now. *Ahlan*. Welcome." Sittu closes the bedroom door behind her.

I jingle the knob to see if she's locked us in, but the door opens and Sittu is standing there.

"Looking for your suitcase?" she says, walking back into the bedroom, rolling all three of our suitcases behind her.

"Thank you—" I say.

"—so much," Deanna finishes.

"Rest now." Sittu closes the door again. I don't trust that she's really gone until I hear her walk away.

"Dibs on this one." Deanna lifts her suitcases onto the bed near the portable closet.

"Deanna, there's no lock on this door," I say, staring at the knob.

"So what?"

"My father told me when he was a kid, his mother would lock him in his room until dinner."

"Yeah, and my mother walked ten miles to school," Deanna says. "Once, she even told me she had to walk through a blizzard. Blizzard! She grew up in Southern California. All parents make up stuff about their childhood so we can see how lucky we have it compared to them. It's their way of shutting us up." Deanna pulls me away from the door. "Your grandmother is really cool, so stop worrying so much. Give her a chance."

"Okay," I say, but I'm not fully convinced.

"Hey, you think I could check email?" Deanna taps Sittu's keyboard.

"Don't touch her computer."

"Hey, Sittu has a Facebook page!"

"You're kidding me," I say, peering over Deanna's shoulder. "Even my grandmother has a Facebook page."

"Your parents said you could have one when you turn sixteen, and that's only a few days away."

I almost forgot about my birthday.

"Too bad her page is in Arabic." Deanna goes back to her suitcase.

"You're going to unpack already?"

"Wrinkles, baby. Wrinkles. If you don't want to iron clothes all the time, you should unpack too." Deanna opens her suitcase. Her clothes have been folded to perfection. She pulls out a light green T-shirt and turns to the portable closet. "This armoire is outrageous." Deanna pulls on the glass handle.

"Armoire. Is that French for *closet*?"

"I guess. Yuck, it smells like your closet at home."

"Mothballs," I say.

"There're only a few hangers," Deanna says, grabbing one and slipping it through her green tee, which she hangs toward the far right of closet. "Hey, look at what's back here."

"Towels?" I say, eyeing the five or so on the one shelf.

"No, this. Isn't it beautiful?" Deanna pulls a bright blue dress from the far end of the rod. She takes it off its hanger. "Look at the gold trim on the neckline and the hem. Feel the material."

I touch the sleeve. "It's soft."

"It's silk. I have to try it on." Deanna pulls off her shirt.

"We should ask Sittu first."

"If she didn't mean for us to try it on, why would she leave it hanging here?" Deanna slides off her jeans. "Help me get this over my head."

I help her put the dress on. Deanna looks at herself in the full-length mirror inside the closet door. "Too bad, the sleeves are too short. It's way too tight around the chest too." Deanna slowly pulls the dress up over her head and tosses it at me. "You try it on."

"No, thanks." I let it fall to the floor.

"I know it'll look hot on you."

"I'm just not so into that look."

"What look?"

"Forget it. I need to unpack. You're right about wrinkles, and there's probably no iron." I roll my suitcase to my bed and lift it up. I feel Deanna staring at me as she puts her clothes back on, but maybe this one time, just this one time, she'll let it go.

"So that's it," she says, walking over to me until she's right up in my face. She's not going to let it go.

"What are you talking about?" I try to open my suitcase, but Deanna pushes me to the side and sits on it.

"What are you doing?"

"What's wrong with you? This dress is beautiful."

I stare at her like that's going to make her move. No way do I want to talk about this with her. It's the same reason I hated the way she did my makeup for the party. I don't want to look like I'm Egyptian. I don't want to walk like one or talk like one or be one. I just want to be what I am: American. Of course, I can't tell her this. Not Miss Cleopatra Wannabe.

"Deanna, get off of my suitcase, please."

"Not until you talk to me."

"Get off." I try to push her this time, but she's holding on tight. She won't budge.

"I will get off as soon as you talk to me," she says.

"*Get off!*" This time I push her so hard that she not only gets off the suitcase, but falls onto the floor and bangs her head against the leg of Baba's desk.

"Oh my God." I drop to her side. "Are you okay? That had to hurt. Deanna?" Her eyes are closed. "Deanna?" I nudge her shoulder. She's not moving. "Oh. Oh my God. Sittu!" I scream.

Deanna sits up and covers my mouth. "Shut up," she says. She waits, looking toward the door. "Thank God Sittu didn't hear you. What's the matter with you?" She pushes me away and stands up, heading back to her side of the room.

"What's the matter with me?" I ask. "You scared me half to death."

"Well, you deserved it." She rubs the side of her head.

"I'm so sorry. Do you want me to get you some ice?"

"It'll be fine. It sounded worse than it is. Hard head." She knocks on her forehead. She takes out a pair of jeans and hangs them on a hanger. She then hangs a T-shirt, another pair of jeans, and her denim skirt.

"You're not going to say anything about this?"

"It's obvious you don't want to talk about it."

I sit on the bed next to her suitcase. "I just don't think you'll understand."

She puts another shirt on a hanger. "No, of course I don't understand what it's like to hate who you are."

I don't know what to say to her, so I wait for her to say something else, to say something to make it all okay again, like she always does. But not this time. She turns toward the closet. I know this time it's up to me to make it right, but I don't know how.

When Deanna looks at me again, I can see she's working hard not to cry. And still, I don't say anything. Deanna shakes her head at me the same way Sittu does and walks out.

I sit there, wanting so much to go home, but at the same time not wanting to go home. I don't want to be around my parents who hide from everything, even my grandfather.

Deanna is my best friend—my only friend—and I couldn't even manage to tell her how I feel. Why am I so lame? I shove my suitcase off the bed and drop facedown onto the pillow, then bounce right up again. I can't. I can't cry anymore. I get up and pick up the blue dress from the floor. I take off my T-shirt and jeans, and look in the mirror. Compared to Deanna, I'm like a walking ironing board. I pull the dress over my head. It slips right on. There's nothing to get in the way. It feels like it actually fits though.

I check the mirror, and for the first time in my life, my nose looks good. Just right. Can a dress actually make your nose look smaller?

I walk to the door. I hope Deanna was right about Sittu wanting us to wear this dress.

chapter NINE

D eanna?" I call out. "Sittu?"

They're not in the living room or the dining room. They wouldn't have left the apartment without me, would they? I push open the kitchen door, but it stops with a thud. "Oh my God—Deanna?! Sittu? Are you okay?"

"My head is pretty hard," a very deep voice says with a British accent. "But you hit me in the backside."

The kitchen door opens all the way.

I look up into the darkest, greenest eyes I've ever seen. Eyes even greener than my mother's.

"I'm so sorry about the door."

"It's an occupational hazard."

Who is this guy in Sittu's kitchen? Her cook?

"What are you doing here?"

"I come to the assistance of beautiful women," he says. From him, this cheesy line sounds like poetry. It's probably the accent. Baba wasn't talking to me very much before I left, but he did make sure to warn me about guys who would try to sweet-talk Deanna and me just because we're American.

When I just stand there, looking suspicious, he says, "I help your grandmother with errands. I was just putting away some fruit."

I peek around his tall, muscular body. The kitchen counter really is covered with fruit. "Mangos? Are those mangos?"

"They don't have mangos in America?"

"My father won't buy them at home. He says the mango is the only thing America doesn't do as well as Egypt."

"I'm sure there are a few other things we do better here too." He pulls a knife from a drawer like he's been in this kitchen before and cuts right into the center of the plumpest mango on the counter. "But our mangos are pretty good." He hands me a slice.

I put it in my mouth. "I've never tasted anything so sweet. It's amazing!"

"Yes, yes, it is." He hands me another slice.

"Wow," I say, biting into the second piece. And this time when I look into his green eyes, I forget all about Baba's warning. All I want is to spend the afternoon eating mangos with him.

"You still here?" Sittu pushes the kitchen door open. He pulls me out of the way before I get hit in the back of the head.

"Thanks," I say.

"I see you've met my granddaughter," Sittu says.

"Well, not formally." He extends his hand. "Hassan."

I shake his hand. "Mariam."

"My pleasure," he says.

I can feel my neck turning red.

Sittu says, "Hassan lived in England, but he's in his first year of university here now. His grandfather owns this building. Watch him. He loves pretty girls."

"You're ruining my reputation." Hassan smiles, and he's even more beautiful.

"Ruining? I'm giving you one. So thank me."

Sittu is flirting with him!

"Oh, and before I forget, please tell your grandfather he needs to fix—" Sittu looks me up and down.

"Mariam, what is that you're wearing?" She sounds upset—very upset.

"I'm so sorry," I say. "I'll change out of it."

"Where did you find that?" She touches the sleeve of the dress.

"In the closet in our room."

"I thought I had taken everything out of that closet," she says, touching my sleeve again. Her voice gets softer. "That's the last dress my *sittu* made for me. The only thing she had left to do was the trim on the right sleeve."

"Wow, this dress is from when you were…"

"Yes, about the same age you are now—a very, very long time ago."

"Not that long." Hassan smiles. "It looks like new."

"I never wore it—I think maybe because it was unfinished and it reminded me too much of her."

"I'm sorry. I'll go change," I say again.

"Wait," she says. "Turn around." She twirls her finger, and I slowly turn.

I feel Hassan staring at me, and my neck feels like it's on fire. I can't tell whether it's a wow-I-think-she's-pretty stare or a wow-she-looks-awful-in-that-thing stare. All I know is that I want to run to my room and hide under the covers.

Sittu sighs as she says something in Arabic.

"Yes," Hassan agrees. "She looks so much like you."

Hassan thinks I look like Sittu? Sittu's beautiful. Okay, now I know I can't trust this guy. It's not like I expect him to say, "She's a dog" even if that's what he thinks, but to say that I look like Sittu? That's an exaggeration.

Hassan avoids my gaze. Is he pretending now to be shy? I'm pretty sure this guy's a big fake.

"Mariam?" Deanna calls out. This time, the kitchen door does hit me in the back. "I'm sorry," Deanna says as she slips around the door to see who she hit.

Hassan is no longer staring at me. He's staring at Deanna. And she's staring at him. They're staring at each other. And it's not the way two people stare when they're thinking, "Who's that?" It's the way two people stare when they're thinking, "Whoever that is, I'm in love."

"See, Deanna? I'm wearing the dress," I say, hoping to divert her attention from Hassan—and get her to forgive me for what happened earlier.

"That's great," Deanna says, but her eyes are still fixed on Hassan.

"Well, I'm going to change now," I say.

"Are you okay?" Deanna asks, finally remembering that she hit me with the door.

"Fine. Just fine."

"Okay, *habibti*—" Sittu starts.

"*Habibti?*" I repeat. I can't believe how much she sounds like Baba when she says that.

"You don't know what that means either?" Sittu asks.

"No, of course I do. *My love*," I say, and I see Hassan in the corner of my eye, staring at Deanna. Now I wish I'd never tried his mango slices.

The phone rings. "Maybe it's your father," Sittu says, and heads off to answer it.

"Deanna, you coming?" I ask, trying to get her away from Mr. Phony.

"Are those mangos?" she asks Hassan. Did she even hear me?

"Would you like to try one?" Hassan smiles at her.

"Mariam!" Sittu shouts.

I leave the kitchen before Deanna can answer, and walk into the dining room, where Sittu's talking on a phone that looks older than I am. "Your *baba*," she says, handing me the phone.

"Baba?!"

"No, sweetie, it's Mom."

"Where's Baba?"

"He was running late for work," she says, "but he said to tell you he loves you very much. Did you have a good flight?"

"It was okay," I tell her. I try not to sound too disappointed that Baba's not on the line. I feel bad about the way we left things between us. Hearing his voice would have made everything feel right again.

"You okay?" Mom asks. "I was worried about you."

"Fine," I say. "I'm just a little jet-lagged."

"Well, I won't keep you, then. Deanna okay?"

I look at the kitchen door. I hope so. "She's fine."

"Her mom called earlier, but there was no answer. She sounded a little worried when I talked with her."

"Customs took a long time," I say. "Mom, I'm pretty tired."

"Well, I love you."

"Love you too." I hang up the phone, and I look up at the apple-shaped clock on the wall. It's 1 p.m.

Sittu's sitting at the dining room table, reading a newspaper. She looks so engrossed I don't want to disturb her.

"Yes?" she asks, taking her reading glasses off and looking up at me.

"I didn't say anything," I say.

"You don't want to ask me something, then?"

"Well, I just wanted to know what the time difference is between here and New York."

"Let's see." She looks up at the apple. "Wintertime, so eight hours."

"So it's only five in the morning there?" So Baba still doesn't want to talk to me. I look over at Sittu. I guess calling Sittu a horrible woman was out of line. I probably also shouldn't have called Egypt a backward country, even if it's true.

Sittu stands up, and without saying a word, she touches the sleeve of the dress.

"The one flaw—" Sittu smiles. "I think it makes the dress more beautiful. But if you want me to have it fixed before you wear it again…"

"You want me to wear it?"

"I have no use for it anymore," she says.

I touch the unfinished sleeve. It would be nice to have it fixed; then, it would be perfect. Instead I say, "It's fine the way it is." I don't know why she thinks a flaw makes the dress look better, but I don't want to make her feel like I don't appreciate it. Besides, I can always get it fixed back home.

*   *   *

The next morning, after we get dressed, Deanna logs in to Facebook.

"I can't believe it!" she squeals.

"What? What is it?" I ask, looking over her shoulder.

"I have a friend request from Hassan!"

"Oh, great." This time, the sarcasm comes through loud and clear.

"What's up with you?" she asks, turning around to face me.

"Nothing's up with me. I'll meet you outside."

"Hey." She stands up and looks me dead in the eye. "I thought best friends don't keep secrets."

"It's just…" I'm about to tell her what I think of Hassan, but I can see from the look in her eyes that she doesn't want to hear it, so I say, "I don't think Sittu likes me very much."

"You're crazy! You're her granddaughter—"

"Girls"—Sittu knocks on the door—"almost ready?" She steps into our room.

"Are we going somewhere?" I ask.

"You sound surprised," Sittu says. "What did you think? That I'd keep you locked up in this apartment all day?"

I don't say that's exactly what I thought.

"The question to be answered is what would you like to see?"

"The mall." I look at Deanna and smile. I can't think of anything that would be more fun for us to do than shop.

"If that's what you want to do." Deanna sounds disappointed.

"You don't want to go to the mall?" Sittu asks.

Of course she wants to go the mall. What could be better than that? It's our favorite place to hang out back home.

"It would be nice to do something more unique to Egypt," Deanna says.

"You have something in mind?" Sittu asks. All I can think about is Deanna and her guidebooks. *Please don't say you want to do some stupid tourist thing.*

"I'd love to see the pyramids," Deanna says.

No! I want to scream. Not the stupid pyramids. Every time Egypt is taught in school, all teachers ever focus on is ancient Egypt, and it never fails, they always ask, "Mariam, would you tell the class what the pyramids are like?" Since my parents are Egyptian, I must be an authority on the pyramids. Well, I've never seen the stupid pyramids, and the last thing I want to do is see them today.

"Is that okay with you, Mariam?" Sittu asks.

"Excuse me?"

"The pyramids. Is it okay that we go to see them today and maybe the mall tomorrow?"

Deanna has her begging eyes on me.

What can I say? "No, it's not okay to go see one of your country's national treasures. I'd rather shop for jeans"?

"Sure," I say. "Let's go to the pyramids."

"Before we go, do you mind if I use the computer for one minute?" Sittu says.

"Of course not." Deanna pulls out the chair for her.

Sittu types something, and I see she's on Facebook, but it's not her page. Still, it's in Arabic, so I can't read what it says.

"Hey, Mar, check this out." Deanna's looking at herself in the mirror.

What, does she want me to see how great her reflection looks? "Look, my T-shirt. See what it says?"

"P!NK. You got it at the concert last October."

"I know it says P!NK, but it's not backward. Words in mirrors always read backward."

"That's a true mirror," Sittu says without looking up from the computer.

"A what?" Deanna and I say at the same time.

"The mirror is designed to show you the way others see you. Your father sent it to me a few years ago. I think he thought I would get a kick out of it. But when you live an hour from the pyramids, it's hard to be impressed by inventions."

Deanna and I study our reflections. "Hey, Mar, see this freckle." Deanna points to her cheek. "It's on this side."

"It's always on that side," I say.

"But not when I look in the mirror. I always see it on the other side. This is so cool," Deanna says. "I can't believe I can see myself the way others see me."

That's the last thing I'd ever want. I turn back to Sittu. She's typing fast, like she's only got one minute before the computer explodes.

"Mariam. Earth to Mariam." Deanna waves her hand in my face.

"Huh?" I ask, looking back at our reflections. "What?"

"I said, are you sure this shirt looks good with these jeans?"

"Fine," I say.

"*Fine?*" She opens the closet.

"No, I mean great. You look great."

"Sure?"

"Positive." Deanna could wear clown pants and a shirt stained with pizza sauce and she'd still look amazing.

"You look great too," she adds.

"Thanks," I say, but it doesn't really matter what I look like. When Deanna's around, all eyes are on Deanna.

"Girls, meet me downstairs. I won't be too long." Sittu's still typing frantically.

I want to ask her if everything's okay, but I never seem to say or ask the right thing.

I'm hoping Deanna will ask Sittu what's so urgent, but she just says "*Yalla*" and heads for the hallway.

chapter
TEN

We wait for Sittu in front of her building. She lives in the suburbs of Cairo, but there are no houses I can see, only apartment buildings. It looks more like a city block, but it's even quieter than my boring street back home. I thought Cairo would be jam-packed, but the only other people around are a woman hanging clothes on a third-floor balcony and two older men sitting in chairs in front of what looks like a barber shop.

"There aren't many people out," I say.

"It's still early," Sittu says, coming up behind us. "It's only eight in the morning."

"In New York, that's rush hour," Deanna says.

"Did you get all your work done?" I say.

"Work?" Sittu says. "I've been retired for a long while."

"I mean on the computer. You looked the way Baba does when he's meeting a deadline for his job."

"Yes, your father was always very serious when it came to his studies. I was just keeping up with the news."

"I hope it was good news," I say.

"*Insh'allah*, it will be," Sittu says.

"*Alhamdulillah!*" Deanna shouts.

Sittu looks at Deanna. "You know *alhamdulillah*?" She smiles.

"Mariam." Deanna turns to me. "Baba taught us, remember?"

Sittu and Deanna stare at me for an answer, but I can't remember. Besides, what's this "Baba taught us" business? What happened to "your *baba*" or "your father" or "your dad"? First, Deanna takes Sittu, and now she wants Baba too?

Sittu turns toward Deanna. "So, Deanna?"

"It means 'praise to God,' but it's what people say when they are thankful for something."

"*Alhamdulillah!*" Sittu hugs Deanna. "Mariam, you should have Deanna give you a few lessons in Arabic." Sittu smiles when she says this, but I'm starting to wonder if she'd rather have Deanna than me as her granddaughter.

"Me? Teach Mariam? She's, like, the smartest kid in school," Deanna says. It's nice that she's trying to make me look like less of an idiot in front of Sittu, but if she'd stop showing off, she wouldn't need to.

"Our ride should be here shortly," Sittu says.

"Salam?" Deanna asks.

"He's off today."

"But Salam is your regular driver?" Deanna asks.

"Well, I let Salam use my car in exchange for driving me places. My eyesight is not what it used to be. I don't feel so comfortable driving anymore."

"You used to drive?" I ask.

"This is shocking to you?"

"No, I just thought women couldn't drive in the Middle East."

"That's in Saudi Arabia," Deanna says.

"Deanna, you can't blame Mariam for what she hasn't been taught," Sittu says. "There is nothing Islamic about forbidding women to drive or hiding them from the world. But we have our struggles here too, like you do in the States." She looks at me when she says this. "In this world, there's a lot of repression in the name of Islam or Christianity or Judaism. Patriarchy will do all in its power to oppress women."

"Sittu, you sound like a feminist," Deanna laughs.

"Is that what I sound like?" She seems offended.

"Sittu's Muslim, Deanna," I say. "She can't be a feminist."

"I didn't mean to show any disrespect," Deanna apologizes.

"My dear"—Sittu takes Deanna's hand in hers—"you haven't offended me at all, but, Mariam…"

But, Mariam? Is she kidding me? What did I say now?

"Feminism and Islam are not like oil and water; they are like the trees and the air." She gestures toward the sky. "One can't exist without the other. Islam is about equality and justice, so I can't see how you can be a good Muslim without being a feminist." She laughs a little. "Mariam, do you know you come from a long line of radical feminists?" Sittu looks at Deanna and smiles. "Have you ever heard of Huda Shaarawi?"

Deanna and I both shake our heads.

"Back in the twenties—that was even before I was born"— Sittu smiles. I don't smile back. It doesn't seem as though she is really even talking to me—"Huda Shaarawi was president of the Egyptian Feminist Union, and after she came back from an international meeting in Rome, she took off her veil and threw it into the sea."

"Was that like burning your bra?" Deanna asks.

Sittu laughs, and it's actually nice to hear, even if I'm not the one who made it happen. "In some ways, yes, it was just like that."

"It's just," I say, "that on the news, Muslim women here are always all covered up and…you know, have no rights…"

"I'm curious, Mariam," Sittu says, "what is it about me that is different from these other women whom you see on television?"

"You're independent and confident and strong."

"The woman at the airport who almost got arrested—she was wearing the whole deal," Deanna says, "and she sure had guts."

"Something happened at the airport?" Sittu asks nervously.

Deanna recounts the story.

"Ahmed said it could have been just about anything that got the man taken away," I add.

"Who's Ahmed?" Sittu asks.

"A man we met on the plane."

"So you talk to strange men on planes?"

"No. I mean, yes," I say. "But he helped us through customs."

"Girls, it upsets me so much that all the conversations about Muslim women are always focused on what we wear and don't wear, and here I am guilty of doing the same. What's important is that you understand no one should be forced to wear anything against her will. But don't make the mistake I did"—did Sittu just say she made a mistake?—"and assume you know a person because of how she looks on the outside." Sittu brushes the back of her hand against Deanna's right cheek. "Many great women struggle against oppression of all kinds, some wearing a burka, while others wear jeans and T-shirts."

Now Sittu touches my cheek. "*Habibti*, you're warm. Are you feeling okay?"

"I'm okay."

"Our ride, finally." Sittu drops her hand and points to the street.

I squint at a blue Herbie the Love Bug pulling up in front of the building.

"Oh, I almost forgot." Sittu pulls a pair of sunglasses even cooler than Deanna's out of her monster bag.

"These are for you."

"Really? *Shukran*," I say.

"I told you—no thanking family." Sittu smiles at me—just me. It makes me almost look forward to seeing the pyramids and maybe even spending time with Sittu.

"Mariam." Deanna pinches my elbow. "Do you see who it is?" she whispers through her teeth.

I put on the sunglasses so I can get a better look at our driver, then I take them off to make sure it's not some mirage. There is Hassan.

chapter ELEVEN

S*abah al-khair!*" Hassan calls to us from the street. He sounds so happy. His voice is sweet. We walk over to him.

"Madam," he says to Sittu, "did you see on Facebook? The call for people to gather?"

"Not today, Hassan."

"Call? Gather?" I ask. "For what?"

"Tunisia has inspired the nation," Hassan answers. "People are calling for all to protest the repression and poverty and corrupt—"

"Not now." Sittu raises her voice. "Tomorrow we fight for Egypt, but today we celebrate my granddaughters' trip to their homeland." Sittu puts her arms around Deanna and me, squeezing us close to her.

"Fight?" I ask.

"Well, a figure of speech," Sittu says. "*Yalla*, Hassan, the door."

"Of course, madam. Please excuse me," Hassan says. "My ladies, your chariot awaits." He opens the back passenger door of his car.

"Out of any other mouth, that would've sounded dorky," Deanna whispers. "But from his..." She shakes her shoulders. "Shivers right up my spine."

She's got it bad. Sure, he's cute; that one dimple makes him look absolutely adorable. But I don't trust him. Baba was clear we should be careful about guys using us because we're American. I can't believe Deanna is falling so fast. Deanna's supposed to be the smart one when it comes to life stuff.

Sittu whispers back, "I see someone is crushing on someone here."

Deanna's so focused on Hassan I don't think she even heard Sittu. "Sittu? Crushing?" I say.

"I may be old, but I'm not outdated."

"*Sabah al-khair*," Deanna says, bending her head as she gets into the backseat. I bend to get in too, but Sittu pulls me back.

"*Habibti*," she says, "I don't like the front seat unless I'm driving. You sit up front with Hassan."

"Really?" I can't believe I finally get to sit up front. My mom still makes me sit in the back because she thinks it is safer. Deanna sticks her head out the door. "I don't mind sitting up front."

"That's kind of you," Sittu says. "But you can keep me company in back."

"I just know Mariam's parents don't like for her to sit in front," Deanna says.

Wait a second! Best friends aren't supposed to sell you out for the front seat, even if they are crushing on the driver.

"Well, Deanna, I'm in charge here. Mariam, *yalla*."

"Sure," I say, with a long look at Sittu. I wonder what she's up to. Maybe she'd rather sit in the back with Deanna, who knows so much more about everything.

"After you." Hassan opens the door for me.

"*Shukran*," I say.

"*Afwan*," he says as he closes it behind me.

When he gets into the car, the top of his head almost touches the ceiling.

"Ready?" Hassan asks.

"Ready," I say.

"Ready," Sittu says.

Deanna doesn't say anything. But I don't have to be in her head to know exactly what she's thinking. She wishes she were in my seat with nothing but the stick shift between her and Hassan. This is probably the first time in my life anyone has ever wanted to trade places with me. It feels good.

Hassan shifts the car into gear and his hand brushes against my thigh. I understand what Deanna meant when she talked about shivers going up her spine. I wonder if he did that on purpose. I look down at his hand. No. There's no way he would like me over Deanna.

"Do you drive?" He catches me looking at his hand.

"No." I move my leg away.

"I'll teach you how to drive then." Hassan looks into his side mirror and changes lanes.

Deanna leans into the front seat. "I'd love to learn too."

"No driving lessons today." Sittu pulls Deanna back into her seat.

Even with the heat blasting, I can hear Deanna sigh.

"Music okay?" Hassan looks into his rearview mirror.

"Of course," Sittu says.

"Wonderful," Deanna says.

"Mariam?" He looks at me.

"Umm Kulthum?" I say, not in the mood for classic Egyptian.

"You know Umm Kulthum?"

"A little," I say.

"Well, she's wonderful. But do you mind if I play something else?"

"Play whatever you want," I say.

Hassan slides a CD into the player.

"No cassette?"

"Egypt may not be as modern as America, but we have a few of the new inventions." He hits the play button. "The quality isn't so good. A friend made it for me."

"I took tabla lessons for two years, but I couldn't drum as fast as this guy if I took lessons for twenty years. He's incredible," Deanna says.

"It's called a darbuka. The artist's name is Simona Abdallah."

"Simona?! A woman darbuka player?" Sittu pops her head into the front seat again.

"*Wallah*," Hassan says. "She's Palestinian and grew up in Denmark. She lives in San Francisco. Her first solo album is coming out in the fall."

"Amazing," Sittu remarks.

"Madam, you like it?" Hassan turns his head to her.

"A woman professionally playing the darbuka? Wonderful!" Sittu taps the top of his head. "Eyes on the road."

"Why is that so rare?" I ask Hassan.

Hassan shrugs. "The darbuka is usually played by men."

"She's incredible," I say.

"She taught herself when she was fifteen." My age.

"She didn't have it easy, but she didn't give up either," he says. "And guess who her favorite singer is?"

"Umm Kulthum," I say, not sure how I know, but I just do.

"How'd you guess?" He turns to me and smiles. I can feel the back of my neck turn red. At least it's not my face that gets red when I'm embarrassed.

"The road," Sittu reminds him.

Hassan quickly turns his eyes back to the road.

"Nice beat," Deanna says. "But do you have any Amr Diab?"

"You know Amr Diab?" Hassan sounds shocked. He adjusts the rearview mirror, and I catch Deanna shifting to see him in it.

"Of course," Deanna says. "I love all Middle Eastern music."

Hassan takes a different CD from the glove compartment and pops it in. Deanna begins to sing along. Must be Amr Diab.

"You have a wonderful voice," Hassan says. "You know Arabic?"

"*Shway shway.*"

"She is modest," Sittu says, and I can hear the smile in her voice.

"I don't know all the words," Deanna says.

"Teach my heart to love. Live with me in my dreams…"

"Your voice is pretty nice too," Deanna says, flirting, ignoring Baba's warning.

I know if a guy were into me, I wouldn't want him to sing some totally obvious love song. It would be something more subtle, like… Well, I don't know exactly, but I know he would choose something special. A song just for me.

✳   ✳   ✳

It's bad enough that for most of the drive out to Giza, Deanna and Hassan sing like they've been a duet for years, but when Sittu joins in, I want to yell, "Stop the car!" so I can get out and walk. I keep my face turned toward the Egyptian countryside flying by my window, pretending to be fascinated.

Deanna finally stops singing. "Look! The pyramids." She rolls down her window, letting all the hot air out and the cold air in.

"Welcome to the Pyramid of Khufu," Hassan says, pulling into the parking area.

I don't turn from my window. What's the big deal? Three big triangles. So what?

"They're more than four thousand years old," Deanna says with awe. "They're one of the Seven Wonders of the Ancient World, the only one that still exists."

OMG, she's like a guidebook now.

"This is the biggest of all the pyramids in Egypt," Hassan says as we get out of the car.

"There are more than these?"

I give Deanna a look she doesn't notice. Why is she playing dumb? She knows more facts about pyramids than the ancient Egyptians who built the stupid things.

"Almost a hundred," Hassan says.

I walk behind Deanna and Hassan as they exchange pyramid trivia, even more grateful for the sunglasses Sittu gave me—no one can see my eyes rolling.

"So, *habibti*, what do you think?" Sittu locks her arm through mine.

"About what?" I ask, distracted by the banter in front of us.

"The Great Pyramid." Sittu tilts my chin toward the sky.

I have to stop walking and just stare. The pyramids really are the most awesome sight I've ever seen.

Every teacher who ever went to Egypt on vacation always insisted on showing me their pyramid shots. Like they wanted to show the little Egyptian girl they understood her, prove that they had traveled to her homeland. I used to think they could've saved the airfare and walked five blocks from the school if they really wanted to see where I'm from. But now, looking up at this spectacle, I'm completely stunned. I wonder if those teachers just wanted to share their experience with someone they thought would get it, someone who'd seen them, and would know how no photograph or video could do it justice.

"Sittu, I don't remember a lot about Egypt when I was here as a little kid, but I can't believe I would have forgotten this."

"Giddu wanted to take you, but your *baba* never wanted to go. He used to joke if you've seen one pyramid, you've seen them all. And your mother didn't feel comfortable letting you go without your *baba* going."

"You didn't want to go?"

"I had seen these pyramids so many times in my life, on so many school trips, I had no desire to push the issue. Besides, I thought you'd appreciate the experience more when you were older."

"The pyramid's a lot taller than the pictures make it look."

"One hundred and thirty-nine meters, or, as you would say in America, about four hundred and fifty feet," Hassan says, joining our conversation. "It used to be the tallest structure in the world until the French built the Eiffel Tower."

"Actually, the spire of Lincoln Cathedral was built first," I say, surprised at how annoyed I sound.

"Oh, well, I stand corrected."

Deanna and Sittu lift up their sunglasses and look at me.

I'm about to apologize when Hassan says, "I'll be right back. I'm going to get tickets."

"You know, Mar, I've been to DC, and no way is it that tall," Deanna says.

"That's the Lincoln Memorial," I say, still irritated, but at Deanna for defending Hassan.

"Well, it must be nice to know so much," Sittu says.

I look at Sittu and Deanna, then run to catch up with Hassan.

He waits for me to speak.

"Thank—*Shukran*, I mean, for driving us here today. This really is pretty amazing."

"*Afwan*." He nods at me, and it's clear he knows I'm apologizing. That cute dimple, right there in the middle of his chin, makes me think he forgives me. Maybe he's not such a bad guy after all.

chapter TWELVE

We meet Hassan at the base of the pyramid.

"Ready to go inside?" he asks.

"If you don't mind, my darlings," Sittu says, sitting down on one of the pyramid's base stones, "I will wait for you here. I've made this climb more times than I care to count."

"So we have to climb up through that entrance?" I ask, pointing to a hole in the side of the pyramid.

"Yes," Hassan says.

"Is it a long climb?"

"It's a bit steep," Hassan says.

"Oh." I don't like heights.

"Would you mind watching my pack?" Deanna asks, pulling her cell phone from her backpack before handing it over.

"You want to call the mummies?" Sittu asks.

"It has a camera too. This way I can take photos without looking like a nimrod tourist."

"Nimrod?" Sittu laughs. "Noah's great-grandson?"

"If someone calls you a nimrod, they're calling you an idiot," Deanna explains.

"And you, *habibti*?" Sittu turns to me. "You don't want to look like a nimrod either?"

I'm used to it, I think. "I don't like taking pictures."

"Good. Better to live in the moment than to snap at it like a turtle," Sittu says, just as Deanna clicks her phone at Sittu's face.

Deanna shows Sittu the screen. "This is a great picture of you."

"You can make a call and take a photo?" Sittu asks.

"And upload it to the Internet if I actually had a connection here." Deanna's obviously not getting that Sittu's playing with us. Sittu surfs the Internet, but she doesn't know phones have cameras inside them? I don't think so.

"Technology is too crazy for me, but I will be very happy when they make a phone that can cook."

Deanna laughs as she takes her first step up. "Can you believe one of these stones weighs almost two tons?" She grabs one of the huge stones to help her climb up onto the next. "It took over two million of them to make this thing."

"Shall we?" Hassan says.

"You know, I think I'll stay and keep you company, Sittu." I don't even like climbing a stepladder.

"*Yalla*," Deanna calls down to us. She's halfway to the entrance already. Several tourists with cameras banging against their tank tops turn to look at her. She's right: they do look like nimrods.

"You'd better get up there before Deanna cracks the stone with her yelling," Sittu laughs.

"I'm a little tired," I say. "Maybe another time."

"Are you sure?" Hassan asks.

"Very," I say.

"She's going. Stand up and go with Hassan."

"But, Sittu…"

"Stand up," she says.

Even though I don't want to, I follow directions.

She grabs my hand. "You listen to me: never, ever let fear stop you from living life. Trust me," she says. "Every fear you don't face bites your ass in the end." She looks over at Hassan. "Excuse my language."

"No problem," Hassan says.

"Do you understand me?"

"I didn't say I was afraid."

"You're not?"

Before I have a chance to answer, Sittu says, "Hassan, take her up."

Hassan and I climb to where Deanna is waiting. I keep my eyes focused on his cute butt, so I don't think about looking down.

"Hey, you okay?" she asks, and I'm sure she sees I'm trying very hard not to cry.

"What happened?" Deanna looks at Hassan.

"I don't want to do this," I say, tears escaping down my face. Sittu pulls a handkerchief from her pocket and hands it to me, and this brings the tears in full force.

"Why are you crying?" Deanna asks, lifting up my sunglasses.

"Her sittu insists she climb to the top with us," Hassan says.

"You're afraid?" Deanna asks.

I nod.

"Then you don't have to come with us." Deanna puts her arm around my shoulder. "I'll talk to Sittu."

"You have a lot to learn about this culture," Hassan says.

"What's that supposed to mean?" Now I'm surprised by how irritated Deanna sounds.

"My intention wasn't to offend, but Mariam needs to understand her *sittu* acts this way because she loves her."

"Loves me?" I say.

Hassan takes the handkerchief from my hand. "Trust me." He wipes my cheeks. "She loves you."

"Well, maybe she should love me less… *Shukran*," I say, taking back the handkerchief.

"Listen, Mariam," Hassan says, "I know it's hard for you to understand. You may live a world away, but you mean the world to your grandmother."

"I have no idea what you're talking about." I wipe my face.

"Well, I think Hassan is trying to say maybe Sittu's afraid to love you too much because she knows you're going to leave."

"Excuse me, Deanna, but Sittu already loves Mariam 'too much.'"

Deanna and I just look at Hassan.

"I think," he says, taking off my sunglasses and looking me in the eyes, "your *sittu* loves you, but she just may not show it in a way you understand. You see, sometimes we are hardest on the ones who mean the most to us. Our expectations are higher."

I think I understand what he's getting at. It's not all that different from the way Baba and Mom treat me sometimes. They have such high expectations for me that I never feel like I'm living up to them.

"Well, for the record, it's not just an Egyptian thing. My mother's on my case all the time," Deanna says.

"I suppose this may be one of those universal principles." Hassan smiles at Deanna. I can see from the way she looks back at him that all is forgiven.

I blow my nose in Sittu's hankie.

"Are you calling the mummies to life?" Hassan jokes.

I can't help but crack a smile.

"*Yalla*?" Hassan asks.

I look up, and from this angle, the pyramid looks even taller. I've never felt smaller in my life.

"Look, you don't have to do this," Deanna says. "I'm sure she'll understand."

"No, she won't."

"Just breathe." Hassan takes my hand in his like Sittu did. "You can do this. You're Egyptian."

"Egyptians aren't afraid of heights?"

"Well, I thought I'd give it a try." Hassan laughs in a kind of goofy way, then covers his mouth, embarrassed.

"Okay, I'll try." As afraid as I may be of heights, I'd rather jump out of a plane than face an angry Sittu.

"*Yalla*," Deanna says, grabbing my other hand. She and Hassan help me take my first step into the pyramid and what I expect to be darkness, except lighting has been set into the walls above us.

Hassan takes the lead. I'm next. Deanna is "the sweep," as she calls herself. I think she's making sure I don't turn around and run.

"There's a chamber below. Shall we go there first?" Hassan asks.

"Let's go to the very top first," I say.

"Really?" Deanna says.

"Really. Let's get it over with."

"To the top," Hassan says.

"Upward!" Deanna shouts, and the pit of my stomach feels the same way it did when Baba made me ride the Dragon Coaster with him at Rye Playland. As we got to the very top and it was time to fall, and fall fast, I looked down—and promptly threw up on the people in the car in front of us.

"Hold on to the side poles."

"Okay," I tell Hassan, but not before I touch the stone walls on both sides of me. The passageway is narrower than I thought. Hassan has exactly five freckles on the back of his neck, and together, they make the shape of a tiny banana. *Focus on the banana and you will be fine*, I think.

We begin to climb. Before I take my third step, I trip and fall into Hassan.

So much for fruit.

"You okay?" He grabs my hand to help steady me.

"Yeah." I look down at what I tripped over.

"The slats are there for safety, so we don't slide down," Hassan says. I am probably the only one who has ever tripped on the safety devices. I hold on to the poles, wishing I could hold on to Hassan's hand the whole way instead.

"This is harder than climbing to the top of the Statue of Liberty," Deanna says, "but just as hot. It's like there's no air in here."

"No air?! What do you mean?!"

"Calm down. There's plenty of air. I just meant it gets hot in here. It must be so much worse in the summer."

"Someday, I have to climb the Statue of Liberty," Hassan says.

"You must."

"Well, we'll see if I can get a visa."

"You can stay with my mother and me," Deanna offers, crowding me in an effort to get closer to Hassan.

He's already using Deanna to come to the States.

"Please—claustrophobic." I elbow Deanna to get her to move back.

"Sorry."

"That's very kind," Hassan says, "but my brother lives in New Jersey, and he would be very insulted if I didn't stay with him."

His brother? "You have family in the States?"

"My brother and his family live in Paramus. Do you know the place?" He looks over his shoulder at me.

"The Paramus mall," Deanna says, jutting her head over my shoulder. Hassan stops climbing and turns. Their faces are so close, I think they're going to kiss with me stuck between them.

"Why are we stopping?" someone shouts from behind us. The accent sounds French.

"Great mall," Deanna says.

Hassan continues the climb.

"Hassan, why wouldn't you get a visa with your brother already in the U.S?"

"Your government makes it hard for people like me to travel these days."

"People like who?"

"Young Arab men."

"You're Egyptian," I say.

"Well, your country doesn't really see the difference."

"Egypt is in Africa," I say.

"Well, yes, but we are still Arabic-speaking people and mostly Muslim."

"But that doesn't mean you're Arab."

Hassan stops climbing again and turns to me. "You say *Arab* like it's a bad word."

Startled, I stumble and Hassan grabs my arm and pulls me to him.

"Careful," he says.

"I didn't mean to offend." I guess whether it's coming out of some TV reporter's mouth or Karen's mouth back at school, *Arab* always sounded like a dirty word.

"Mariam, please understand, Egyptians are not from the Arabian Peninsula, and our histories and cultures are very different, but when it comes to—"

"WHAT IS THE HOLD UP?" echoes up the staircase.

"Hold your horses!" Deanna snaps.

"Alas, this is not the place for such a discussion."

Hassan picks up the pace. We don't talk, and as I take each step, I think about Hassan and how he seems like a guy who only wants to help.

I start to think I'm glad Sittu made me do this when the ceiling drops so low that I have to bend over. It's so dark that I can barely see Hassan.

"Deanna, I want to go back." I turn to her. "Please. I can't breathe."

"What?"

"It's too hot! I want to go back down. Now!" I reach out, accidentally grabbing Deanna's right tit.

"Ow!"

"You have to get out of my way. Now."

"Mariam, you can't go back now. You've come so far." She won't get out of my way. "You know you'll so regret not finishing this."

"Please! Get out of my way. I want to go back down!" I'm struggling with Deanna, my voice getting louder and louder.

"Let her go back down already, so the rest of us can go up!"

"Take deep breaths," Deanna says, ignoring the voice from behind us.

"Deanna, I'm freaking out. I can't breathe."

"She wants to go back. Please. Let her go," Hassan says from the dark.

"Fine. I'm coming with you," Deanna says. "Excuse me," she says over and over, pushing people to the side.

"It's scarier going down." My eyes are burning and I'm gasping for air.

"Hold my hand," Deanna says, "and stop panting. You'll pass out."

I take a deep breath, grab Deanna's hand tightly, and, focusing on the back of her light green T-shirt, let her lead me to safety.

chapter THIRTEEN

When we leave the Great Pyramid, we find Sittu sitting exactly where we left her, and she's arguing with a man holding a camel by its reins.

"*Emshi!*" she shouts.

I rush toward her, thinking she's in trouble, when Hassan pulls me back. "If he sees us, he'll want to raise his prices."

"For what?"

"*Emshi?* Doesn't that mean 'walk'?" Deanna asks.

"In this context, it's like saying 'get walking' or 'get lost.' She's negotiating a better price for the camel ride."

"Camel ride? I'd rather walk," I say. The last thing I want to do is get up on something that high off the ground that doesn't have a seat belt.

"It looks like fun," Deanna says. "But I don't want to look like a geeky American tourist."

Hassan raises his eyebrow, like, *Are you kidding me?* but instead, he says, "You look beautiful."

"And you're pretty good-looking yourself," Deanna says, looking into his eyes.

I turn away. *Get a room already.*

We watch the guy walk away with his camel, but he only goes a few feet before he returns to Sittu. He says something that I can't hear, and again, Sittu yells, "*Emshi!*"

Again, he walks away with his camel, only to come back a few moments later. This time, Sittu stands up, and Hassan says, "I think she's done."

The three of us walk over to her. "Ready?" Sittu says.

I'm not ready to climb up on that beast, but I'm even less ready to argue with Sittu about it. "Sure," I lie.

The camel guy looks Deanna and me up and down. "American," he says. I think he's just figured out that he's been duped.

He waves over another guy with a camel.

"My name is Hakim, and this is George."

"George?" Deanna and I say in unison.

"Yes, George," George says.

"Okay, George. I'm with you," Deanna says. "This is going to be great! Thank you, Sittu." Hassan and George help her into the saddle, and she looks so graceful, you'd think she's ridden a camel a million times before. The camel spits and shakes his head, but otherwise doesn't seem to mind too much.

"Mar, it's amazing up here," Deanna calls as George walks the camel around in a circle. "This is so much more fun than riding a horse."

Okay, but I've never ridden a horse.

"Ready?" Hassan turns to me.

The saddle is way too high up; I'd so much rather walk. But

when I look at Sittu standing, arms folded, tapping her foot in the sand, I don't even bother to argue.

"Okay."

"Put your foot into my hands," Hassan says, "and we'll hoist you up on the count of three."

I nod, not wanting my voice to quiver, and lift my foot in the air, trying not to fall back.

"*Waahid*," Hassan starts.

"*Itnein*," Hakim continues.

"*Talaata*," they finish the count together, and before I know it, I'm up on the camel, but I lose my balance and start to slip down the other side. George leaves Deanna and runs over just in time to push me back up.

"You okay now?" Hassan asks, biting his front lip, trying not to laugh. Sittu's covering her mouth, and Deanna's looking down at the ground. But George and Hakim aren't holding anything back. They're cracking up like I'm the funniest thing they've seen in years.

"Aren't you going to ride?" I ask, looking down at Hassan and Sittu. "I thought Egyptians weren't afraid of heights."

"Not heights. Big teeth." Hassan grins, showing us his teeth. I didn't notice before, but he has one crooked tooth on the right side. From the way Deanna's staring at him, she must think it makes him cuter. It does.

"You've ridden one camel, you've ridden them all." Sittu slaps her thigh; she cracks herself up. "We're going to drive the car around and meet you both in front of the Sphinx." I hear Umm

Kulthum coming from Sittu's bag. Sittu pulls out her phone and looks down. "A tweet," she says. "Hassan, it looks like tomorrow will be the day."

"The day for what?" I ask.

Sittu looks up at me, but before she gives me an answer, Deanna says, "Sittu! You have an iPhone. I should've known you were messing with me." She pulls out her own iPhone and shows Sittu. "When we get back, I'll show you my apps. I have some great games. I can even check my horoscope."

"You can let the stars—or your iPhone—guide you, but I think the camel will get you closer to your destination." Sittu smiles. "*Yalla*, Hassan." Sittu and Hassan walk in the direction of the car. George and Hakim walk us toward the Sphinx.

"Isn't this amazing?" Deanna calls out to me. "This is, like, the best day of my life."

"I'm happy for you," I yell back, holding the reins as tight as I can. I don't want to fall off and break my neck.

"Oh my God, did you see that? My camel just spit all the way across…Mariam! Are you listening to me?"

I can't listen and be terrified at the same time. "Are you upset about not climbing to the top of the pyramid? It's not a big deal—"

"Just not having the best time," I say.

"Egypt is so amazing!"

"I was referring to this moment, on this animal, but if you really want to know how I feel…" I stop myself. Dumping on Deanna isn't going to make anything better. It's not going to get me home, it's not going to get my *sittu* to like me, and it won't even get me off this stupid camel. We don't both need to be miserable.

"Tell me." She leans so far in my direction I'm afraid she's going to fall off her camel and onto me.

George and Hakim shout, "Careful!"

"Deanna," I snap, "sit up straight!"

"Tell me what you're so pissed about, then."

"I'm just tired."

"The truth." She leans so far toward me that I reach for her, thinking she's going to fall, and almost slip again.

"Please!" Hakim and George both shout, running to my side.

"I'm okay, I'm okay."

"See, Mar, if you don't tell me, we'll both fall off these camels and break our necks."

"You had me up half the night with Hassan this and Hassan that!" I finally say, looking straight ahead.

"Well, excuse me." She sits up straight again. "I was just excited. Sorry. I wanted to share that with my best friend."

"I'm happy for you. I really am. I'm just tired."

"Are you jealous?"

"Miss, here is the second pyramid," Hakim says as they stop the camels so we can take a longer look.

"*Shukran*," I say to him. "Are you crazy?" I say to Deanna.

"Beautiful, no?" George asks Deanna.

"Very," Deanna says to him. To me she says, "Don't call me crazy!"

"Why would I be jealous?"

"Maybe you like him," Deanna says.

"Well, I did see him first." Why did I just say that? Hassan is cute and all, but I can't imagine my first kiss being with him.

"Oh my God." Deanna puts her hand over her mouth. "You're right."

"Are you okay?" I ask.

"We go?" Hakim asks.

"One minute, please," I tell him. "Deanna, are you okay?"

"You saw him first. You saw Hassan in the kitchen. You had first dibs. And I didn't even ask you if you liked him. I'm sorry… I'm so sorry." Deanna's starting to sound like I did in the pyramid.

"It's okay," I say.

"It's not okay. I'm your best friend, and best friends don't…" Her voice cracks as her eyes tear up.

I want to reach out to her, but I'm afraid I'll fall off the camel.

"Deanna, please. It's fine. I don't know why that even came out of my mouth. Maybe I am jealous. But not because I like Hassan. It's just you're so into each other and…"

"What do you mean 'but not because I like Hassan'? What's wrong with him?"

"Nothing…"

"Then why don't you want him for yourself?"

"He's cute—okay, gorgeous—but he's into you."

"He put his hand on your knee."

She doesn't miss a thing. "That was probably an accident."

"You sure you don't like-like him? Maybe he's not your type, but I'm sure he has a friend."

"Deanna, I don't want Hassan's friend."

"See? You do want Hassan."

"No, I don't want Hassan. I mean, okay, he's cute and not sleazy—"

"Sleazy?"

"You remember what Baba said about Egyptian guys? How they just want one thing from American girls?"

"Of course he said that. He's your father. If you were going to Italy, he'd say it about Italian guys."

"I wish sometimes he wouldn't say anything."

"He cares about you." Deanna pets the side of her camel. "That must be kind of nice."

"Having a father who doesn't trust you?"

"Having a dad," she says, looking me straight in the eyes. I feel awful.

"But how many kids can say their mom wanted them so much she went and had them on her own? Most people just have kids. Your mother *really* wanted you," I say.

"Still, not having a dad can really suck sometimes."

"Do you know anything about your dad?" I've never asked her about him before. We've hung out every day since last summer, but I assumed since she never talked about it that she really didn't want to.

"We don't call him that. He's just the sperm donor," Deanna says. "My mom said she picked him because his eye color, hair color, those sorts of things, matched hers. She wanted me to look as much like her and her family as possible. Except for this"—she points to her face—"I do look a lot like my mom."

"You are both so beautiful."

"Thanks," she says. "So are we cool?"

"Of course," I say.

We ride in silence for a minute. I can tell Deanna's thinking about Hassan. I listen to Hakim and George talking to each other in Arabic, and I can actually pick out a word here and there. *Bamiya*. That's okra—one of the few Egyptian dishes Baba makes. I wonder if they're hungry.

"Hey, Mar?"

"Yeah?"

"What you said…do you really think it's true?"

"What's true?"

"That Hassan's into me?" Deanna sounds unsure of herself, which is about as unusual as me riding a camel.

"Of course! He stares at you like you are the only thing he can see. He called you beautiful. What more do you want?"

"He hasn't held my hand. He held yours."

"He didn't want me to hyperventilate and cause an international incident," I tell her.

Deanna laughs.

"What?"

"How would it look for an American tourist to pass out and roll down the side of the pyramid?"

Deanna's eyes look as if they're straining to smile.

"You must really like this guy. I've never heard you sound so *fine*," I tell her.

"Freaked out, insecure, neurotic, and emotional?"

I smile.

"I've never been in love before." She sighs and when I look at her, I can see how right I am. She really is in love.

"We go faster?" both George and Hakim ask, tapping their wrists as if they are wearing watches.

"I think we're on the clock," Deanna says.

We start to pick up the pace, and I think about what is really bothering me. "Deanna, what do you think Sittu was writing about on Facebook?"

"Brangelina," Deanna laughs.

"Come on, I'm serious. There is something going on that she doesn't want me to know."

"Like what?"

"I don't know, but remember when Hassan said something about tomorrow being the day?" And Salam too, he was talking about a tweet and she shut them both up. "What does that mean?"

"Mar, Sittu's really great, and she totally loves you. So why don't you just trust her?""

"You're right." I smile at her. "Thanks, Deanna." I turn to Hakim and George. "Okay, guys, *emshi*. Fast!" I say, surprised that I know yet another word in Arabic.

"You're really starting to get into this," Deanna says.

"Giza's cool."

"Well, you are one hundred percent part Egyptian."

"Yes, I am," I say, surprised that it feels good to say that. If it weren't for the tourists clicking pictures around us, it would feel as if we were living in a different time, as if Deanna and

I were Cleopatra and Nefertiti, princesses of the pyramids. We both would've had princes who would become kings and make us queens. Strike that. We would be rulers ourselves.

I look over at Deanna. Maybe for now, being two girls on a dorky camel ride is enough.

chapter FOURTEEN

Sittu and Hassan are waiting for us at the Sphinx. Deanna gets off her camel first. She hardly even needs help from George. I, on the other hand, am way too afraid to move, so it takes George, Hakim, and Hassan to get me down.

Deanna makes us take about a dozen pictures of her and the Sphinx from different angles. Right profile. Left profile. Foot to paw. "I'm going to put these all over Facebook," Deanna says. "Didn't Beth—or was it Karen?—call me Sphinx Face?"

It was Karen. "They didn't mean it as a compliment, Deanna."

"Of course not. But look how amazing this thing is." Then she makes me take a photo of her and Hassan and the Sphinx, of her and Sittu and the Sphinx, and then she makes Hassan take a picture of her and me and Sittu and the Sphinx. They are mostly profiles of the Sphinx, with a few head on. Sittu explains that Napoleon didn't shoot off the Sphinx's nose, like we thought; it was a man named Muhammad Sa'im al-Dahr, who got really mad that people were worshiping the Sphinx and leaving offerings at its base to ensure they had a good harvest.

"It's getting late. We should head back home," Sittu says.

It can't be later than noon, but I don't question her. Time seems different here. What's late feels early and what's early feels late. I don't get it, but it doesn't really matter. I'm just glad we're here.

"I'll go ahead and bring the car," Hassan announces, and then hurries off.

"Slow down!" Sittu shouts. "That boy is always rushing. He also thinks I'm this old lady. The car isn't far."

"Well, we're a little tired," I say, hoping to make her feel better.

"Yes, it can be exhausting to climb to the top of the pyramid," Sittu admits.

I'm about to tell her the truth when Deanna yells, "Ahmed!"

Five different guys turn around.

"That Ahmed!" Deanna points to our friend from the airport.

"Girls!" He waves to us and we run over to him.

"I thought we'd never see you again," Deanna says, giving him a big hug.

"It's so good to see you." I hug him too.

"Well, it's a small world, but Egypt is even smaller." Ahmed asks, "So what do you think of the pyramids?"

"Amazing," I say.

"Ahmed," Deanna says, "I don't get it. If you were raised in Giza, haven't you been to the pyramids, like, a million times?"

"Still asking questions! Let's just say I have a lot of family—a lot of family. And sometimes I need some time alone to appreciate my family's greatness. So this is where I come to think, appreciate, and breathe." Ahmed laughs. "Sometimes it's easier to clear one's head in the presence of what we know well."

"Very true," Sittu says as she walks up to join us.

"*Izzayyik?*" Ahmed says, bowing slightly toward Sittu.

"Very well," Sittu says.

"Ahmed, this is my *sittu*," I say.

"Madam, you are too young to be a grandmother." He is sweet, but I don't think his cheesy line is going to work on Sittu.

"And you, I see"—Sittu glares at the silver band on Ahmed's ring finger—"are too married to be talking with such a sweet tongue."

You go, Sittu. My *sittu* knows how to put a cheesy guy into the grater.

"I mean no disrespect," Ahmed says, stepping back. "I am a widower."

"You didn't tell us," I say.

"I was married for so many years, sometimes I forget she's no longer in this world." Ahmed smiles, but his eyes look sad.

"I understand what you mean," Sittu replies. "I was married for close to forty years."

"May God's blessings be upon him," Ahmed says, and he bows to her, but his expression has changed, and he looks at Sittu longer than is really polite.

Sittu nods. "*Shukran*. And may Allah's blessings be upon your wife too."

"Sittu, Ahmed is the one who helped us through customs," I share.

"Then I thank you for all of your generosity." Sittu touches her heart.

Ahmed nods, but it seems like he's not really listening. "Tell me,"

Ahmed says, sounding surprised and pleased at the same time, "did you by any chance attend the University of Cairo?"

"Why, yes, I did," Sittu says. She moves closer to his face. For a moment, she just stares. Then she says, "Ahmed! *Izzayyak?*"

"Egypt really gets smaller all the time," Ahmed says cheerfully.

"You know each other?" Deanna asks.

"We were at university together," Ahmed explains.

"You were great friends with Gamal," Sittu says.

"He lives in Dubai now." He shrugs. "You go where there is work."

"And Suad?" Sittu asks.

"Ahh, I married her."

"May Allah's blessings be upon her," Sittu says. "She was a good woman. Great sense of humor."

"That's why she married me." Ahmed laughs, and Sittu laughs too. Ahmed turns to us. "Your grandmother was quite the firecracker in those days. She led student protests. She was steadfast—never feared going to prison."

"You were arrested?" I exclaim. My eyes must be the size of dinner plates again. I wait for Sittu to explain.

Instead, she cuts off Ahmed, who looks like he's about to tell another story, simply saying, "The energy of youth."

Deanna tugs on the back of my shirt. I know exactly what she's thinking: Ahmed and Sittu would make a great couple. Maybe they would. They are both widowed. They went to college together. But playing matchmaker for my grandmother is too weird. Besides, she wouldn't like any idea that came from me.

"Well, it was the pleasure of all pleasures to see you again, madam," Ahmed says. Sittu doesn't say a word, but I think she's blushing. "Girls, I hope our paths cross again."

Deanna tugs on my shirt so hard this time I fall back a step. "What?" I whisper, as I turn to her.

"Don't you think we should take Ahmed for coffee or lunch or something, to thank him for his help?"

"That is very sweet of you but not necessary," Ahmed says.

"Of course. Where are my manners?" Sittu says. "After all you did to help my granddaughters, it is I who should take you for lunch. I will be offended if you refuse."

"Well then, how can I refuse? I must get back to see a cousin today, but any other time would be wonderful," Ahmed says. "I'd love to take you all to the National Museum. You know, I did my master's work in Egyptology; ironically, that was in America," he laughs. "Tomorrow? Though, tomorrow that area may be a little dangerous because of—"

Sittu cuts him off. "We live in Heliopolis. We can meet there."

Deanna raises her eyebrows like now she understands what I meant about Sittu keeping something from me. "What's happening there?" Deanna asks.

"It's January twenty-fifth—"

"We shall meet in Heliopolis then," Sittu interrupts again.

"New Cairo." Ahmed smiles, going along with Sittu.

"Not so new anymore, but there are some nice places in the area. Do you drive?" Sittu asks.

"I rented a car."

"Sittu, maybe you should give Ahmed your number," Deanna says.

"Of course. A pen." The normally composed Sittu fumbles in her bag. "I know there should be one in here…. Here we go." Sittu lets out a breath as she pulls out a pen. "Oh, paper."

"Here, I have something." Ahmed pulls a receipt from his pocket and gives it to Sittu.

"Lean on me." Deanna turns, and Sittu rests the receipt against Deanna's back to write.

Sittu hands the paper to Ahmed, who puts it back in his pocket.

"Until we meet again." Ahmed bows and then walks in the direction of the Sphinx.

✻   ✻   ✻

On the drive back, I insist Deanna ride up front. For most of the ride home, she and Hassan sneak glances at each other while Sittu stares out the window with a smile on her face, as if she were sixteen again.

It must be nice to be in love.

chapter
FIFTEEN

I don't know how long I've been asleep when Deanna's snoring wakes me up.

"Deanna," I whisper. No response.

"Deanna," I say louder, but she doesn't wake up. She's in too deep a sleep to hear me. Climbing pyramids and falling in love take a lot out of a person.

My thoughts turn to all that happened during the day. What is Sittu hiding about tomorrow? What would I Google? Egypt? January 25? Maybe find something on Facebook? But it's not like I could find any information on an American website, and here, they'd all be in Arabic. For the first time in my life, I wish I actually knew the language.

I look over at Deanna, still snoring, and I think about how I had worried for nothing about her not having a good time. And how after we'd finished dinner, Hassan and Deanna talked about American and Middle Eastern music until Sittu announced it was time for all of us to go to bed and politely kicked Hassan out. I meant what I told Deanna about being okay with the two of them getting together. But that doesn't mean it's easy to live with.

When Sittu came in to say good night, I was about to ask her about what she'd said when we were with Ahmed, but just then Deanna asked if she could call her mom. Sittu, of course, said yes and took her to call in the other room. I fell asleep before Deanna came to bed.

Now I roll over and stare at the ceiling. Whatever is happening tomorrow, I'll find out soon enough. At this moment, I just want Deanna to stop snoring. I didn't know girls could snore that loud.

I quietly go over to her bed. She has one of her romance novels open on her chest. This one has some super-cute guy wearing one of those traditional Arab headdresses that men in movies wear when they are supposed to look like some rich Arab oil business-person. Of course, the guy is on a camel, and his arms are wrapped around an anorexic-looking chick wearing a long, flowing dress.

This kind of thing really flips Mom out. She says it's racist garbage. She starts to say "crap" but stops herself. I always thought pictures like this made Arabs look better than the long-bearded guys you see on television screaming, "Death to America."

I put the book on the nightstand, making sure to turn the cover face down, so Sittu won't see it. I have a feeling she'd find the stereotypical Arab and damsel-in-distress portrayal offensive—or at least stupid.

I nudge Deanna's shoulder. Her snoring just gets louder, so this time I shove her a bit.

"What?" She waves her hands in the air like she's swatting at a mosquito.

"You're snoring."

"Sorry," she mumbles, instantly falling back to sleep—wonderfully silent sleep.

I climb back into bed and close my eyes; two seconds later her buzz saw starts right up again. Now I'm thirsty.

I drag myself out of bed again. As I'm pushing open the kitchen door, Sittu calls to me from the balcony.

"Mariam, come here."

She's still awake? I go out to join her on the balcony.

"Take a seat." Sittu pats a chair that looks a lot older than her. Its plastic cover is cracked down the middle.

For a long while, Sittu doesn't say a word to me. I'm too afraid I'll say something wrong, so we just sit in silence, watching the cars go into and out of the traffic circle. I've never seen anything like it. Cars enter the circle from five different roads, but they can only exit from one road at a time, and it's not always the same road. The exit road seems to alternate every few minutes.

"It is so much busier here at night," I say.

"Is traffic this crazy in New York?" Sittu asks.

"In the city."

"It must be a beautiful place, New York."

"Sittu, how come you never come to visit us?" I ask.

"Your *giddu* didn't like to fly," she says. "And I never felt good about leaving him alone."

"It's been almost ten years since Giddu—"

"I'm an old woman now," Sittu says.

"Ahmed certainly didn't think so." I try to make her smile, but she's looking down at the street.

"Ahmed?" she says, like she doesn't know who I'm talking about. But it's obvious that she does.

"You know who I mean—the man we met at the pyramids. The man you're taking to lunch."

"Of course," she says, turning toward me. "See, my memory is going—a sign of aging." She looks back at the road. "He won't call for a while if he calls at all."

"Why wouldn't he?"

"He's still wearing his wedding band." Sittu rubs her own band as she says this. "He's still very much married, so it will take some time for him to feel right about having lunch with another woman, even if that woman is an old friend and only talking about lunch."

I don't try to convince her otherwise. What do I know about men? What do I know about *sittus*, for that matter? For several minutes, we watch cars below.

"You can't sleep?" she finally says. "The time difference takes a bit of adjusting."

I shrug. "Deanna's snoring pretty loudly."

"Your *giddu*, now he was a snorer. I think I spent the first year of our marriage sleeping on the couch. In time, you adjust. After he passed, I couldn't sleep because I missed his snoring." She smiles so wide she's actually showing teeth.

"Did my *baba* and Giddu not get along?" I ask, thinking about how Baba never talks about him.

"They had their 'stuff,' as you kids call it," she says, her smile disappearing. I don't have the guts to ask what kind of stuff.

"I wish I could remember him," I say, then catch myself. "Sorry,

Sittu. I know I acted like I remembered him when we were looking at the photos. We just don't have a lot of family pictures around. We mostly have paintings—copies of Monet, Van Gogh, Picasso. My favorite is the guy who did the giant green apple."

"Magritte," Sittu says. "He's one of my favorite artists too. I gave your parents a print of that painting for your room when you were born."

"I didn't know that. It's hanging in the living room."

"Well, it was a gift to you, so it should be in your room," she says.

"I like that we all can share it."

"You are very generous in spirit," Sittu says. "Remember, don't give away so much that you are left with a hole in your heart."

"I have a painting in my room that I found in our storage area. It's by an Egyptian artist—an original. It's an oil painting. Very cool." I tell her all this, hoping to impress her. "It's pretty abstract, but it makes you feel like you're on fire. You look at it and want to go out in the world and make something happen."

"You don't know this artist's name?"

"The painting isn't signed, and when I asked Baba, he just said, 'some guy.' I don't think it's his kind of thing. He didn't even want me to bring the painting into the apartment, but Mom convinced him to let me have it." I shrug. "Mom needed more storage space for all the stuff she never gets rid of. You know," I say, trying again to make Sittu laugh, "she still has shoes from when I was in first grade."

"The painting that made you feel on fire—was it blood orange and canary yellow with stripes of red?"

"That's the one! How did you know?"

"It's your *baba*'s painting."

"Baba?! I've never seen him paint or do anything creative at all."

"When he was younger, one of his favorite things to do was go to the Egyptian Museum and sketch."

"The ancient artifacts?"

"No, the tourists. Your father loved to sketch people, and then he'd come home and make abstract paintings, like the one in your room."

"You mean that painting is of a tourist?"

"Or inspired by one."

"Probably an American." I laugh.

"Why do you say that?" Sittu asks, but her chuckle shows she knows exactly what I mean.

"Deanna says American tourists are loud and obnoxious and always pissing people off, which makes locals want to punch them in the nose."

"Not all American tourists," Sittu says with a smile. I wonder if she thinks of me as a tourist, though I guess that's what I am.

"Would it be okay for us to go to the Egyptian Museum?" I ask.

"Of course we can." Sittu smiles wide at me. "I'd be very happy to take you."

"How about tomorrow? I mean today. It's already tomorrow."

"Today, it might be best to stay near home instead."

"Is the museum very far? As far as Giza?"

"It all depends on traffic."

"We can just go for a little while—"

"You are like your father—persistent." She sighs, looking out into the night.

"I'm sorry."

"*Habibti*." Sittu touches my cheek. "Don't apologize for asking for what you want. I would love to take you, and we will go, but the museum is at Tahrir Square, and tomorrow…" She pauses. "Well, it's best to be closer to home tomorrow."

"What were you going to say? What's happening at Ta…Ta…"

"Tah-rir," Sittu says.

"Does it have something to do with Tunisia?"

Sittu pulls her shawl tighter around her body. "Do you want to get a sweater?"

"I'm not cold," I say, frustrated that she's changing the subject. She's doing exactly what my parents do—treating me like a child.

Sittu just nods. At least she's not trying to tell me how I should feel—"You must be cold" or "You must be hot" or "Put on a sweater anyway. Trust me"—like my parents do.

"You know," she says, forcing a smile like that's going to make me forget about my question, "when your *baba* was a kid, we would all sleep out here in the summer. Your *baba* called it balcony camping."

"Sittu, please tell me what's going on tomorrow," I say.

The expression on her face makes me want to run back to bed and pull the covers over my head.

Instead of answering my question, she says: "'I've come here to Cairo to seek a new beginning between the United States and Muslims around the world, one based on mutual interest and mutual respect; and one based upon the truth that America and Islam are not exclusive and need not be in competition.'"

What is she talking about?

She continues, "'Instead, they overlap and share common principles—principles of justice and progress, tolerance and the dignity of all human beings.'" She pauses. "Mariam, do you know who said these words?"

I'm sure she can tell from the clueless expression on my face that I have no idea. I shake my head.

"Your president."

"Wow, Obama said that about Muslims? That's so cool."

"The summer he took office, he addressed the world from Cairo. It was an important, historic speech—and you don't know this?"

If Sittu is trying to shame me, well, it's working. I don't want to tell her that Baba always shuts off the world news.

"It was important that your President Obama won the election and that he made this speech, but words without action are like those cars down there when they're out of petrol: they get us nowhere. Since your president made his speech last summer, conditions in Egypt have only gotten worse, much worse. For Muslims and Christians—for everyone."

"President Obama has something to do with what's happening at the square today?"

"Tahrir Square," she says, sounding like Baba when he's lost patience with me. "The United States has given Mubarak a lot of aid over the thirty years he's been in power, but it goes into his pockets and those of his corrupt police force."

"Mubarak, he is the president, right?"

She slams her hand on the railing. "A president is elected. In the thirty years that he has been running this country into the ground, Mubarak has never been elected. The elections we have here are not real."

"They're fixed?" I say, remembering the conversation from yesterday.

"More like broken!"

"Well, if President Obama knew this—"

"Mariam, don't they teach anything in those American schools? Doesn't your father talk to you about what's going on in this world? I didn't raise my son to turn his back on his country."

"My father loves America."

"Your father's country is Egypt!" Sittu shouts.

She must see that I'm totally confused, because she takes my hand and says, "For the past thirty years, this man has kept all the money America gives us. So our streets stay dirty and food prices soar. Parents can't feed their families. And our people grow more humiliated and angry. Do you see this?" she asks, showing me her palm.

It looks like a hand. I'm not sure what I'm supposed to see there.

"The dirt. It's from pollution—pollution that only gets worse as the streets get filthier, as the people become hungrier and their shame deepens, all because of this man who calls himself the president."

Sittu's anger and my confusion are making me tired and cold, and I suddenly just want to go to bed.

Sittu turns her head toward the traffic. "When your father was at the university—"

"I had no idea Baba went to college here."

"Yes, before he went to America. He had one semester left before he would have graduated. But during a student demonstration against the government—"

"He was arrested, like you were?" I ask, not believing that my father would have ever done anything illegal.

"It was much worse for your father."

"Why?" I ask.

"*Habibti*, forgive me. I don't know why I'm talking of such things."

"Please tell me," I plead.

"I can't tonight."

"You're treating me just like my parents do." I stand, snagging the back of my nightshirt on the cracked plastic of the chair back. "Please don't."

Sittu looks up at me, and instead of the tough-ass grandmother I'm used to seeing, she looks fragile, breakable.

"It's too much right now." She looks away.

"Please, Sittu. Talk to me."

She sighs. "He was interrogated."

"You mean, like, he was tortured?" I sit back down, not sure I want to hear any more but desperate to understand this piece of my father's life that I've never heard spoken about before.

"The protest, like the others, was peaceful. Students were chanting, holding signs on the campus. I believe they were protesting against the government for arresting a writer."

"Like the bloggers who were arrested?"

"Yes, except writers wrote for printed newspapers at that time." Sittu clears her throat and shifts in her seat. "Your father was one of many students arrested that day, and all of them were beaten very badly."

"Baba's scar," I say. "The one over his right eye. He always says he doesn't remember how he got it."

"Yes, the scar comes from that time, but not from a police baton. Your father would never tell me what happened in any detail, just that it was a…burn."

We sit without talking for what feels like longer than the flight to Egypt. I break the silence first. "Sittu?"

"Yes," she says, still not meeting my gaze.

"Is that why Baba wanted to leave Egypt?"

"My son," Sittu says, turning to me, "never wanted to leave. It was his father and I who forced him to go. We were too afraid of what might happen if he stayed. But your father didn't want to go. I don't think he's ever forgiven his father—or me." Sittu wipes her eyes with the back of her shawl. I don't see tears in her eyes, but it looks like she's been crying for years.

"I didn't mean to upset—"

"Mariam, my love, there are many things that upset me right now, but you, *habibti*, are not one of them."

I think about what I said to Baba, calling Sittu a horrible woman, and now I want to beg her to forgive me.

"It was a peaceful demonstration—no violence. Then the police came and beat the students and used tear gas on them."

"You did the right thing," I say quietly. "You wanted him to live in a country where people don't risk going to prison for speaking out."

"Oh, Mariam. To me, they teach history in America the same way they teach it here—with many distortions."

"What do you mean?"

"You're a smart girl. You will understand someday."

"Sittu, what's happening tomorrow? Please tell me."

"Tomorrow is a national holiday for the police." She shakes her head. "There is a call for people to gather and protest the police's abuse and oppression we experience every day in this country, as well as all the other things we have talked about tonight. *Habibti*, this is a very hard time for Egypt right now, and, well…Egypt needs to take care of Egypt."

"Is that what you wrote about online?"

"I blog a little." She half smiles.

"I don't even have a Facebook page."

"Your parents."

I nod.

"Well, maybe when you're sixteen. Isn't that the day after tomorrow?" she asks, looking happier now.

"Do you want to go to the protest tomorrow?" I ask. Now I'm the one changing the subject.

"*Habibti*, this is for the youth of Egypt."

"Should Deanna and I go?"

"No!" Sittu looks upset, but this time I don't take it personally. I know this isn't about me. She clears her throat. "Miss Deanna seems to be having a good time in Cairo."

"A great time," I say, realizing this is the first time Sittu and I have been alone since Deanna and I arrived.

"Love makes everything great—even the mediocre."

"Hassan seems to like Deanna a lot too."

Below us, brakes screech. Then there's a large bang. I jump to my feet to peer over the balcony's railing.

Right below us, three cars have crashed into one another in an exit from the traffic circle.

"Sittu! Should we call someone?"

"Soon there will be more someones to help than will be helpful. Just sit and watch."

Sure enough, Sittu is right. The drivers get out, inspecting the damage to their cars, but so do all the drivers and passengers of all the other cars that are stopped in the traffic circle because of the accident.

"Back home, they call that *rubbernecking*. But people don't get out of their cars or anything. They just slow down to look. My mom calls them *looky-loos*."

"Looky-loos," Sittu says. "I like that. There are those who live life and those who stand by and comment on it. Here in Misr, it's not enough to just look. Everyone needs to give advices."

"Advice," I correct.

"No, I meant advices," she says. "You see, in Misr everyone gives advice in the plural. Everyone knows how to best live everyone else's lives, you know? The problem is there aren't many people who have any idea how to best live their own life. But who knows? Maybe tomorrow there will be less advices and more action."

"Advices," I say. "I like that."

"Do you mind some more advices from your old Sittu?"

"Okay," I say, now wanting to hear everything she has to say.

"First loves are a very powerful and all-consuming phenomenon. It is stranger than politics. Deanna will seem for a while like she's from another planet. Just know it's not space invaders or you; it's just crazy love."

"Like crazy drivers?"

"Exactly. You think you know where you're going, and you're happy getting there until, one day, you realize you haven't any idea where you are or how you got there."

"I understand that," I say.

"Oh?" Sittu says, arching her eyebrows. "Why is this?"

"No reason." Could I sound any less convincing?

"I 'fessed up,' as they say in your country, about all that happened with my son and me. Now it's your turn. My lips are sealed to others. You can trust me."

I believe her.

"Well, Hassan…"

"You like Hassan."

I nod.

"Maybe love?" she asks.

"I don't know," I say.

"Do you feel crazy?"

Looking down at the street and the people who just had the accident and everyone who gathered around them sharing advices, I realize that's exactly how I feel. "Like crazy traffic."

"But you are willing to step aside for your friend," Sittu says.

"It's clear he likes her, and she's so into him."

"Remember what I said about giving away too much?"

"That I'll end up with a hole in my heart."

"You are a good friend, Mariam, and maybe your friendship with Deanna is strong enough to fill that hole." Sittu pauses before she says, "Life doesn't always give us what we want."

I nod. I know this very well.

"But sometimes, Mariam," Sittu says, grabbing my hand, "life gives us exactly what we need, though we don't always know we need it until we get it."

"I'm feeling kind of tired now."

But Sittu keeps talking. "Sometimes we expect more from those who are closest to our heart. They reflect back so much of ourselves. Of course, this isn't always the best. But like I said, in Misr, we all know how to best live your life, yet we are never too sure how to live our own. You understand me, *habibti*?"

I nod, but I don't know what it is I really understand—except that just now I could hear her love when she called me *habibti*.

"See," she says, pointing at the traffic, "everybody's back in their cars and traffic is moving again. Sooner or later, we always get back to it.

"And, Mariam, if you'd just gone a few more feet in the pyramid today, it would have gotten so much easier. It's still hot, but the ceiling is almost forty feet high, and there's much more light. Sometimes if you force yourself to keep going, you find the most amazing surprises." She shrugs. "But we all are ready in our own time."

She knew all along. Of course she did.

As I kiss Sittu good night, she whispers one last piece of advice in my ear: "Roll Deanna on her side. She'll snore less."

Back in my room, I move Deanna so she is facing me, and the snoring stops. I stare at her and wonder if Sittu is right. *Will love make her act crazy?*

chapter
SIXTEEN

"Mar, wake up!" Deanna screeches from in front of the computer. With one eye open and the other half-shut, I grumble, "Let me sleep."

"Do you hear that singing? All the voices echoing each other?"

"It's the *adhan*—the call to prayer." I rub my eyes. "There are a lot of mosques nearby," I say, realizing I do remember some things from when I was here as a kid.

"I love this place," Deanna says. "To wake up to a symphony every morning…" She turns to the computer.

"I'm going back to sleep," I mumble, rolling away from her.

"You have to see this," Deanna says.

I ignore her. She keeps talking.

"I checked out Hassan's Facebook page. I wanted to see if he, you know, mentioned anything about yesterday or me in his update."

"And?" I try to sound disinterested, but I jump out of bed so fast I bang my knee into the edge of the nightstand, knocking the book with the pseudo-Arab lover boy on the cover onto the floor.

"Ow!" I rub my knee as I wobble over to Deanna.

"You okay? That had to hurt."

"So did he say anything?" I ask, more focused on the computer screen than on the pain in my leg.

"I don't know. His update is in Arabic. But look at this page—there's this group with eighty thousand fans. It's huge. They're calling for today to be the Day of Revolt. It's officially some national holiday for the police, who they say torture people and stuff."

"Yeah, I know about it." I turn away, catching my reflection in Sittu's true mirror, still not seeing how I look any different than I do in any other mirror.

"You knew about the protest, and you're just telling me now?"

"Sittu just mentioned it last night."

"When? You were asleep when I came to bed."

"Well, someone woke me up with her snoring—" I say, but Deanna interrupts me.

"What is this? Wait until Deanna goes to sleep, then talk about all the juicy stuff?"

Ignoring her, I put my suitcase on the bed. I still haven't unpacked.

"We're going, right?" Deanna comes to sit at the edge of my bed, watching me pull out everything while trying to find a T-shirt I don't completely hate.

"Where are my jeans?" I ask, tossing a pair of shorts in the air.

"Right here." Deanna holds up the wrong pair of jeans.

"Not those. The jeans that don't make my butt look fat."

"Your butt never looks fat," Deanna says, shaking her head at me. "Just wear these."

"Don't tell me I forgot to pack them," I whine.

"Mar, stop freaking out. Who cares about your butt right now? People aren't going to be worrying about what your butt looks like when we're protesting for freedom."

"Protest?" I grab the jeans from her, then drop them on the floor. "That's the last place I want to be today. Do you even know why they're protesting?"

"Corruption, soaring food prices, half the population lives below the poverty line, making less than two dollars a day…"

Okay, so she knows. "People can get hurt," I say, pulling out more T-shirts. I hate them all.

"I went to tons of demonstrations with my mom when we lived in San Francisco, for gay marriage, women's right to choose, education, equal pay for equal work. They were always completely safe. No one ever got hurt. And when people got arrested, they were let out right away."

"Deanna, that was San Francisco. This is Egypt." I think about mentioning what Sittu said about what happened to my dad but decide against it out of respect for Baba. "Hassan's going, isn't he?"

"I don't know. Look, you have to see this video link." Deanna goes back to the computer. "Come here and look at this."

I look over her shoulder. "Hassan has 1,122 friends. Popular guy. Wow, and he's friends with some very pretty girls."

"Just look at this." Deanna clicks the video, and a girl in a headscarf who looks younger than us starts talking in Arabic.

"Who is she?"

"Her name is Asmaa Mahfouz."

"What is she saying?"

"How do I know? I didn't learn that much Arabic from your dad. But it's not what she's saying; it's how she's saying it. Look at the expression on her face. She's talking about some serious shit. The video's from January eighteenth, but I think it has something to do with today's protest. And this group, the April Sixth Youth Movement—that's the name of one of the groups calling for action today—they have a huge number of fans."

"'We are all Khaled Said.'" I read from the list of Hassan's favorites.

"That's another group. It's named after this young guy the police beat to death last year."

"That's horrible." And I think about how this could have happened to Baba.

"See why it's so important we go and show our support?"

"It's too dangerous."

"If it weren't for our country's money, this Mubarak jerk wouldn't be able to keep hurting people."

"You can't blame America for what's happening here," I say, but I think about what Sittu said last night, and I know Deanna has a point. But if I tell her that, she'll keep pushing that we go. "You only want to go because you think Hassan will be there," I snap.

"You know that's bull," she says, and I don't think I've ever heard her so angry with me before. Maybe I'm not being fair. Deanna really does care about saving the world. She's always getting me to sign some petition to save the whales, the air, kids in Africa. But those petitions are different. Here, speaking out against the mainstream, against politics is dangerous, and it's not our fight.

"What's your problem with Hassan?" she asks.

"I don't have a problem." I walk back over to my suitcase and busy myself with finding a bra.

"Wait a minute." She gets up from her chair and pulls the bra from my hand. "Look at me."

"Yes?" I turn my face to her but avoid making eye contact. She pulls my chin to try to make me look at her. "I knew it. You were lying yesterday. You do like Hassan."

"Give me a break." I turn to the mirror and hold a blue T-shirt against my chest, pretending I'm really interested in how it looks on me.

"When are you going to be straight with me?"

"A bunch of students are going to demonstrate," I say. "Teenagers. Like us. They're not revolting or overthrowing the government. It's no big deal."

"Well, who do you think starts revolutions? Did you ever hear of Tiananmen Square?"

"Of course I have. And do you know how many people were killed there?"

"Okay, so maybe that's not a great example, but my point is, young people can change the world. Look at what young people did in our country. They stopped the war—"

"We went to war with Iraq twice, and we're still there," I say, surprising myself. I do know some things about politics.

"I'm talking about the sixties—how young people protested in Washington and helped stop the Vietnam War."

"Fine, Deanna. When we're back home, if you want me to go

to some rally, I will, but not here. This isn't about us. It's not our fight. Can I please just get dressed now?" I grab my bra out of her hand.

Deanna returns to the computer but keeps on lecturing me: "How can you say that? Fighting for people's rights and freedom isn't about us? You saw them take away that man at the airport. You're the one who wanted me to call my mother to help him, and now you're saying it's none of our business. And you're Egyptian!"

"I'm American. Why can't you understand that? You calling me Egyptian is no better than what Karen and Beth do to me, making me feel like I don't belong and I'm some foreigner."

"That's not what I mean, and you know it," she says. Now she's really pissed off.

"Deanna?"

She doesn't even answer me.

"I'm really sorry. I shouldn't have said that about Karen…"

"Forget it," she says, but I'm not convinced she means it.

"Even if I wanted to go, Sittu won't let us."

"What?" Deanna swings around. "After all she told us about the long tradition of strong women you come from?"

There's a knock on the door. "May I come in?" Sittu asks.

Mom never knocks. Baba only began to knock when I started wearing bras.

"Of course," Deanna says.

"You are up early. It's not even light yet," Sittu says. She's wearing a white scarf loosely over her head.

"Praying?" Deanna asks.

"Soon," she says. "I just finished my ablutions."

"What?" Deanna asks.

"It's washing up before you pray so you're clean when you stand before God," I tell her.

Deanna looks at me like she can't decide if she's impressed or confused that I know this.

Sittu turns to me. "You pray?"

"I used to, with Mom. It's been a while."

"Your mother doesn't pray anymore?"

"She does—"

"But you don't pray with her?"

I shake my head.

"Well, it's good your mother doesn't force you to pray."

"My mother's not very religious," Deanna says. "We don't pray, but I'd like to learn how you do it. I've watched on the news when all the Muslims pray together at Mecca. It looks so beautiful."

"You are welcome to join me anytime," Sittu says.

"*Shukran*," Deanna says.

"*Afwan*." Sittu smiles. "After we pray, we can take some breakfast and then talk about what we might do today."

"We were just talking about that. Right, Mar?"

I don't say a word, and I hope Deanna doesn't mention the demonstration.

"I made a list of all the places I wanted to see. Mar, would you get my notebook for me?" She turns and points to the nightstand. I pick up her notebook and hand it to her, wondering what she's up to. "Let's see, what did I write down? Go to the pyramids. We've already done that." She flips through pages. "There's really nothing else." This is such a lie. Deanna has pages filled with places she wants to see.

"I guess I have nothing on my agenda for today. Mar, you were talking about going to Tahrir Square, weren't you?" Her eyes are begging me to back her up. I really do want to. Deanna has always been there for me, but I can't ask Sittu to take us to this protest, not after all she and I talked about, not when I know how she suffered over what happened to Baba.

"The mall," I say. "Is there one nearby?"

"The mall?" I can hear Deanna straining to keep her cool.

"Of course," Sittu says. "It may not be fancy-schmancy." I try not to laugh at the way Sittu says *schmancy*. It sounds like she's heard the word in a movie and isn't sure if she's using it correctly. "It's no Mall of America, but they do have an ice-skating rink."

"In Egypt?" Deanna and I ask at the same time.

"If Jamaicans can compete on a bobsled in the Olympics, Egyptians can ice-skate at the mall. I'll leave you girls to get some more rest. It's still very early, and the stores won't open for a while." Sittu heads toward the door.

Deanna calls to her, "Sittu, can you tell me what this girl is saying?" Deanna hits the video link on Hassan's page.

Sittu watches for less than a minute, then reaches over Deanna to pause the video. "Her name is Asmaa Mahfouz."

"That much I know," Deanna says.

"You've heard of her?" Sittu looks surprised, but in a good way.

"It says her name right there in the clip." Deanna points to the screen. "What is she saying?" She keeps her eyes on the frozen image of Asmaa.

Sittu takes in a deep breath and slowly lets it out. "She's talking about the people who set themselves on fire."

"On fire? Are they crazy?" I say.

"That's what the government would want you to believe, but no. They're not crazy. Some would say heroic, and others say desperate. One man couldn't feed his daughter. Asmaa made this video on the day one of these men burned to death. She called for people to join her at Tahrir Square. That was on January eighteenth. It's hard to believe that was only a week ago."

"Why meet there?" Deanna asks.

"The Parliament buildings are there, and other government buildings. She was very upset when people started posting that this man had committed a sin for killing himself when she believed he was doing this for Egypt, like people in Tunisia had done. She asked people to join her in protest against what our government is doing—for people to stand up for their rights. She told people who worried she would set herself on fire that they needed to meet her there and save her from this. She is a very smart girl.

"'I, a girl, am going down to Tahrir Square, and I will stand alone.'" Sittu sounds like she's reciting the Pledge of Allegiance. "'And I'll hold up a banner. Perhaps people will show some honor…'"

Sittu stops. She looks over at me, and then she looks down at Deanna. "Yes, she wanted people to show some honor and join her. I must have watched that video a thousand times."

"Did they?"

"Three people. And security forces and police stopped them, pushing them into a building. In this video"—Sittu points to another link on the screen—"she talks about what happened and asks people to join her for another demonstration, a demonstration of peace, on January twenty-fifth."

"Today," Deanna says.

"Yes, today."

Sittu's iPhone beeps. She pulls it from her housecoat pocket and starts to type.

"You're texting?" I ask.

"Twitting," Sittu says.

"Tweeting." I smile.

"About the protest?" Deanna asks. "We should all go, right?"

"It's not the best plan for today," Sittu replies.

"Please," Deanna pleads, "think about what this would mean. It's our chance to fight for Egypt! We can't let Asmaa do this alone."

"*Habibti*, she won't be alone. Many youth will be there, I'm sure. Youth groups are the reason I'm on Facebook. When I see what these young people are doing, they give me hope."

"Back home, we use Facebook to tell our friends what song we just downloaded—so lame," Deanna says.

"The youth here are doing that too, *habibti*."

"But they are also talking about trying to make a difference," Deanna says. "We should help them."

"Deanna, stop pushing. Sittu doesn't want us to go, and we need to respect her decision."

"She never said she didn't want us to go. Right?" Deanna looks up at Sittu, her eyes so wide I'm afraid her eyeballs will pop out of their sockets.

Sittu's quiet for a long moment. Sittu can't seriously be considering giving her permission? How totally irresponsible would it be to take us to some protest—especially after what happened to my father—when she's supposed to keep us safe? Sittu walks over to the mirror. I've never noticed it before, but Sittu and I have the same full cheeks, large round eyes, and classic Egyptian nose. My lips aren't as full as hers, and there is green mixed into the brown of my eyes, but I look like her—a lot. Except the features that look so beautiful on Sittu don't do anything for me. She adjusts the barrette holding her hair. The movement feels so familiar. Maybe I do have memories from my last visit. Sittu's hair is all white, and yet she looks so young to me right now. "I would love to go to the protest today."

"You can't do that!" The words just burst out of me.

"I can't?" Sittu snaps at me. "You are telling me I can't?"

"Last night you told me about Baba getting arrested and tortured!"

"Your father was tortured?" Deanna sounds as shocked as I was.

"Mariam." Sittu moves closer to me, and I flinch.

"Do you think I would ever put my hand to you?" she asks.

"You just sound so angry."

"Mariam." Her voice is softer now. "I may do Facebook, but I'm very old-school about some things. A granddaughter yelling at her grandmother about what she can or can't do is disrespectful."

"I didn't mean—"

"I know, I know." Sittu holds my chin in her palm. "But think before you speak."

"So then we're going?" Deanna is so smiling inside.

Sittu drops her hand. "I love your spirit, Deanna. You remind me very much of a dear friend of mine."

Now I know Deanna's beaming inside.

"But, *habibti*, Mubarak's security forces are also looking at these tweets and Facebook updates and all the communication about the protest. They know exactly where people plan to gather, and they will have these areas blocked off. Look at what happened just last week to poor Asmaa—only three people and so many security forces. It's wonderful that there are so many young people trying to make change, but this will be one more demonstration in a long line of useless demonstrations."

"Really?" Deanna sounds crushed.

Sittu's phone beeps. She ignores it, but it continues to beep. Finally she reads the message on the screen then says, "Deanna, may I please sit at the computer?" Sittu sits down, and we watch as she pulls up another video of Asmaa.

"Is that new?" Deanna asks.

"Yes. From last night." Sittu hits play.

"She looks happier in this video," Deanna comments.

"Shush, please," Sittu says.

We're silent as Sittu listens to the girl speak in Arabic. Asmaa seems more passionate than she did before; she looks as if whatever she's saying is the most important thing in the world. And from the way Sittu is so attentive and still, I think she must feel the same way.

When the video ends, Sittu shuts down the computer. "Okay, I am going to do the morning prayer, and then we can have a little to eat, unless you want to sleep more."

"But what did she say?" Deanna asks.

"More words."

Last night, Sittu said words without action have no meaning. I can't help but wonder if this applies to Sittu too, or if she's excused from this.

Sittu pauses. "Okay, I'll tell you, but then no more talk of this today."

Deanna nods, but I can't believe she'll let this go.

"She talks about how people have been working very hard for today's protests. Children under fourteen and older people in their sixties and seventies, old people like me"—Sittu half smiles—"all working to spread the word about the peaceful protest. She says if we all stand together against the security forces and the police, we can demand our rights—that we must demand our rights."

"Please, let us go and support her and Egypt." Deanna sounds like, any minute, she's going to get down on her knees and beg.

"You agreed: no more talk," Sittu says. "I believe you are a woman of honor."

"Fine," Deanna says, and when I look into her eyes, I realize this is the first time I've ever seen her look defeated.

"Thank you for your love of this country." Sittu kisses Deanna on the forehead, and I'm feeling jealous. "If I could," Sittu continues,

"I would give you an Egyptian passport, though unfortunately, your American passport gets you treated far better here. Still, in my eyes, you are Egypt."

For the first time, maybe in my whole life, I wish I were Egypt too.

"Okay, my loves, it's getting late. I need to pray." Sittu walks out of the room, closing the door behind her.

"What happened, Mariam?" Deanna asks.

"I didn't tell Sittu not to take us," I defend.

"No, but you didn't fight for us to go either."

"How can I ask Sittu to take us after she told me what happened to my father?"

"Mariam, this isn't about your father, and Sittu isn't afraid, for her or for us. Sittu's not going to the protest today because she's lost hope. And here you are, her only granddaughter, hating everything about yourself, the culture that's a part of you. If I were her, I'd feel hopeless too. When are you going to wake up and see what matters?"

Deanna stalks out of the room, slamming the door behind her.

I want to yell after her, but the things I want to say I cannot say in Sittu's house. So instead I get dressed for the mall, putting on a blue T-shirt and the jeans that make my butt look fat.

chapter SEVENTEEN

D eanna, can you believe it?" I point to a girl standing in front of the electronics store. "She's wearing the same T-shirt you gave me."

Deanna ignores me. She's still not talking to me. Like it's my fault she can't go and save Egypt.

"What girl?" Sittu asks.

I point.

Sittu pulls my hand down. "Don't point."

"Sorry. She's wearing the pretty lavender hijab. See? Her shirt has the word *lipstick* painted with pink glitter across the chest… I haven't gotten to wear it though."

"Your parents?"

"Yes."

"Well, if your shirt is that tight, I wouldn't let you wear it either."

It's awkward to hear my grandmother talk about this, so I change the topic. "Her hijab is beautiful. The ones I see people wearing back home are usually pretty boring. Right, Deanna?"

"Is this mall always so empty?" Deanna asks as if I weren't there. She's right. Maybe everyone is going to show up to support Asmaa this time.

"Times are rough," Sittu says. "There's not a lot of money to spend." She pulls us in front of a store window. "What do you think about these jeans?" she asks me, nodding toward the mannequin.

"Those are kinda cute," I say.

"What do you think? Shall we go in?" Sittu asks.

I glance at Deanna, who is still pretending I don't exist.

"I guess," I say, but I feel strange about shopping for jeans while Asmaa might be at Tahrir Square alone. What if the mall is empty because everyone is at home for the holiday, not because they are going to protest?

We all walk into the store. Usually, Deanna would be all over this place, wanting to try on everything, but right now, she looks bored.

"You girls look around, and I'll see about getting someone to help us."

I start thumbing through jeans folded on a shelf but can't find my size. "Mar, come over here," Deanna calls.

I'm so excited she's talking to me I practically skip over to her.

"Aren't these beautiful?" Deanna asks, standing in front of a display of hijabs. "The turquoise one is to die for." She picks it up. "Touch it. It's silk, like Sittu's dress."

"Feels nice," I say.

"Turquoise is feminine but not too girly. What do you think? Should I get one?"

"For what?" I ask.

"To wear, of course."

"Why on earth would you want to cover your pretty hair?"

"The saleswoman will be with us in a minute," Sittu says, returning to us.

"Sittu, she wants to buy one of those head things."

"They're beautiful," Deanna says.

"If you would like to get one, you should," Sittu says.

"If Deanna wears that around her head, people are going to think she's Muslim," I say.

"So what if they do?" Deanna asks defensively.

"Well, I just don't know why you would want people to think you are if you're not."

"Mar," Deanna says, "I'm used to people assuming things about me."

"Are you really going to wear it back home? I don't know why anyone would if they didn't have to. I'm just lucky my parents aren't that backward"—I put my hand to my mouth. Sittu's eyes narrow—"I didn't mean…"

"Don't say you didn't mean what you did mean." Sittu has the same hurt look on her face Baba did when I told him I didn't want to go to Egypt.

"But I didn't mean to upset you."

"This I know, *habibti*, but I'm not sad for myself."

"Would you like me to show you how to put it on?" the saleswoman asks Deanna, who's still holding the turquoise hijab in her hand.

Deanna looks at Sittu.

"If you like, be my guest." Sittu smiles, and I'm surprised she doesn't have a problem with Deanna wearing the hijab.

"*Shukran*," Deanna says to the saleslady. "That would be great."

The woman pulls the scarf around Deanna's head and under her chin so tightly it's like she's making it hurricane-proof.

Deanna looks in the mirror. "Beautiful," the saleslady says.

"The color is very nice on you, Deanna," Sittu says.

I pretend to look at some long skirts hanging on the rack nearby. It's one thing to want to go to some protest, even to pray with Sittu, but now she wants to wear the hijab? What's she trying to prove?

"*Shukran*," Deanna says.

"*Afwan*," the saleswoman says. "Shall I wrap it for you?"

"Let us have a minute," Sittu says.

"Of course," the saleswoman says, walking over to a woman who's offering her child a lollipop to get him to stop crying. Of course, it's not working. I don't know why adults always think offering kids something they don't want will make them stop wanting the thing that they do want.

"Do you really like it?" Sittu asks.

"Very much. It's a beautiful color," Deanna says.

"True, but you do understand it's not just a fashion statement when you wear one of these? It's your choice, of course."

"Well, maybe I'll think about it some more," Deanna says. "Can you help me? It's on a bit tight."

When I turn back to them, Deanna is folding the hijab and placing it back on the shelf.

"Did you want to try on some of those jeans?" Sittu asks me, sounding like everything is cool between us again.

"They only have big sizes—like in the thirties."

Sittu and Deanna laugh, and even though I'm the target, it's nice to hear Deanna's laugh again.

"What? What am I clueless about this time?"

"Those are European sizes," Deanna says.

"So what would an eight be?"

"You are not an eight, Mar," Deanna says.

"I can't be a ten," I say. "I don't think I've gained any weight."

"Come here." Deanna pulls me in front of the mirror. "You're, like, a size two. Smaller than me. Look at your pants! They're all baggy on you."

"It's true," Sittu says. "We have to get some meat on your bones. I can't send you back to your *baba* looking like I've starved you."

Sittu's bag starts to sing, "She wears short skirts. I wear T-shirts…" She rifles through her purse and pulls out her iPhone. "What?" she says.

"Taylor Swift?" Deanna and I both say in unison.

"It was a free download, and it has a peppy beat," Sittu says, looking down at her phone. "I need to get this… *Aiwa?…* Good to hear your voice too… Just a minute," she says. "I can't hear you too well." Sittu presses her phone closer to her ear, covers the other ear with her hand, and walks out of the store.

"I bet it's about the protest," Deanna says.

"You're not going to let it go, are you?"

"Don't you think Sittu wants to be at Tahrir Square instead of some stupid mall? Doesn't it make you feel bad that the only reason she's probably not there is because she's worried about us?"

I shrug.

"Listen to me." Deanna stares into my eyes like she's trying to hypnotize me. "Your grandmother has waited all her life to see change happen in this country—"

"No, you listen to me," I say, surprising myself. From Deanna's half-open mouth, I can tell she's a bit shocked too. "You can blame me all you freakin' want, but did you ever think maybe after she lost her son, she may be a little nervous about something happening to us?"

"Your father's not dead."

"Well, he may as well be. He never comes to see her. He didn't even go to his own father's funeral. After my father was tortured, Sittu and my grandfather forced him to leave the country, and he never forgave them."

"Then why did he come back when you were a baby? Maybe your father hasn't visited because of 9/11 and how hard your government makes it for Muslims to travel."

"I was six when 9/11 happened. I'm sure the only reason my father came when I was a baby was because my mom made him. Sittu doesn't want to risk our safety for what will probably be yet another useless demonstration. People will get arrested, interrogated, and nothing will change."

"Okay, I get it," Deanna says. "It must have been a huge deal for your father to even send you here." We both look over at Sittu, who's standing by the down escalator. "Do you think it's your father?"

I remember how Baba isn't talking to me and feel a moment of sadness.

Before I can respond, Deanna says, "No, it can't be your dad. Look at her, she's talking to some guy she's crushing on."

"How do you know?"

"See the way she's smiling? That's not just any smile. That's an I'm-really-into-this-guy smile. If there's one thing I know, it's smiles."

We watch Sittu finish her conversation. When she rejoins us, she still has that silly smile on her face. Maybe Deanna's right. It wouldn't be the first time.

"So who was that?" Deanna's tone is so obvious. Why doesn't she just sing, "Sittu and some guy, sitting in a tree…"?

"It was Ahmed."

"Ahmed who? There are a lot of Ahmeds in Cairo," Deanna says.

"You know which Ahmed." Sittu's actually blushing. I can't believe it.

"What did he want?" Deanna asks.

"To meet for coffee today, but I told him I was spending the afternoon with my granddaughters at the mall. Now, should we go and see about those jeans or try another store?"

"You should have coffee with him," Deanna says. "Right, Mar?"

"She should do what she wants. What do you want?" I ask my grandmother.

"Oh, throwing my own words back in my face. You are my granddaughter," Sittu says.

"Well, what do you want?" I ask again.

"I already told him I couldn't."

"I'm sure there's a café in the mall," I say.

"Have him meet you here," Deanna suggests.

"He did say he was in the area." I can hear from her voice that she really wants to see him. "But I didn't get his number."

"Can I borrow that?" I snatch the phone from her hand before she has a chance to respond, and I hit the last number in her call log. "It's ringing," I say, handing her the phone.

Sittu takes the phone back from me. "You are hardheaded like your father."

And like my sittu, I almost say, but I'm pretty sure she knows this.

"Ahmed? Yes, it's me. It turns out I can meet... Why don't you meet me here...in fifteen minutes?" Sittu looks nervous.

Deanna and I nod and mouth, "Yes. Say yes."

"Yes, that would be fine. *Wa-Alaikum-Salaam.*" She ends the call. "What are you girls getting me into?" she says.

"It's coffee," Deanna says. "Just coffee. You may want to refresh your lipstick though."

"Oh, you." She nudges Deanna's arm. I've never seen her so playful.

"Is there a bathroom nearby?" Deanna asks.

"Need to refresh your lipstick too?" I ask her.

"Need to pee," Deanna says.

"There's one over there," Sittu says, pointing to the WC sign.

Sittu and I take a seat on a metal bench outside the bathroom. We sit for a few minutes before I finally say, "I'm really sorry."

"Why are you always sorry?" Sittu asks.

"I know I upset you with what I said, and I didn't mean to say people here are backward."

"*Habibti*, you didn't upset me."

"You said you were sad."

She takes my hands in hers and rests them both on her lap. "I'm sad for you, my love."

"Me?"

"It must be very hard to be ashamed of who you are."

I pull my hands back. "I'm not ashamed."

"Then I apologize for making a false judgment. That was my observation. It just seemed that being Muslim, being Egyptian, was the problem for you, not the hijab."

"I don't have a problem with—" I stop myself. There's nothing I can say to Sittu that could convince her I'm okay with being Muslim and Egyptian, because the truth is I'm not okay with it. It would be so much easier if I were Christian or Jewish or even an atheist.

"It can't be easy, *habibti*, to feel different from everyone around you."

"But I'm not different," I say. "Kids at school treat me like I am, but I'm not."

"Well, this is true. You care about your clothes and boys and—"

"Sittu!" Now I feel my face turning red.

"Okay, no talk about boys, but do the kids at school say things to make you feel like you don't belong?"

"Some of them do," I say. "They call me names."

"And what do you tell them?"

I don't respond. I can't think of anything I've ever said to stand up for myself—to Karen or Beth or anyone.

"You have never answered them back? Do you walk away?"

"No. I guess I just stand there and take it."

"Why do you think this is?"

"I don't know."

"Are you afraid of these people?"

"No. I'm not afraid of them."

"So then you want to be like them? Accepted by them?"

"No. Well, maybe I did, but Deanna's showed me they're really jerks."

"Deanna sounds like she's a good friend."

"She's the best."

"Not so smart, though, huh?"

"She's totally smart."

"Well, she's kind of different herself, with her face not working."

"Sittu." I stand up. "I don't mean to disrespect you, but what makes Deanna different from those jerks at school is that she's beautiful and brilliant and—"

I stop talking. She's got me again. "Okay, I get it," I say, sitting back down.

"What do you get?"

"I should care about what people like Deanna think and not what those idiots think."

"Well, you're close."

"What don't I get?"

"You're smart. You will figure it out."

I'm silent for a long while, but I'm not trying to figure anything out. I'm just feeling guilty about how wrong I was about Sittu and how I hurt my father. When I can't take it anymore, I blurt out, "Sittu, I have something to confess."

"Do I look like a priest?" She smiles.

"Well, I don't know if you know this, but Baba's not talking to me."

"I had my suspicions something was not right between the two of you."

"Well, he's very mad at me because…"

"I know all about the party. It wasn't very smart of you to get caught up in such a mess and to lie to your parents. But I'm sure you learned your lesson, and for my own selfish part, I'm glad this incident brought you to me."

"Sittu, I'm glad too. I really am. But Baba's not mad at me because of…" How can I tell her what I'd said about her?

"Look at me." Her tone is serious, the way it was the first day we arrived. "Do you believe I love you?"

"Uh, yes."

"What is this 'uh'? You hesitate?"

"No, of course I know you love me."

"So nothing you say will change that. It may make me angry or hurt my feelings or break my heart, but it won't make me love you less."

"I said some awful things about you and Egypt."

"Now you know me and Egypt a little more. Do you still believe the things you said?"

"No. No, I don't."

"Maybe just a little?"

"Maybe. I don't know. But not about you."

"Then we have nothing to talk about. I don't fault ignorance."

"Baba does."

"Your father, he's very much like your *giddu*. Soft hearts make for strong heads. But he will forgive in time."

"You said he still hasn't forgiven you. And you're his mother."

"I wasn't ignorant. I knew what I was making him give up, and I understood the consequences of my actions. But to have him safe, well, I thought it was worth losing him. Was it the right decision? I don't know. We're only human and that means we are destined to make mistakes. Some greater, some lesser. I do not think your mistake is so great. It just feels that way. You learn."

I kiss her on the cheek.

"What is this gift for?" She touches her cheek.

"You're pretty cool, that's all."

"Actually, I'm feeling a bit warm, but you, *habibti*, are the very coolest," she says, wiping her forehead with the back of her hand. I wish I had the handkerchief she gave me at the pyramids. She's really sweating. I guess she's nervous about meeting Ahmed. It's kind of sweet.

"The hardest thing for you will be patience," Sittu says.

"With Baba?"

"With yourself."

She takes my hand as if she's going to tell my fortune. "Love, whether it be for a child or a parent or a very cute boy, is difficult, but you can't let it beat you down."

"I'm fine," I say.

"Well, you make sure you find yourself something beautiful to wear for your birthday tomorrow."

"I guess so much has been happening, I forgot."

"I didn't." Sittu puts money into my palm, closes my fingers over it, and lets go.

"Baba gave me money," I say, trying to give it back to her.

Sittu clicks her tongue at me and I know I better not argue. "*Shukran*," I say.

She smiles, and says, "You know, I think I will take some of Deanna's advices and put on some lipstick." She stands. I go to follow her, but she tells me to wait for Deanna and walks toward the escalator.

"Sittu," I call to her. "The bathroom is right here."

She stops and turns to me. "I'll use the one in the café downstairs. When you're done, meet me there. It's at the far end of the food court."

"We will," I say.

She steps onto the escalator. "*Habibti*," she calls to me.

"Yes?"

"Take your time shopping." She winks, and then she's out of sight.

chapter EIGHTEEN

W here's Sittu?" Deanna asks a moment later.

"She went to meet Ahmed."

"Already?"

"Well, you've been gone a long time."

"Do you really want to know what I was doing in there?"

I wrinkle my nose. "Ew. Maybe you should eat more fiber." Deanna glares at me and I change the subject. "Sittu seemed a little nervous."

"How cute!"

"She said we should take our time before meeting her in the café."

"Then let's take our time. Hey, there's a movie theater over there."

We walk over to the entrance. "Wasn't this out, like, two years ago?" I point to the poster advertising the Hannah Montana movie.

"I saw it," Deanna mumbles. It's actually kind of nice to see that even Deanna has a dorky side. "Well, it wasn't my choice. My mom doesn't like to take me to R-rated movies, and it was the only thing playing in the theaters at the time."

"Your mom will take you to demonstrations, but she won't take you to R-rated movies?" I regret this as soon as I say it.

"You just don't get it." Deanna starts toward the escalator.

"I'm sorry!" I run after her and catch her before she gets on. "I didn't mean to bring it all up again."

"Look, Mar, when you say such clueless stuff, it just makes me mad. So let's stop talking about demonstrations and justice and Egypt and pretend nothing is happening outside this mall. Okay?"

"Deanna, I want to understand. I really do. But I guess I never cared enough about something to consider protesting or marching."

"You sign all those petitions I email you."

"That's because you're my BFF and I love you."

"Well"—Deanna puts her arm around me—"I guess I love you too." I can hear her smiling.

"Hey, Sittu gave me this," I say, opening my palm. "She wants me to buy something nice for my birthday.

"Then let's find you an awesome outfit. Let's check out the lower level." Deanna drops her arm and steps onto the escalator.

I go to follow her but pull back. Ever since I was four, when I tripped and fell on one, I hesitate to take the first step.

"Mariam, come on!" Deanna shouts up to me. She's already halfway down.

I try to step again, but I can't do it.

"Don't rush me!" I shout to her. "You know I hate these things."

There's a woman and a little boy waiting behind me. I move out of their way. The boy, who can't be any older than three, jumps on and runs down a few steps until his mother catches him. I was never that fearless. Why am I such a wimp?

The next thing I know, Deanna is climbing up the escalator.

"What are you doing? Are you crazy?" I yell to her.

"If you won't come down, I'm coming to get you."

Deanna passes the boy and then his mother; then she is at the top, reaching for my hand, stepping in place like she's on the StairMaster in her basement.

"This is stupid," I say. "I can do it. I just need a second."

"Of course you can do it. You climbed up the freakin' Great Pyramid."

"I turned around."

"Well, you almost made it to the top and you climbed down, and that was a lot harder than this. Listen," Deanna says, breathing heavily, "climbing up this thing in the wrong direction is one thing, but stepping off it in the wrong direction is dangerous. So if you don't want me to fall and cut up my face at the bottom, you'll suck it up and step on." She reaches out for my hand. "Trust me."

I grab on to her hand. I hold on to Deanna for dear life until we reach the bottom and get off safely.

Deanna slaps me on the back.

"*Shukran*," I say. "Aren't you tired of always saving my ass?"

"Friends don't leave friends behind," she says.

There's a big ice-skating rink in front of us.

"Sittu wasn't kidding."

"I guess not," I say. "But it doesn't seem very popular." The ice is completely empty, and as we get closer, I can see that it's so smooth, it looks like it's never been skated on.

"You want to skate?" I ask.

"Why not? How many kids back at school can say they went ice-skating in Egypt?"

"I don't think many kids at school can say they've done anything in Egypt."

We walk over to the ticket booth, which has a sign in Arabic and English: Skate Rental.

"There's no one here," I say.

"Maybe it's closed for the holiday?"

I don't respond. I don't want to go back to arguing about why we're here and not at Tahrir Square.

"Well, there's the food court," Deanna says, looking toward the other side of the rink. "Let's get a juice or something."

Sittu said she was meeting Ahmed at a café, and the last thing I want to do is mess up her date. We are walking away from the skate rental booth when a man starts shouting at us.

"Madams! Please, one moment!"

By the time he catches up to us, he's breathing so hard I'm worried he may have a heart attack.

"You're open?" Deanna asks.

"Too much *ful*," the man says, huffing and puffing and patting his huge belly.

"What's *ful*?" Deanna asks.

"Fava beans," I say.

"Fava beans?" The man sounds insulted. "*Ful* is Egypt's national dish. So much more than just fava beans."

"Mar, all the times I've eaten over at your place and we never had *ful*?"

"I'm allergic to it," I say, knowing what's coming next.

"What?" the man says. "You're not Egyptian, then?"

"She is," Deanna says.

"Egyptian and allergic to *ful*…" The man sounds as disappointed as if he had been told he couldn't eat *ful* anymore.

"So can we rent skates?" I ask.

"Of course."

Deanna and I try on several pairs before we find ones that fit and have blades sharp enough to use.

"You have to put these on." I hand her skate guards.

"What for?"

"You need them to walk," I say.

"We're only going a few feet to the ice." She stands up and, after one step, falls back to the bench.

"Don't say anything," she says. "I get it."

I help her put her guards on, then quickly put on mine. "Ready?"

"I guess."

"It'll be fun," I reassure her.

Deanna grabs my arm to steady herself. The two of us wobble our way toward the ice. "We're having so much trouble, and we're not even on the ice yet!" Deanna laughs so loud, she sounds like a foghorn.

"We're having trouble?" I laugh. "I'm not the one holding on for dear life."

"Okay, fine. But this was your idea."

"Guards off," I say.

"Wouldn't it be easier if we just left them on?"

I shake my head.

"Fine," she says.

"Come on. I'll help you." I step onto the ice, and now it's me reaching out to Deanna. For once, it's nice to be able to help her. Deanna grabs on to my hand but has too much forward momentum, so we both fall on our butts.

I hear laughter, and when I look up, a group of guys are watching us from the food court on the far side of the rink. My first thought is to get off the ice, like, now, but then I think, *Who cares what these idiots think?* My second thought is that the mall isn't so deserted after all, and now I'm even more worried about Asmaa.

"You said you had me."

"Well, let me lead." I stand up, then reach down and help her up. "You can hold on to me for balance, but try not to lean into me too much, or we'll both land on our butts again."

"Okay," Deanna says, and I think it's the first time I've ever heard her sound hesitant. "Are those guys still watching us?"

"Forget them," I say.

"Don't let go," she says as we scrape slowly along the ice.

"You're doing it," I say.

"Still, don't let go."

"I won't."

We manage to make it around twice. Both times we pass the boys, our audience claps. Then the owner shouts to us that we have ten more minutes before our time is up.

"Thank God," Deanna says.

"It's not that bad," I say. "You want to try and go solo?"

"Okay."

When I let go, Deanna skates about two steps and then she's down.

"Let me help you up." I reach for her hand.

"No, I'm just going to crawl my way to the edge."

"You can't crawl on the ice. Please, take my hand."

I lead her off the ice.

"We still have time," she says. "Show me what you've got."

I make sure Deanna has her guards back on properly before I get back on the ice and fly. I've missed this. I used to skate a lot. I took lessons when I was younger. Baba loved to take me skating on Saturday afternoons. He never tried it himself, but he said it made him happy to watch me. I think he secretly wanted me to be an Olympic figure skater, but he never pressured me. Maybe because he was so pressured as a kid. Yet the way he looked when I'd wave to him as I skated around the ice, I could see he had big hopes for me.

"Way to go," Deanna shouts as I speed skate by.

I feel like I can do anything. I skate to the center of the rink. Maneuvering backward, arms stretched out wide, I spin and pull my arms into my body. I spin faster and faster, then do the one thing I've never been able to do: stop without losing my balance. I stop exactly on my mark.

I did it! Baba would always call me his ballerina on ice, but I never felt like one until now.

I hear applause. When I look up, the group of guys has grown. They're watching me and shouting what seems to be the Arabic equivalent of "Go, girl! GO!"

I bow. I'm never this bold, but hey, I just did a scratch spin for the first time in years.

"*Shukran!*" I shout to the guys. They're all dressed pretty much the same—jeans and short-sleeved polo shirts, but there is nothing uniform about their sizes. The two bookends are close to six feet and string-bean thin. Two inner guys are probably only a few inches taller than me, and they're apple shaped. The guy in the middle is monster size: basketball-player tall and football-player wide.

They applaud again, and I turn to make my way toward the exit, not wanting to blow my moment of glory by falling on my face, when I see him—Hassan.

He's sitting in the food court, and he's not alone. He's with some girl who's wearing a blue hijab. If he were any closer to her, he'd be sitting on her lap. I stop and stare. That's when he kisses the girl, right there, on her hand. And it's in that moment I know I'm really not into him. Sure, he's cute—and yes, what a sexy dimple—but not even one tiny jolt of jealousy hits my heart. I really couldn't care less. But I look over at Deanna. She's looking in Hassan's direction. *Please, oh, please, don't see him; don't recognize him.* As I skate closer to her, I can tell from the way she's staring that she's noticed him.

Maybe Deanna feels like I do and couldn't care less. When I reach her, I jump off the ice.

"Ready to go," I say. I take a step and trip into Deanna.

She stops me from falling this time. "Don't forget to put on your guards," she reminds me, handing me a set. She sounds sad. As I fix my skates, she asks, "Do you see who's over there?"

"Who? Where?" I ask, no longer concentrating on my feet.

"He kissed her hand," she says. It's clear her heart has been Tasered.

Hassan is now laughing with the girl. Baba was right after all: avoid Egyptian guys. "I'm sorry."

"Is my mascara smeared?" she asks.

I look closely at her face. I've never seen her cry before.

"No, not at all. Bet you're glad you paid extra for the waterproof kind," I joke, trying to lighten the tension.

"I know you want to make me feel better, but you're kinda sucking at it." She runs her hand lightly over her cheek to double check. "They're probably freakin' engaged. But he was so flirting with me! Sittu had to make him go home. He was into me, right?"

"Of course he was," I try to reassure her.

"Come on. Let's go find Sittu at the café."

She nods, but when we go to turn in our skates for our shoes, the guy who eats too much *ful* is nowhere to be found.

"This is just great," Deanna says, leaning into me for balance, and I can see in her eyes she's really hurting—the kind of hurting crying doesn't help. "Where is that guy?"

"He's probably in the food court," I joke, but Deanna isn't finding anything funny right now.

"You know, if I had a cell phone that worked here, we could just call Sittu so we wouldn't have to find her," Deanna says.

I know what she really means. We wouldn't have to walk through the food court and pass Hassan on our way to meet Sittu at the café.

"Didn't Sittu say I could buy a phone at the mall? But first I need my shoes. Where did that guy go?"

"Listen. Sit here." I help Deanna sit down on the bench. "I can

walk faster in these things than you. I'll look around for him."
Deanna looks over at a young couple standing in front of the
skate rental booth. They're not kissing or even holding hands,
but you can tell from the goofy smiles on their faces they're really
into each other.

"You know, Mar, what hurts the most is that for the first time in
my life, I felt like I could just be me. I even felt pretty."

"Pretty? Deanna, you're beautiful."

"I'm a freak. I was a freak back home, and I'm a freak here."

"You're not a freak. And if you were, so what? Who says freaks
aren't cool? I'm a freak too."

"Okay, Mar, we're cool. It's just some days I hate looking like this."

"*Stop it*," I say. The couple looks at us. "They're closed," I snap.
They walk away.

"Mar, calm down."

"No, I'm tired of being calm. You're one of the most beautiful,
brilliant—no, not one of. You are the most beautiful and brilliant
person I know. Are you going to let some guy make you doubt that?"

"Now you sound like me. Mar, you always treat me like I'm all
that, and you don't get how scared I am inside, just like you."

"But, Deanna, you're so much braver than I am. You'll go up to
anyone and just start talking to them. You tell people exactly what
you think," I say.

"I have to. Look, I act all tough because I got tired of being
bullied. Do you know what it was like at my last school? People
think everyone in San Francisco is all hippie and nice, but kids in
San Francisco are mean too. Do you think Sphinx Face is an insult?

You should have heard the other names I've been called. They all thought I was stuck up and wasn't friendly because I wasn't smiling at them, then when they found out I just can't smile, they felt sorry for me. And no one wants to be friends with someone they feel sorry for."

"I never felt sorry for you." I want to say something more to make Deanna feel better, but then I remember why I stopped telling my parents when I was sad—it's exhausting to have people trying to cheer you up.

"Hey." Deanna grabs my hand. "Thanks. Really."

"For what?" I ask.

"For getting it. And for thinking I'm perfect when I'm not."

"You know," I say, "you may talk tough, but you don't just talk, you act. You have guts. You wanted to go to the protest today. To stand up for what's right. I was the one who was scared, too scared to do the things that matter."

Deanna sighs. "You should go and find the skate rental guy."

I nod, thinking how Deanna needs our friendship as much as I do. "I'll be back soon," I say, clopping away.

"Hey!" Deanna shouts after me.

I turn to face her.

"When you find Mr. Ful, tell him I want a *ful* refund!"

chapter
NINETEEN

The entrance to the food court is blocked by a huddle of ten girls. They're all about my age, all wearing jeans and long-sleeved T-shirts. They look exactly like the cliques back at my school, except about half of them are wearing hijabs and a few have Arabic writing across their foreheads. *What a weird place for a tattoo*, I think. I'm expecting things to go as they do at home—that is, any minute, someone will hassle me.

"Excuse me," I say. I'm trying to play it cool. "Do any of you know the guy who runs the skating place?"

When no one answers me, I'm not surprised. It's what I expect. Cliques are cliques in any culture, but then I realize maybe they don't speak English. As I start to wobble away on my skates, one of the girls asks, with a heavy accent, "You're American?"

"Yes," I say, "visiting my *sittu*."

"So you are Egyptian." A girl with curly red hair steps in front of me. It's almost as curly as Deanna's, but not nearly as beautiful.

"Yes," I say.

"I have family in New Jersey," she tells me.

"Jersey is nice," I reply, because I don't know what else to say. The only time I've been to New Jersey was when Baba accidentally drove over the George Washington Bridge on his way out of Manhattan.

"I'm going to visit next summer," she says.

"That's great," I say, trying to slip around Miss New Jersey. Maybe one of the food court workers can help me.

"Do you go to university?" a girl with an Arabic tattoo on her forehead asks.

"High school."

"Do you know *High School Musical*?" another jumps in.

"I've seen it," I say, looking over at Deanna on the bench. I would never have admitted it to anyone before, but now I know Deanna saw the Hannah Montana movie, so why not?

"I love it very much. *High School Musical 2* is not as good, but not bad."

"You look older." Jersey girl is back in my face. "I like your shirt." I have to look down to see which one I am wearing.

"*Shukran*," I say.

"*Afwan*." She smiles, launching into what sounds like the story of her life, all in Arabic.

"Excuse me." I try to interrupt, but she talks for several more sentences before she pauses to take a breath.

"I don't understand Arabic. Only a few words."

Jersey girl looks disappointed for a moment, but then she says, "So you will learn. I can teach you Arabic, and you can teach me English."

"That would be nice," I say, again not knowing how to respond. These girls have never met me, and they're acting like I'm their cousin visiting from America. I have to admit it's kind of nice to be liked without having to work for it.

"Is that your friend?" High School Musical asks, gesturing toward Deanna. "She doesn't look very happy."

I start to tell her she just can't smile, but then I remember Deanna isn't happy. She's miserable.

"We have to go, and the man who runs the skating rink has our shoes."

"He disappears all the time," Jersey says. "He's probably hanging out over at the *kushari* shop, at the other end. Do you know *kushari*?"

"The lentil, rice, and pasta dish," I say.

"My brother will take you. Omar, *yalla*." She waves at the group of guys who'd been watching me skate. From the way they are moving their hands and raising their voices, they seem to be arguing about something. Not one of them looks over at us, so I have no idea which one is Omar.

She turns to me. "We never made introductions. Safi." She extends her hand to me.

"Mariam," I say taking her hand.

"A pleasure," she says as we shake. Then she introduces me to all the other girls. Pointing to each one, she says their names: Hoda, Mona, Hala. By the fourth girl, I've lost track of who is who, but I keep shaking and responding, "A pleasure."

"Omar!" Safi calls again. This time, one of the guys looks up. He's about my height and definitely the cutest one in the group.

Actually, he's one of the cutest guys I've ever seen. He's so hot he could be on the cover of one of Deanna's romance novels.

"*Yalla*," she says, waving him over.

He gives her a why-are-you-bothering-me? shrug.

"He drives me so crazy. The youngest is always spoiled."

"I'm the youngest," Hoda says. At least, I think it's Hoda.

"Exactly my point." Safi laughs, and the other girls, including Hoda, join in.

"Pardon me, Mariam. I will be right back," she says, and before I can stop her, she's marching over to her brother. I can't hear what she's saying, but from the way all of the guys step back, it's clear she's being taken seriously.

"What happened with Omar?" one of the girls asks Hoda. "Are you not together?" I wonder whether she's talking in English because she's being polite or because she wants me to know the deal.

"Always politics," Hoda says. "Yes, it's important, but it would be nice if he took a minute to say how beautiful my eyes are." She and the other girls laugh so hard and loud, all of the guys stare.

"What did I miss?" Safi asks, returning with Omar trailing behind her.

"*Ahlan*." Omar nods to the group, but from the way he stares at Hoda, it's clear their breakup wasn't what he wanted and their relationship isn't quite over.

"Omar, this is Mariam, from…?"

"New York." I turn to him and extend my hand, but he's still so focused on Hoda, he doesn't notice. Embarrassed, I quickly drop my hand to my side.

"I appreciate your help," I say, "but I'm sure I can find the man from the skate rental on my own. No problem."

Both Omar and Safi click their tongues, the same way my parents do when they don't want to say a simple no, but an are-you-out-of-your-mind? no, a no-freaking-way no.

"You'll never find him," Omar tells me. "He's always hiding out, playing backgammon in the back of the store. Come, I'll take you."

"We have to leave," Safi says. "But we hope to meet again, Mariam."

"How will I get downtown?" Omar asks his sister.

"I told you we only have two cars." I can't imagine how they will fit all these girls into two cars. "Take the bus with your friends."

"The bus—" He mumbles something in Arabic.

"And take this." She hands him a flyer with Arabic writing on it.

"I know where people are meeting," he says, handing it back. "Are you going?" He looks at Hoda.

"You know my parents," she says.

"They should be going too!" Omar says. "This is a time when we all need to stand together."

"*Khalas!*" Safi says, shaking her head. "Save it for when you get to the protest."

"Come." He motions to me with his head. We start to walk, and I stumble into him. He grabs my arm to steady me. "You are a lot smoother on the ice," he says, and I think I see a smile.

"I'm sorry. I forgot I was wearing these."

When we get to the *kushari* place, Omar says, "Wait here."

My ankles hurt so badly from walking, I have to take off the skates. I sit down at a table to unlace them. I feel so much better, it's totally worth looking like an idiot as I walk around in my socks. I tie the laces together and sling them over my shoulder.

When Omar comes out, he says, "He's at the shawarma place. Come on, we have to hurry." He starts to walk, but after a few steps, he stops, looking down at my feet. "Nice socks," he says, then resumes at a pace even faster than before.

"I'm really sorry for taking up your time."

"Don't worry about it. There are just fewer rides because two people who were supposed to drive canceled at the last minute. No guts."

"You're going to Tahrir Square," I say.

"Where else?" He walks faster. I'm sliding around in my stocking feet and can barely keep up.

"Hey." He stops. "Do you have a car?"

I shake my head.

"Of course. God is not smiling on me today," he says. "This is the place. Be right back."

I'm really thirsty now, so I follow him inside to get a juice. As I wait in line, I watch the man behind the counter. Wearing a meat-stained apron, he's shaving shawarma with a small saw right onto people's plates.

"Looks delicious," the guy behind me says. I turn to him. "Hungry?" he asks in a very heavy Egyptian accent.

"Getting juice," I tell him. He's taller than most of the guys I've seen around here.

"You were the girl skating," he says.

"What gave me away?" I nudge the skates slung over my shoulder.

"It's your eyes," he says. "I would never forget eyes so beautiful."

I know this is a totally cheesy line, but I can't help but smile.

"My name is Muhammad."

"Mariam." I extend my hand. "Pleasure," I say now, used to the routine.

"I tried skating once—more like falling." He laughs. It's a sweet laugh. An honest laugh. He's not half as cute as Omar, but there is something about this guy I like. "There are some things that just aren't natural," he says.

"Like an Egyptian on ice," I say.

"Like anything that requires me to have coordination. I have two left feet and hands. You're American?"

"Yes, from New York." The line moves forward, and it's my turn to order. "*Itnein*." I hold up two fingers.

"You must be very thirsty," Muhammad says.

"One is for my friend." Deanna is probably starting to freak out. I've been gone for a while.

"*Itnein*—?" The counter guy asks.

I don't know how to say *guava juice*. "Excuse me"—I turn to Muhammad—"how do you say *two guava juices*?"

He steps up to the counter and says, "Two guava juices."

The guy nods.

"Oh," I say, embarrassed. "I guess he speaks English."

"Enough to sell his juices."

"To go," I say, and the man looks at me like he doesn't understand. "Is it my accent?" I ask Muhammad.

"Takeaway," Muhammad says to the man, who nods again.

"Thank you—I mean, *shukran*," I tell Muhammad.

"The pleasure is mine." He smiles, and one of his front teeth is crooked. Now I think he's twice as cute as Omar. "I've been to New York a few times. It's an amazing city."

"I live outside New York City," I say. "It's boring, not amazing like the city."

"Sounds like the village I'm from," he says. "Everybody knows your name, and you wish half the people didn't."

"More than half," I say, thinking about a lot of the kids at school.

The man puts the juices on the counter. Muhammad pays him before I can even get my hand out of my pocket.

I try to hand him the money. "Thank you, but I can't let you pay."

"Please, you are a guest in my country. It would make me very happy to do this. I rarely get a chance to practice my English," he says.

"Your English sounds pretty good to me," I say.

"So you can practice your Arabic, then," he says.

"I really can't let you pay." I try to hand him the money again. He gently pushes my hand away. "*Shukran.*"

"See, you are already practicing your Arabic!" He smiles, showing two deep dimples, and it makes me feel nice. "When I come to your country, you can buy me a juice."

Is he flirting with me?

Omar comes running out of the back room, shouting something in Arabic to the guy behind the counter, who reaches up and turns on the television.

"Look!" Omar grabs my arm like his team just won the Super

Bowl—or here, I guess it would be the World Cup. "Do you see how many people are there?"

"Is that Tahrir Square?"

"Thousands already!" Omar shouts, grinning. I have no idea what the news commentator is saying, but from the way Omar and Muhammad, and everyone else, are smiling, it must be good.

"I must go," Omar says. "But the guys in back said the ice-skate man has already returned to the booth. So you can get your shoes. It was nice to meet you." He grabs my hand and shakes it. "You're American, right?"

I nod.

"You should join us. It is important for the world to see Americans support us." He pauses. "You look too much like an Egyptian. People won't be able to tell you're American. Still, join us. The revolution starts today, and it may not be televised, but it will be tweeted!" he shouts, running out of the store.

"Your expression is very sad now," Muhammad says, looking into my eyes. "Did you want to go with your friend?"

"Omar? No. It's just my *sittu*—I think if she wasn't worried about me, she would have gone to this," I say, looking up at the television. The camera is on two small girls, no older than six, holding hands and swinging their arms. They look so happy.

"I have to find her and tell her we should go." I want to run to the café, but in socks and with the skates banging against my chest, it's just not happening.

"Let me carry these for you," Muhammad says, picking up the juices from the counter.

"That's okay. I can manage." I take the juices from him. After two steps, I realize everything will fall—drinks and skates—so I turn to him and say, "*Shukran.*"

He takes the juices.

"Didn't you need to order something?" I remind him.

"For some reason, I'm not hungry anymore." He smiles, and we walk back toward the rink.

Right before we make it out of the food court, someone shouts Muhammad's name. We both turn. It's Hassan and his blue-hijab girl.

"Mariam," he says, "I didn't realize it was you. What a nice surprise. Where is Deanna?" I look over at the bench by the ice, and she's not there. All I can imagine is Deanna crying her eyes out in the restroom, and without thinking, I grab one of the plastic cups from Muhammad's hand and throw the juice in Hassan's face.

Well, at least that's what I would have done had it not been wrapped so tightly in cellophane that nothing spilled out—not even a drop.

Hassan, Muhammad, and the girl all have the same expression on their faces: another crazy American.

But right now, in this moment, I don't feel crazy, even if I am walking around in socks, carrying skates over my shoulder, standing in a food court next to a skating rink in a mall in Egypt. And I definitely don't feel American. I feel like I come from a long line of strong women like Sittu who stand up for their best friends.

Hassan's expression is priceless—so innocent!

"Hassan, you almost had me convinced you were one of the good ones."

"Good ones? Good what, Mariam?" Hassan is very convincing. "Is everything all right?"

"Is this your girlfriend?" I roll my eyes, giving her a huge, fake smile. I guess Karen and Beth have taught me something.

"His girlfriend?" Muhammad says.

"Samia," she says, extending her hand to me. "Hassan's sister."

"Hassan's sister?" I repeat. I give the plastic cup back to Muhammad. "Hassan's sister!" I grab her hand in both of mine and shake it hard, up and down. "I'm so happy to meet you."

"My pleasure," she says, pulling back her hand.

"Excuse me. I'm just so excited Hassan has a sister."

"Well, I don't know if I've ever gotten that kind of enthusiasm for being a sister, but I've heard a great deal about you and your friend, so it's nice to meet you too."

"Why were you going to throw juice in my face?" Hassan asks.

"It was just a joke. See?" I point to the cellophane. "Sealed tight."

"Well"—he smiles—"you did surprise me—"

"Thousands are already there," Muhammad tells Hassan. "We just saw the news."

"Thousands?" Samia says, then looks at Hassan.

Hassan shakes his head. "You can't, Samia. Mama suffered too much. She wouldn't live through it again."

"It looks peaceful," Muhammad says.

"For now," Hassan says. "You know that won't last."

"Well, I think we all need to be there, standing together," Muhammad says.

"Don't tell us what we need to do." Hassan sounds on edge. "My sister has given a lot for this country. She lost her baby in prison. No more."

Samia says, "Hassan, please!"

"Forgive me, Samia." Muhammad puts his hand to his heart and bends. He reminds me of a younger version of Ahmed. I wonder how Ahmed and Sittu are getting along, and whether she knows what's happening. Thousands. Asmaa Mahfouz doesn't stand alone.

"I know how much you suffered. I hope you can forgive me if I made you feel like you owed anything more." Muhammad looks at Samia like she's his hero.

"Muhammad." She takes his hand. "You, my friend, have known more suffering than all of us. Still, you are willing to risk going today."

"I see that look," Hassan says to his sister. "Please don't go. Please." He sounds like a little boy.

"*Habibi*"—Samia turns to Hassan—"for our mother, I am not going, but for Egypt, my heart is breaking not to be there for her when she needs us the most."

"Thousands are there," Muhammad says. "Egypt will be fine."

Finally, I remember Deanna. I have to find her.

"Excuse me, but I must go and find my friend," I say to them.

"Is she okay?" Hassan asks.

"I hope so. She wasn't feeling well when I left her, and I don't see her on the bench now."

"We will all go," Samia says.

"We can help you find her," Muhammad says.

"Thank you. *Shukran*."

The four of us go to the ice-skate rental place. There's Mr. Ful. "I wondered where you went," he says. "I thought you took off with my ice skates."

I hand him back his skates. "Did you see my friend?"

"The serious girl. She asked me to give you this."

It looks like the same flyer Safi tried to give Omar.

"What does it say?" I ask.

"It has instructions about where to meet—the real places to gather," Hassan says. "On Facebook and Twitter, people gave other information so the police would go there. The real meeting place for the protest was spread by word of mouth."

"There's something on the back," Hassan says.

I turn it over.

Mar,

I'm going to Tahrir Square. I just have to. Don't worry. Don't feel bad about Hassan. Hey, I'll get over him. He's just a guy, right? Love you. Tell Sittu I love her. I know she'll understand.

With Love,

Sphinx Face

"What does she mean, 'Don't feel bad about Hassan'?" Hassan asks, reading over my shoulder.

I don't answer him.

"I bet it has something to do with the juice." Muhammad smiles, showing his crooked tooth.

"I hope she'll be okay," I say.

"It looks peaceful," Muhammad reassures me.

"Just saw an update on my mobile," Mr. Ful interjects. "The police are starting to use tear gas."

"She'll be okay," Hassan says, but I know he's as worried as I am.

"Can you show me where the café is? Sittu is there."

"Of course," Hassan says. "It's down another level."

This time I run down the escalator. Hassan, Muhammad, and Samia follow.

"Where is it?" I ask, stepping off the escalator.

"This way," Muhammad says.

We follow him into a restaurant that reminds me of the set from a fifties detective movie. It's empty.

"Where is she?" I say, not even trying to hide the panic in my voice.

"I'll check the WC," Samia says.

"Thanks."

A man who looks like he may be a waiter says something to us in Arabic.

Hassan says something back, and from his hand gestures, it looks like he's describing Sittu. The waiter talks to him for a few minutes, and from both his and Muhammad's facial expressions, I know something is wrong.

"She's not in there," Samia says, rejoining us.

Muhammad responds in Arabic. Samia looks at me, and I want to cry, her expression is so sad.

"What is it?" I look from Hassan to Muhammad. "Where's Sittu? What happened to her?"

"Mariam," Hassan says, "an ambulance took her to the hospital."

"The hospital? I just saw her an hour ago. What happened?"

"We don't know exactly. The waiter said Sittu and Ahmed were eating when she stood up and just fell over." Hassan reaches out to take my hand, but I pull it away. I don't want to be touched right now. "The waiter said she came to after a few minutes. She wanted to go home, but Ahmed insisted they call an ambulance."

"The hospital's very close to here. I can take you," Muhammad says.

"Please," I say. Then there is shouting on a television by the cash register. I look at Hassan. "Deanna," I say.

"Go to the hospital with Muhammad. I'll find Deanna."

"But—"

"He will be fine." Samia half smiles. "Hassan's not like me. He's good at keeping out of trouble."

"Thank you," I say to Hassan and Samia. I turn to Muhammad. "Can we go now?"

"Of course. But first," he says and winks at me, "you should put on your shoes."

chapter
TWENTY

I'll wait out here," Muhammad says when we reach Sittu's hospital room.

"Thanks." I want Sittu to meet Muhammad. I know she'd like him. But I think she's had enough surprises for one day. I still have no idea what to tell her if she asks me where Deanna is. *Oh God, please make Deanna be okay.*

"Sittu?" I say, pushing open the door. The smell of bleach stings my eyes.

"Mariam." Ahmed jumps to his feet and wraps his arms around me. I don't know how I should respond, but when I feel him trembling, I hug him as tight as I can.

"I am so relieved to see you," he says, stepping back. "She wanted me to go and get you girls, but I didn't want to leave her alone."

"It's okay. I'm here." I walk over to Sittu's bedside. She's sleeping.

I raise my eyebrows at the ancient bed they have her in, and at her heart monitor, which looks like it might be the first one ever made.

Ahmed catches my look and says, "They fix things here; they don't throw them away."

"You sure it works?"

"Just fine."

"What's that for?" I whisper, pointing to a tube hooked into her nostrils.

"Oxygen."

"Ahmed, what happened?" I ask.

"We were eating and talking, and everything was fine. Then she said she was feeling a little nauseous. I thought it was something she had eaten, but as soon as she stood up, she went right down."

I look at the IV in Sittu's arm. I hope it doesn't hurt.

A nurse wearing all white, including a white hijab, comes into the room with a blood pressure cuff.

"Can you tell me what's wrong with her?"

"The doctor will be here soon." She wraps the black cuff around Sittu's arm and pumps. Sittu doesn't react. I've had my blood pressure taken a few times at the doctor's, and it always makes me cringe. It feels like the cuff is trying to squeeze off your arm.

The nurse says something in Arabic to Ahmed.

"This is her granddaughter," he responds, "visiting from America."

"Welcome," she says, keeping her eyes fixed on the gauge.

"Is her pressure okay?" I ask as she uncuffs Sittu's arm. She gives me some numbers that mean nothing to me. "Is that good?"

"Low. The doctor will be here soon," she says again as she leaves.

"Ahmed? You okay?" I ask. He looks pale.

He nods, but I don't believe him.

"Please, Ahmed, sit down."

"No, no, you sit." He nods to the chair by the window. I'm surprised that I don't hear any of the traffic noise from the street below, but what kind of hospital hangs dusty drapes instead of blinds?

Neither of us sits down. We both just stand at Sittu's side, watching her like she's going to open her eyes any second now.

There's a knock at the door.

"Mariam." Muhammad pushes the door open a crack.

"Come in, please," I say.

"*Asalaam alaikum*," Muhammad says to Ahmed.

Ahmed doesn't respond. He just keeps staring at Sittu.

"Mariam, can I talk to you for a minute?" Muhammad asks. "Outside?"

I follow Muhammad into the hallway.

"Your grandfather looks very worried."

"My grandfather died years ago." I glance back toward Sittu's room. "Ahmed is a friend. This was their first date."

"Well, I guess it's true what they say. Love is not on the clock."

I've never heard anyone say this before. I wonder if it's the translation.

"Thank you—for everything," I say.

"You don't need to thank me. *Insh'allah*, she will be well."

I try to smile, but I can't. "It was very good to meet you." I extend my hand.

He takes it, but instead of shaking, he just holds it. I feel a jolt, not in my heart, but in my stomach.

"Are you asking me to go?"

"I thought you were saying good-bye."

"Not at all," he says. "I just needed to tell you…"

A woman holding a clipboard and wearing a white coat and a stethoscope walks past us into Sittu's room.

"That must be the doctor. Excuse me, please." I pull my hand free, though I wish I didn't have to, then follow the doctor.

"Excuse me," I say. She looks up from the clipboard hanging on the end of Sittu's bed. "Are you the doctor?"

"I'm Dr. Nassif," she says, extending her hand to me.

"I'm her granddaughter, Mariam."

She shakes my hand.

"She's going to be ok?" Ahmed's voice startles us.

"Are you the husband?" Dr. Nassif asks.

Ahmed looks confused. I can't blame him. What are you to a person you haven't seen in decades but might be in love with?

I jump in and say, "He's a close friend of the family."

The doctor nods but doesn't look convinced. "Well, we can't say for certain until we run the necessary tests—"

"No." Sittu's eyes open. "No tests!" She tries to sit up but can't.

"Easy, madam." Dr. Nassif approaches Sittu, removing the stethoscope from around her neck, and says *pardon* to Ahmed, who is hovering over Sittu like he's her guard dog. He moves back some, but barely.

The doctor presses a button on the side of the bed until Sittu is in a sitting position. I guess the bed isn't that old; it uses electricity, not a manual crank, like Hassan's car windows.

"May I take a listen?" Dr. Nassif places her stethoscope on Sittu's chest before Sittu has time to answer.

"Doctor," Sittu says, "I feel fine."

"Good to hear," the doctor says. "You were taking medicine for your heart?" Sittu turns her head toward the IV stand.

"Sittu, please, you have to answer the doctor," I say.

"The medicine made me feel worse." Sittu turns back to the doctor, sounding more like a little kid than herself.

"Madam," Dr. Nassif says, "we believe you had a heart attack."

"Oh my God." I put my hand to my mouth. Sittu reaches up and pulls it away.

Ahmed sits down with a plop.

"It's important for us to know what kind of damage has been done."

"Of course," I say.

"No," Sittu says. "No tests."

"The tests will help the doctor know how to help you." Ahmed gets up from his seat and puts a hand on her arm.

"All I need is some water."

"Of course, of course," Ahmed says, looking relieved. I have to wonder whether it's because he's glad to help in some way or because he has a reason to leave.

"*Shukran*. Now please go." Sittu waves him away.

As soon as Ahmed walks out, Sittu says, "He's a very kind man but too serious. Taking me to the hospital—what was he thinking? I would have been fine."

"He had you brought here by ambulance. He saved your life," I tell Sittu.

"Ambulance? I don't remember any ambulance."

"Sittu, that's because you passed out."

She looks at me and then at the doctor as if she's trying to figure out if we're lying to her. "I want you or one of your nurses to get my clothes. I'm going home now."

I want to yell at Sittu the way she'd yell at me if I was acting this stubborn, but her hand is shaking, so I grab it and hold on.

"Madam," Dr. Nassif says, "this is your choice, of course." I'm impressed by the doctor's calm. Sittu is acting so rudely, and Dr. Nassif just shakes it off. "But you must know, if the problem is as serious as I suspect, you may not survive another attack like this."

"My heart has taken a lot. It can take a lot more."

Dr. Nassif shakes her head. Her expression tells me Sittu isn't her first stubborn patient. "I still have a few other patients to see. I will give you some time to think about this, and then I will be back."

"I won't be here," Sittu says.

Dr. Nassif turns to me on her way out. "I hope you can reason with her."

Me? Talk sense into Sittu? Me trying to convince Sittu of anything would work out as well as my convincing Deanna not to go to Tahrir Square today. "Sittu, please—"

"I'm tired," she interrupts me. "No talking now."

"Mariam?" Muhammad sticks his head in the room. I forgot he was waiting for me.

"You are?" Sittu asks.

"Pardon me, madam." He enters the room and gives Sittu a small bow. "I didn't realize you were awake."

"Well, I am. *Yalla*." Sittu waves him over to her. He comes and stands next to her bed, directly across from me. He really is pretty adorable.

"I hope you're feeling better," he says.

"I was never feeling bad. I just got a little dizzy, and now these doctors want to run tests. They want my money is what they want."

Muhammad doesn't say a word as Sittu continues to rant about the medical profession, but he never takes his eyes off her. Sittu likes him; I can tell by the way she goes on and on.

Then Sittu stops midsentence. She looks at me and then again at Muhammad. "So you like my granddaughter?"

"Sittu," I say through clenched teeth.

"Very much," he says.

Did he just say "very much"?

"Where did you meet her?"

"He's a friend of Hassan's," I say, not wanting Muhammad to tell her I started the conversation at the juice bar.

"Why are you interested in my granddaughter?"

"Sittu!" I turn to Muhammad and say, "Please, you don't have to answer."

"I need to answer," he says. "It would be disrespectful otherwise."

I really have been loving Muhammad's Prince Charming–like ways. But now, not so much.

Sittu turns to me and grins. It's hard to believe this same woman was unconscious less than ten minutes ago.

"Mariam's beautiful, of course, but it's clear from the way

she worries for you she has a huge heart," Muhammad tells my grandmother.

Sittu turns to me. "Don't you worry for me."

Muhammad says, "It's hard not to worry about those we love."

Yes, I think. I'm worried about two people right now. Sittu and Deanna. I hope she is safe.

Muhammad's phone startles us with its loud, old-fashioned ring. The sound makes Sittu smile. "Now we have phones that imitate phones. What a world."

"*Allo*," he says. After listening and nodding, he clicks off his phone. He widens his eyes in my direction like he needs to talk to me now. "It was a pleasure to meet you, madam, and I do apologize. I must take my leave." He puts his hand to his heart and bows.

"You must come again," she says. "I think my granddaughter likes having you around."

"SITTU!" Can she be any more embarrassing?

"You can't run from the truth—or a *sittu* wanting to have some fun," Sittu says.

"Sittu, if you don't mind, I will walk Muhammad to the elevator."

"Of course, but, Muhammad, would you mind giving me a moment with Mariam first?"

He nods. "May Allah's blessing be with you," he says; then he turns and walks out of the room.

"Sittu, why did you have to embarrass me like that?"

"If the truth makes you blush, so what? You'll survive. Besides, he likes you, and I think you like him."

"I just met him."

"It's wise to use your head, but in some cases, you have to let the heart lead. This is something you can learn from Deanna." Sittu looks toward the door like she expects Deanna to walk in. "Where is she, by the way?"

I hesitate, trying to find a place in the middle between the truth and a lie. "We split up for a bit, and I came down to the café to see you—"

"You left her by herself at the mall?"

"No, with Hassan."

"Get my phone from my bag and call Hassan. Tell him to bring Deanna here."

I can't call Hassan in front of Sittu. What if she wants to talk to him and he tells her he's looking for Deanna in the middle of the demonstration? I see Sittu's purse behind the chair where Ahmed was sitting, but I don't think it's in Sittu's view.

"Where is your purse?" I ask, opening the drawer of her night-stand and pretending to search around the room.

"I hope it wasn't left at the café."

"I'm sure Ahmed knows where it is. We can ask him when he gets back. But Muhammad will let me use his phone."

"Okay, *habibti*," she says, closing her eyes. "I think I'll take a short rest before we go home."

I open my mouth to tell her she has to take the doctor's tests, but before I get a word out, she says, with her eyes still closed, "No talking about tests now. Go call Hassan."

I bend down and kiss her forehead, and then I rush into the

hallway. Muhammad's nowhere to be seen. Could he have left? I head to the nurse's station, where I see Muhammad standing by the elevator, talking to Ahmed. They both look like it's the end of the world.

"Hey," I say. "What's going on?"

Ahmed has three bottles of Safi brand water in his hands. "You can't tell Sittu Deanna is lost."

"She's not lost," I say.

"Mariam, that was Hassan on the phone. He can't find Deanna anywhere," Muhammad says. "The square is getting more and more filled. Things are getting hot."

My heart starts to pound. "Let's go, then," I say.

"Where?" Ahmed asks.

"Tahrir Square. Muhammad, you'll take me, right?"

Muhammad and Ahmed look at each other. Then Muhammad says, "We think it would be best for you to stay here. I will go and help Hassan look for Deanna."

"Muhammad, you don't even know what she looks like, and no disrespect to you or Hassan, but I know Deanna better than either of you. If anyone can find her, it's me." I don't know whether I really believe this, but I know I have to try. Best friends are supposed to have each other's back. Always.

"Mariam," Muhammad says. "Things can get crazy. And dangerous."

"If you won't drive me, I'll take a cab or a bus. I'll walk if I have to."

"Okay, okay, I'll take you."

"We can't worry your *sittu*," Ahmed says.

"So we won't. She's resting now. When she wakes up, just tell her we couldn't reach Hassan by phone, that his battery died or something. Tell her we went to the mall to pick her up."

Ahmed looks so scared, I'm afraid he's going to vomit.

"Don't worry," I say, grabbing both his forearms. The Safi bottles jiggle together softly. "We'll be back soon, I promise. Just, whatever you do, don't let Sittu leave the hospital. She needs to take those tests."

"She's a very determined woman," Ahmed says, looking even more freaked out than he did a minute ago.

"She's not the only one." Muhammad looks at me, and I can't tell whether he thinks this is a good thing or whether he's wishing he'd never bought me that juice.

"Ahmed, listen, all you have to do is tell her that you are waiting for me and Deanna to get back before we can leave. Then, when Deanna and I get back, I'm sure together we can all convince her to listen to the doctor."

I'm surprised by how easily these plans are coming to me. I guess a lot more of Deanna has rubbed off on me than I thought.

Ahmed nods. "You are the dream team," he says, almost smiling. "Here." He hands Muhammad and me a bottle of water. "You may get thirsty."

We're not going on a journey into the Sahara. We're only going downtown. But it is very kind of him. "Thanks," I say, leaning over to kiss him on the cheek. "I'm so glad you annoyed Deanna on the plane."

Both Muhammad and Ahmed look confused, but I don't take the time to explain.

"Come on, *yalla*," I say to Muhammad. "We have to find Deanna."

chapter
TWENTY—ONE

Muhammad leans on his horn, but no one moves out of our way. Not one driver even turns to look. We roll forward slowly, then stop.

"It would be faster if we crawled," he says just as some guy jumps on the hood of the car. Muhammad rolls down the window and shouts, waving for the guy to get off. The guy turns around and smiles at us.

"Is this the way you hitchhike here in Egypt?" I look at Muhammad to see whether he gets my joke, but he beeps his horn again. Still, the guy doesn't move off the hood.

"I'm sorry I got you into all of this," I say.

"Too many people. We're going to have to walk the rest of the way," Muhammad says as he puts his foot on the brake. The guy slides off the hood but leaps right up again and moves into the crowd along the side of the street. "When you get to know me better"—Muhammad takes the key from the ignition—"you'll understand I don't do anything I don't want to do. So please, no apologies."

He's planning on me getting to know him better? Awesome.

Muhammad sets the emergency brake. "We'll walk." He opens his door.

"It's okay to just leave the car in the middle of the road?" I ask.

"No one is moving anymore, and I think the police are otherwise occupied," he says.

My stomach starts to hurt. Until that moment, I wasn't worried that Deanna was in real danger. She usually manages to take care of herself, but the one thing she can't do is keep her mouth shut. That doesn't make you popular in a police state.

"How far do we have to walk?"

"It's about half a kilometer to KFC."

"You're hungry? I thought we were going to Tahrir Square."

"It's on the square. We're meeting Hassan there." Without locking his car, Muhammad starts to walk, and I follow. He's walking through the crowd, and I can hardly keep up with him. I think maybe it'd be safer if I held on to the back of his jacket, but when I reach for it, some random guy who's not Muhammad turns around.

"Excuse me," I say, moving past him, thinking the next guy must be Muhammad, but after a few yards, I realize I've completely lost sight of him. I can't see anything except the people right next to me. It really sucks being so short.

I jump and shout, "Muhammad!" Several men turn around, but none of them is my Muhammad. *My Muhammad.*

Where is he? I jump again. I don't see him, but then again, maybe I do. I have no idea what the back of his head looks like. I can't remember the color of his jacket or whether he was even wearing a jacket. I'm starting to feel more anxious. Even though I'm used to the crowds in New York City, there are so many people around me now that it's getting scary. And it's not just young people, like Sittu thought. There are old people too. There's even a woman in a wheelchair with an older man pushing her along.

I wonder how Sittu is doing. I haven't felt much like asking God for anything in a long time because I didn't believe God was listening. But now, when I pray for Deanna, Muhammed, and Sittu, I truly hope God is hearing every word.

The crowd's moving faster, pulling me along like I'm on one of those moving airport sidewalks. I have no choice but to go forward. Did Muhammad say the square was half a kilometer away? How far is that? I always get metric measurements mixed up. Is a kilometer three and a half miles? Or is a centimeter three and a half inches, and a kilometer is about a mile? I hear sirens like the ones in French movies—a *whaa-a whaa-a* sound. It's getting louder. I wonder again how far I am from the square.

Muhammad, where are you? How I wish I were the little boy next to me, sitting on his dad's shoulders. Then I could see what's ahead. I wonder what Baba is doing now. Seeing all of these people here standing up for Egypt would make him happy—a real happy, not the kind of happy he pretends because he doesn't like me to see him sad.

The sirens grow louder, so we must be getting closer. My heart pounds so hard, I think it's going to rip through my chest.

Breathe. Breathe. What am I worried about? I'll just go to where Muhammad said we would meet Hassan. OMG, I can't remember what he said. My brain is, like, shutting down. What is wrong with me? I come here to find Deanna, and now I'm lost.

What if I never see Muhammad again? I didn't even get to thank him for all his help. To kiss him. He's the only guy I've ever felt like I wanted to kiss—I mean *really* kiss. And then I lose him in less than two minutes. Why am I so useless?

Think, Mariam. Think. What would Deanna do if she were here? She'd pause, breathe, and… That's right, I remember: it was a fast-food place—American. Pizza Hut? No, no, what was it? Maybe if I see the place, it will come to me. It's on the square, right? So how many fast-food places can there be?

I push my way through the crowd. People let me by. No one pushes back or curses me out. The sirens are loud, but everyone around me is chanting in Arabic. I don't understand, but it's like when I heard the morning call to prayer. It feels like there's something greater than me, that something, well, spiritual is happening. The chanting pulls me forward, and I don't stop until I have no place to move. Everyone stands like we're at an outdoor concert in Central Park (which, of course, I've only watched on television since my parents never let me leave the apartment), but instead of music, there's chanting. I must be almost at the square now, because I can hear someone leading the chant over loudspeakers.

"Excuse me," I say to a girl who doesn't look too much older than I am, chanting with so much force her face is as red as ketchup. I touch her arm to get her attention. She turns to me. "Do you speak English?" I ask.

"A little," she says.

"Can you tell me where we are?"

She raises her eyebrows, and I'm about to ask someone else when she asks, "Are you a tourist?"

"I'm Egyptian," I shout, and for the first time in my life, I don't feel shame. I feel awesome.

She gives me another look, this one more confused than the last. "Tahrir Square, of course. The regime must end." She points up at the buildings in front of us, and when I see all of the banners and Egyptian flags that people are waving, I start to chant too.

Well, I try, but I can't quite make out the words, so after I mumble a bit, I say, "*Shukran*" and start moving through the crowd again. It takes me forever, but I finally reach an area where there seem to be stores, and there it is: KFC.

That's it! KFC. Muhammad said KFC. I make it to the front of the restaurant, but I don't see Muhammad or Hassan. When I go inside, the only person there is a man standing behind the counter. He shouts to me in Arabic, waving a sandwich like the people outside are waving flags.

I couldn't eat even if I had the money to pay for it, which I don't. No money, no cell phone, no contact information for anyone I know here, and I can't even remember the name of the hospital Sittu is in. I'm probably the worst-prepared protester Cairo has ever seen.

Am I a protester? Did I really just call myself a protester? I came here today to find Deanna, but now all I want to do is join her. I want to join all of these people. Deanna was so right; this is history happening right here and now. And it's Sittu's history and Baba's history. And it's my history. I don't have to watch it happening on television, because I'm here. I am Egyptian.

The man says something to me in Arabic.

"I don't understand," I say. "I'm sorry."

"Please, take this food."

I put my hand in my pocket and pull out not even a piece of lint.

"No, here. Here. For free, no money." The man runs from behind the counter and puts the sandwich in my hand. "Today we all need our strength. Today is the beginning of our freedom. Eat."

"*Shukran*." I take a bite. It tastes like nothing I've ever eaten at KFC or anywhere else. It's delicious. "What is this?" I ask.

He smiles. "You like it?"

"Very much." I smile back.

"Chicken and *ful*—"

"*FUL*?!" Oh my God. I roll up my sleeves, looking for the hives. I clear my throat, expecting it to close any second.

"Where's the WC?"

I'm sure he hears the panic in my voice, because he leads me to the bathroom, almost sprinting. He opens the door for me. There's no mirror.

"I need a mirror," I say.

He looks as freaked out as I feel, but he shows me to a back room where there is a mattress on the floor, one chair, a small table, and, on the wall, a full-length mirror. I examine my face, my ears, my neck, but I don't see one hive. Not one. I've been allergic to *ful* all of my life. How can there not be one hive?

"Is there a problem with my sandwich?" the man asks.

"Allergic," I say, scratching my arm for emphasis, not because it itches.

"Allergic to *ful*?"

"Yes, I'm Egyptian and allergic to *ful*," I say before he can comment like the man at the ice-skating rink. "It's been years since I've had any, but when I was a kid, I used to break out in a rash all over my body. But now, nothing," I say, sticking out my tongue again in the mirror.

"Maybe you're not allergic to *ful* made in Egypt!" he says, grinning so wide I'm afraid he may put a crack in both his cheeks.

"Maybe."

"I'm glad you are well," he says.

"Me too," I say, walking out of the room and right into Hassan.

"Hassan!"

"Mariam!" We both jump up and down.

"I can't believe I found you." Hassan looks at me like he's never been happier to see another person in his life. "When Muhammad showed up and said he lost you in the crowd, I was so worried. Well, actually, I was angry. How could he lose you like that?"

"Muhammad? Where is he?"

"He went to find you."

"Why didn't he just wait here?"

"You're American. How could you find your way?"

"Well, I'm Egyptian too, and now we don't know where he or Deanna are."

"I found Deanna," Hassan says, sounding more worried than excited.

"Is she okay? What happened to her?"

"I'm sure she's fine." I can hear a loud *but* coming my way.

"She was part of a sit-in. More of a lie-in—"

"What does that even mean?"

"All these people were lying on the ground, refusing to move until Mubarak steps down…"

"She was lying on the street? The dirty street?"

"They were chanting, 'End the regime,' and I heard her voice."

"In English?" I say.

"Arabic."

Deanna can chant in Arabic. Why is this not a surprise to me?

"She wouldn't come back with me. I begged her. I finally had to tell her about Sittu in the hospital. That's when she got up and shouted, 'This is for Sittu!' and ran into the crowd. I've been trying to find her ever since." Hassan lowers his head as he says this.

The KFC man tries to give him a sandwich, but he refuses, leaving the KFC man looking sad.

"He's not hungry now, but I'm sure he'll eat it later." I turn to Hassan. "Take the sandwich," I whisper.

"*Shukran*," Hassan says.

I crumple what's left of my sandwich in my hand so the KFC man doesn't see it. "Now we have to go find our friends," I tell the man.

"*Asalaam alaikum*. May you find your friends safe."

"*Alaikum salaam*," Hassan and I say. When we step out into the street, my eyes sting like someone just squirted lemon juice into them.

"Cover your mouth and nose." Hassan hands me a handkerchief. "Tear gas."

Blinking hard against the smoke, it's hard to believe it was only yesterday when Deanna, Sittu, and I were standing in the bright, clear sun at the pyramids.

The line of policemen ahead of us is a blur, though I can see they look stern, like the guys at the airport, only here they have helmets with plastic visors over their faces and they are holding up shields. They swing their batons in the air as they move through the crowd.

"We should leave," Hassan shouts over the noise.

I pull the handkerchief from my mouth long enough to say, "Not until we find our friends."

"The police are not going to stop," Hassan says, and almost on cue, a tank shoots water into the crowd. We stand off to the side, but I can still feel the force.

"I have to get you out of here," Hassan says into his sleeve.

Now some people are running—not away, but toward the police. The crowds of people head toward the tank, pushing against the force of the water.

"Look, Hassan," I say. "The tank is moving back."

"I can't believe what I'm seeing," he says. "The police are retreating."

Hassan watches a guy run right at the line of police, his body his only weapon. "What courage."

"Oh my God! It looks like Omar!"

The police pull him to the ground and start beating him with their batons.

"What?" Hassan asks over the roar of the crowd.

"Omar!" I shout and run toward him, but Hassan soon catches me and pulls me back.

"I have to see if it's him," I say.

"Mariam! Stop," Hassan says as I struggle to get free of his grip. "This is not your cause."

Abruptly, I stop struggling. "I don't care," I shout. "The police are beating Omar to death. We have to stop them!"

Hassan moves his mouth like he wants to say something, but when his eyes shift to what's behind me, he doesn't utter a sound. I turn around. There are hundreds, maybe thousands, of people, moving in on the police. In response, the police shoot more tear gas into the air. Tears stream down my face and Hassan's. But when we look at each other, we know it's not the gas making us cry.

"I'm sorry, Mariam. I didn't mean what I just said."

"Forget about it," I say, grabbing his hand. "Don't let go. We can't lose each other." I lead us deeper into the crowd, trying to see what happened to Omar, or if it really is Omar. But there are too many people pushing. The police have stopped their retreat and are swinging their batons, hitting everything and anyone in their way.

There are now more people screaming than there are chanting, and as we push ahead, I trip over a woman sitting with a young girl on her lap. The girl's head is bleeding. I bend down and give her my handkerchief.

"Hassan!" someone shouts, and Hassan yanks at my hand, pulling me in the opposite direction from the bleeding girl. He pulls me toward a woman. It's Samia, his sister.

"What are you doing here?" Hassan asks. "You promised!"

"When I saw what was happening on television, I had to come," she says. "Did you ever think we'd see our people stand up and fight together for freedom? We are going to bring down Mubarak and his regime. Nawal El Saadawi is here!" Samia grins at Hassan and me like she just saw P!nk or some Egyptian superstar. I wait for her to explain who that is, but she doesn't.

When Hassan doesn't smile back, she puts her hand on his arm and says, "*Habibi*, I have to be here."

Hassan sighs and shakes his head but says nothing more.

Samia says to me, "Thank you for being here." She kisses me on both cheeks as hard as Sittu did at the airport. "It's important the world see Egyptian-Americans like you here, supporting us."

"*Shukran*," I say.

"You mean *afwan*, 'you're welcome,'" she says.

"No, I mean *shukran*."

Samia smiles at me, but I don't know if she really understands why I'm thanking her. I want to tell her I'm thanking her for her courage and her love of Misr, a place that, until this trip, I didn't want to know, but now I never want to forget. Ever. But she's gone before I can get another word out.

"Mariam, if this is all over the news, we have to go back to Sittu," Hassan says. "She's going to be so worried for you."

"She thinks I'm at the mall."

"Mariam." Hassan shakes his head. "This is Sittu we're talking about."

Of course he's right. She will know Deanna came here and that I came to find her. Just like she knew she couldn't have stopped me if she'd tried. This is Sittu. She just knows things.

"But what about Deanna and Muhammad?"

"Muhammad can take care of himself, believe me, and I'm sure Deanna…"

"Yeah, she's okay," I say, wanting to believe that my friend, the girl who isn't afraid to tell you want she thinks or feels, who stands up to bullies and always has my back, can take care of herself now. But this may be more than even Deanna can handle. There's a noise like firecrackers in the distance, and now everyone is screaming and scattering in different directions.

"They're shooting," Hassan says, pulling me with him and running until we reach his car.

chapter
TWENTY—TWO

A hmed, please!" Sittu's voice is loud and strong, even through the closed door of her hospital room.

I turn to Hassan. "Wait here. If she sees you, she'll ask for Deanna, and I want a minute before I tell her."

Hassan agrees.

In the room, Ahmed is hovering over Sittu, trying to fluff her pillow.

"Stop your fussing!" Sittu has the same exasperated tone I've heard from Baba so many times. I run to hug her, and squeeze her like I never want to let go. Immediately the ancient heart monitor beside her bed beeps loudly.

I jump back like I've been electrocuted, and Sittu and Ahmed smile at me as a nurse comes into the room. She walks straight to Sittu and, without looking at me, fixes the piece of Velcro wrapped around Sittu's pointer finger.

"Did I hurt something?" I ask the nurse.

"We just have to keep this on her finger." She looks at the machine behind Sittu, which flashes numbers. "It's how we monitor her heart."

"My heart is fine." Sittu raises the tip of her finger. "I'm E.T." She smiles, and I try to smile back, but I can't. I'm too upset. "You get the joke?"

"Is that the alien with a glowing finger who rides a bicycle?" I ask, watching the nurse press a button on the machine. The beeping stops.

"You never saw *E.T.*?" Sittu sounds surprised.

I shake my head.

"I think I have the tape of it. We can watch it when we go home."

"That would be great." This time, I manage to force a smile for Sittu. I don't want her to see how worried I am about her.

"I will be back to take your pressure soon," the nurse says, and walks out of the room.

"Not necessary!" Sittu shouts after her, and coughs.

"How are you feeling?" I ask.

"How are *you* feeling?" Sittu counters. "So serious. What took your smile?"

I'm thinking Deanna's somewhere out there, lost in Cairo. I always thought she was okay and didn't care what other people thought of her. I can't believe that I needed her to tell me what she was really feeling. Was I too self-centered to see the truth? Maybe Deanna worked so hard to protect me from her pain that I couldn't see it. Just like Baba has tried to protect me from his pain all these years. Now, here is Sittu lying in this hospital bed, pretending like all is okay when obviously it's not. I can't let her try and protect me too.

"Stop the serious." Sittu puts her hand to my face and tries to push my cheeks up into a smile. "Remember, there are many things Egyptians are known for—some good and some bad—but the best is our sense of humor. We always try to find a way to keep ourselves laughing."

"That's when we're not crying," Ahmed says, and then he laughs. It feels good to hear him happy.

"Well, no crying today." Sittu drops her hand from my face, and I hold the smile for her. "Today is a new beginning for us, a true revolution." She grins, looking happier than I've seen her. "I only wish I could have been there with you today."

It's hurting to keep this forced all-is-great expression on my face. I must now tell her about Deanna, the police, the tear gas, and the shooting.

"Sittu."

"*Habibti?*"

"I have to tell you something about…"

Sittu looks past me for a moment and says, "Deanna?!"

I turn and Deanna's standing right behind me. Hassan's beside her. He looks at the machine above Sittu's head, then walks to the other side of Sittu's bed and takes her hand. He says something that I can't hear because Deanna is giving me a huge hug. I don't know whether I want to kiss her because she's safe or shake her for worrying me so much.

"Hassan told me you were there too—" Deanna puts her hand over her big mouth.

"Sittu knows we were there," I say.

Deanna looks relieved, and then steps toward Sittu and kisses her on the forehead. "I wish you'd been with us." Deanna's unnaturally bubbly, as though she were talking about going to a street fair. "It was amazing."

Hassan just shrugs, as confused as I am.

"I'm glad you're back," Ahmed says from his chair next to the window. I'm just noticing how tired he looks.

"Did Mariam tell you about it?" She glances over at Ahmed, but when he doesn't respond, she turns back to Sittu.

"Ahmed told me a little bit"—Sittu coughs a few times—"of what the news was showing." Sittu looks weary now but still happy.

"Thousands of people!" Deanna says. "Protesting peacefully. There were even street performances—people doing skits, making fun of Mubarak. Everyone was laughing." She sounds like she had this great time. Does she not remember the tear gas? The gunshots? The beatings? Is Deanna just trying to focus on the positive to not upset Sittu?

"I told you, Egyptians never lose their sense of humor." Sittu smiles.

"Actually, humor is often our only weapon." Ahmed laughs; he cracks himself up.

"I wish you could have been there, Sittu," Deanna says again.

Okay, now I know she's hiding something. She's not looking Sittu in the eyes, and the only time she does that is when there's something she doesn't want to think about—like whenever anyone asks why she doesn't have a dad.

"I wish I had been there too, *habibti*," Sittu says. "At least my two granddaughters were there to represent the family."

"Tomorrow, you can join us," Deanna says.

"You're not going back there," Hassan says.

No kidding, I think.

"Don't tell me what to do." Deanna makes eye contact with Hassan for the first time since they walked into the room.

Sittu looks from Hassan to Deanna like she's trying to work out what's going on between them.

"Someone has to look out for you," Hassan says. He doesn't raise his voice, but it's clear he's angry. Sittu raises her eyebrows at this.

"That someone is you?" Deanna sounds so angry she could spit.

"Who else?" Hassan says.

Who else? Now he's pissing me off. "What about me?" I ask. "I found my way there with no help from you." This makes me think about Muhammad, and my stomach hurts. I'm worried about him.

"Please, Mariam, I don't mean to offend, but it's not like you're the best—"

"Because she's a girl?" Deanna asks.

"No, because she listens to everything you say without question."

I lean over Sittu. I'm so mad I want to poke him in the chest, but he steps back so I can't reach him. "You know, Hassan, maybe that was true yesterday, but not today. And I wasn't the one who found her and then lost her."

"That's right," Deanna says. "And who are you to talk to my friend like that?"

"Who am I?" Hassan asks.

Deanna and Hassan shout at each other. Hassan yells about American girls who think they know everything, and Deanna yells back about Egyptian guys who think they just have to snap their fingers and any girl they want will kiss their feet. (I'm sure if Sittu weren't here, Deanna would've said "ass" instead of "feet.") Then they both get really loud and stop making any sense at all.

Ahmed stands up, but Sittu waves him back down. She looks amused, watching Hassan and Deanna go at each other. Sittu is one strange bird sometimes.

"Did you tell Sittu about how you were lying on the ground?" Hassan asks, lowering his voice.

"A lie-in," Sittu says. "Very nice."

Hassan looks at Sittu like she's out of her mind. "Sittu, they tear-gassed us. The police were shooting."

"Tear gas?" All signs of joy drain from her face. "Move this bed upright now!" I've heard Sittu mad before but not like this. Both Deanna and I fumble around, looking for the button at the end of the bed to help Sittu to a sitting position.

"Hassan, step out of the way. I want to see my silent friend over there." She says this with a motion of her head, indicating she means Ahmed.

Without hesitation, Hassan steps back.

Ahmed opens the heavy drapes, peering out the window to avoid Sittu's gaze. "Hey, I can see my car from here," he says, pointing down at the street.

"Why didn't you tell me about this?" Sittu demands. "Ahmed, look at me."

Ahmed comes to Sittu's bedside. Hassan gives him a slight pat on the back, which means either "It's okay" or "May the force be with you."

"Well?" Sittu asks, quieter now but somehow sounding even more upset.

Ahmed reaches for her hand, but she pulls it away and slips it under the sheet.

"I didn't want to worry you," he says.

"Am I a child?" Sittu's now coughing and can't seem to catch her breath.

"The doctor said you're not supposed to get upset."

Sittu stops coughing and spits out, "What a great job you've done."

The machine starts to beep, and the numbers flash red. Something's very wrong.

"We need to get the doctor," I say.

Hassan and Ahmed both race into the hallway.

Sittu grabs Deanna's arm and says to us, "You two stay here."

I look at Sittu's monitor. The numbers are lower, but it's still beeping.

"Deanna, you're very courageous," Sittu says.

Deanna stays quiet.

"I remember how scared I was when the police—" Sittu begins.

"It was fine," Deanna says, looking away.

"You were brave," Sittu says, "but I don't want you girls going back there. Okay?"

I nod.

Deanna doesn't answer, but she keeps her head down.

"Deanna! You have to agree! You call me selfish. You're the one who's selfish. You're going to make my grandmother sicker—"

"Mariam!" Sittu slaps me across the face.

I don't know whether I start to tear up because she just hit me or because she looks like she put all her strength into that slap and I barely felt it.

"Don't ever call me sick."

To Deanna, she says, "You have no plans to go back."

"No," Deanna says, then adds, with her head still bowed, "I don't want to go back."

"So why didn't you just say that?" I ask.

Deanna shakes her head, and I can see she's crying. Her tears are falling onto Sittu's hospital gown. Sittu pulls Deanna to her chest, and Deanna cries like she's in physical pain.

"You were afraid," Sittu says, patting Deanna on the back.

Deanna nods against Sittu's chest and tells her, "It was wonderful at first." She uses her hand to wipe at the tears, but they just smear. "There were a lot of people, but not like later, when the square was so packed it felt like you couldn't move." Deanna sits up and stares out the window.

"Deanna, please. Just tell us what happened today," I say.

Sittu reaches out and touches my forearm. "Deanna is telling us in her own way."

Deanna looks from me to Sittu and back again. "I have never been so scared in my life." Her lip starts to quiver.

"It's okay." Sittu takes Deanna's hand and holds it. "It's like a bad dream. If you talk about it, some of its power will go away."

Deanna looks at Sittu like she doesn't believe her.

"You'll feel better," I say. "I promise."

It's another moment before Deanna starts to speak. "When I first got to the square, there were a lot of people, but it wasn't too crowded. For a while, it felt like I was walking around sightseeing. People were holding up homemade signs, probably ones they'd just made on the spot, mostly in Arabic. But some were in English and said 'Down with Mubarak' and things like that. But people were happy. One group was drumming and—"

"What were the police doing then?" I ask.

"That's the thing. They were there, wearing helmets and all, so you couldn't miss them. But they weren't doing much—just waiting, I guess. The police at the airport freaked me out a lot more than the ones in the square. These policemen didn't seem that threatening, and there were so many people, they were outnumbered anyway. I mean, Mar, you were there! Did you see how cool everyone was? Little kids were running around, and even though it was intense, everything was peaceful, you know?"

Sittu nods.

"There were rows of people praying, right there in the middle of everything. Did you see them, Mar?"

"No." I shake my head.

"Maybe you came later. You couldn't miss them early on. People were lined up, kneeling or standing side by side."

"When we pray, we don't leave space between us," Sittu explains. "You don't want the devil to stick his head there." She smiles, but she looks tired.

"It was like watching a dance or some other beautiful performance. Someone said they were praying for Mubarak to leave." She smiles at Sittu. "I just kept walking; I wanted to see everything. There was a lie-in, so I lay down and chanted with everyone. I even forgot about Hassan for a while, that's how caught up I got in what was happening," Deanna says. She looks away. "Then he showed up, of course. He said you were in the hospital, and I don't know why, but I thought he was lying to get me to leave with him." She gives Sittu an apologetic look. "I'm sorry. I just never imagined you really would be in the hospital. So I kind of made fun of him and charged into the crowd, shouting, 'This is for Sittu!'

"When I stopped running, I was in front of some government buildings, and there it was, right in front of me—a Sphinx Face, a little Sphinx." Deanna's eyes smile when she says this. "I wish I'd had a camera on me."

"You were outside the museum," Sittu says.

"And that's when I smelled it—it was so awful! My eyes stung, and I felt like I was suffocating, so I ran—but that only made me feel worse, like it got deep into my lungs. A woman handed me a handkerchief and said, 'Don't breathe.'

"So I started freaking out a little. I mean, how do you not breathe? But the whole time people still chanted and yelled at a police blockade. This one guy charged the police line and they beat him...they beat him and kept beating him.

"It got so bad, Sittu." Her voice is barely above a whisper. "Then they shot a boy right in front of me."

"Oh my God," I say, suddenly feeling sick to my stomach.

"He wasn't much older than us."

"Muhammad?"

"*Habibti*, there are many thousands of young men at Tahrir Square," Sittu says. "But *insh'allah*, he's fine."

"He was so close to me I could've reached out and touched his face." Deanna blinks to clear away the tears. "He sank to his knees, and for a second, I thought he was going to pray. It almost looked like he was smiling. But then he fell forward. He'd been shot in the back."

Sittu squeezes Deanna's hand.

"I didn't even hear the shots, Sittu. I was right next to him, and I didn't even hear the shots!" Deanna and Sittu just stare at each other, like maybe they're reading each other's minds, as tears stream down their faces.

It's a long time before Sittu speaks, and when she does, she says, "This will be with you for a long time. I'm sorry for that. But you will be okay, Deanna."

Deanna shakes her head. "All I could think was, 'When the bullet goes through my head, will it hurt?'"

I feel like I can't breathe. Deanna rests her head on Sittu's chest, and I smear the tears across my face. I hope Sittu's right and Deanna feels better after telling us about what happened, but I can't imagine how after all she saw.

"Then I ran and ran and ran until I was far away from the smoke and chanting. I didn't know what to do, so I just kept asking people how to get to the mall until I found it." She pauses. "That's when I found out you really were in the hospital. The waiter at the café said you were here. I'm sorry. I should have come when Hassan told me." She wipes the last of her tears on her sleeve. "Who's Muhammad?" Deanna asks, sounding more like herself.

I don't answer her, not yet ready to change the subject.

"A guy?" Deanna demands. "What guy? Why don't I know about this?" I'm saved by a nurse.

She hits the button that stops the beeping on Sittu's monitor, then adjusts the Velcro strap around her finger. But when she looks at the numbers on the monitor, she frowns and seems worried in a way that she wasn't before. She says to me, "Please, she must rest. The doctor will be here soon."

"I didn't mean to cause you any problems," Deanna says to Sittu.

The nurse turns her attention to Deanna and me, and says, "Please leave. You are disturbing her."

"No, my granddaughters stay," Sittu says, grabbing the IV line attached to her arm. "Or I'll pull this right out."

"Please don't." I reach out to stop her.

"Madam, please."

The nurse reaches out to her too, but Sittu lifts her arm with the IV line dangling from it and says, "I mean business."

"I'll get the doctor," the nurse says. She's pretending not to be angry, but I know she'd have slammed the door behind her if she could. It's not that kind of door though; it just swings open and closed, like a saloon door in the Wild West.

"Sittu, I'm sorry we upset you," I say, guiding Sittu's arm back to her side.

Deanna nods.

"I'm angry you both disobeyed me, but I'm proud you followed your hearts."

Technically, I followed Deanna, not my heart, but when Deanna gives me a look with those eyes of hers, I can see she's beaming inside. We both did what we needed to do, and we both did the right thing. Besides, Deanna truly is a part of my heart.

Sittu tugs at one of Deanna's curls and asks her, "What's going on with you and Hassan?"

"There's nothing going on." It may be easy for Deanna to keep a straight face, but she sucks at playing dumb.

Both Sittu and I shake our heads, and I say, "Give us a break."

"Well, I—" Deanna stops talking and looks over toward the door.

"The girl we saw him with is his sister," I blurt out, finally remembering why she's upset with Hassan.

"That was his sister?" Deanna asks. Her voice sounds as if she wants to believe me, but she still doesn't.

"Sittu, do you know Hassan's sister?"

"Yes, she's a smart girl," Sittu says, "with a lot of courage. Did you meet her?"

"I did, but Deanna didn't."

"Ahhh! Now I see," Sittu says as she widens her eyes. "It's a case of mistaken identity."

"He's not interested in me, anyway," Deanna says.

Sittu pulls Deanna's chin down until their eyes meet, then gives Deanna's chin a little shake. "If you can't see from the way that boy looks at you that he's, as you would say, into you, then you are not the smart girl I thought you were."

Sittu sighs dramatically, drops her hand into her lap, and shakes her head. "*Habibti.*"

"Yes?" I say.

"I mean this *habibti.*" Sittu looks at Deanna. Maybe she should start calling us *Habibti* One and *Habibti* Two. Or *Habibti Waahid* and *Habibti Itnein.*

"I really do like him."

"What am I going to do with you two?" She sits up a bit straighter in bed. "Okay, so I have a few advices," Sittu says.

"You mean *advice*?" Deanna asks.

I shake my head at her. "No, she means *advices.*"

"I know the two of you still have a lot to learn about the ways of this world. But *habibti*"—Sittu looks at Deanna again—"losing yourself gets you nowhere but lost."

Deanna nods like she understands what this means. I think I do. I'm starting to understand Sittu's advices a little better.

"And you," she says, and I think, Where's my *habibti*? "You are cursed with a little bit too much of your *sittu* in you."

I have no idea what she means.

"Before you go running out to save someone, make sure she really needs saving."

Now this, I get.

"But you were being a good friend. And I'm proud of you for that."

"Thanks, Mariam." Deanna's eyes are smiling.

"Friends have each other's backs," I say, beaming.

"I'm not finished with my advices, girls. Remember, the reason two people are attracted to each other sometimes makes as much sense as trying to start your car with a carrot stick. But trying to come between the ignition and the carrot stick will only get you left by the side of the road, so let the heart be what it will be."

We both nod, and I think of Muhammad. In my head, I say a prayer that he's okay.

"So are you going to take your own advices?" I ask.

"What are you talking about?" Sittu asks. She's even worse than Deanna at playing dumb.

"Ahmed—he's really into you."

"He's a nice old man who has nothing better to do than sit around in hospital rooms."

"Whatever you say, Sittu. Whatever you say." I bend down and kiss her on the cheek.

"So you really think Hassan likes me?" Deanna asks.

"*Yes!*" Sittu and I say as one.

Dr. Nassif comes in with the nurse following her. "So, are we ready?"

"For what?" Sittu asks

"Those tests we talked about."

"Please stop your craziness!" Sittu coughs for what feels like forever. "I have a little indigestion from lunch, and you want to turn me into a lab rat."

"Are you okay?" I ask, looking down at her.

"No tests," Sittu says, coughing so hard now, her face is turning red.

"Sittu!" Deanna and I move to her, but she waves us away.

"Please, come with me," the nurse says. And this time, I know we don't have a choice.

chapter
TWENTY—THREE

We follow the nurse to the waiting area. Ahmed's sitting on a gold velvet couch covered in plastic, biting his cuticles. Hassan's banging on a television. The ends of its antenna are wrapped in tinfoil, something I've seen only in old movies.

"Hassan, you okay?" I ask as he bangs away.

Ahmed jumps to his feet. "How is she?"

"She's refusing to let the doctor run tests," Deanna says.

"That woman is so hardheaded." Ahmed starts to pace. "Doesn't she know these tests can save her life? I should bring her to the States. I know one of the best cardiologists in the country."

There's no way Sittu's getting on a plane in her condition, but I don't bother to say it out loud. Besides, I think he's talking more to himself than to us.

"People aren't leaving the square," Hassan interjects, still pounding on the side of the television. "And protests are happening all over Egypt." This time, Hassan wallops the TV so hard he almost knocks it off its stand.

"I know you're angry that you're not there," I say, "but beating on the TV isn't going to help."

"I'm not beating on the TV because I'm angry," Hassan says as he pulls on the antenna and rotates it. "I'm just trying to get some reception so we can see what's happening with the protests." He checks the picture, then moves it again.

Ahmed stops pacing and tells him, "Just turn it off. The government's probably blocked Al Jazeera by now, so the only thing being broadcast is their propaganda."

Hassan shuts off the television and comes to join Deanna and me when his pocket beeps. He pulls out his phone.

"Is that Muhammad?" I can hear the panic in my voice, and Deanna puts her arm around my shoulders.

"It's my sister," Hassan says as he reads the text. "This is incredible. People are protesting even in the poorer parts of Egypt, where they don't have access to the Internet or mobiles or anything."

"Wait—can I borrow your phone?" I ask, reaching out for it. "I really need to call home."

"It's a pay-as-you-go SIM card deal," he says, and slides it back in his pocket. "There isn't enough money on it for an international call."

"Oh—sorry," I say, feeling like an idiot. Things are hard for people here, and I just assume I can make an international call on his phone. What is wrong with me?

"Use mine," Ahmed says, handing me a very low-tech-looking phone. It doesn't even have a camera.

"*Shukran*," I say. Looking down at the keypad, I realize I've never made an international call before.

"Dial zero-zero-one and the number," Deanna says, dropping her arm from around my shoulders.

I dial, then wait. A recording of a woman's voice speaks to me in Arabic. "What's she saying?" I ask, handing the phone to Hassan.

"The circuits are all busy," he says. "My sister says journalists from all over the world are at Tahrir Square broadcasting stories about the protests. People must be trying to get through to their families here to find out what's happening."

"At least they haven't cut off phone service yet," Ahmed says, taking his phone back from Hassan. He begins to pace again and says, "It'll be okay," but he looks like he's struggling to keep it together. "You can try your father again in a while, but for now, we have to try to get your *sittu* to do what the doctor wants."

"Who would cut off the phone service? The phone companies?" I ask.

"No. The government," Ahmed says.

"It's like they think if we can't tweet or update our Facebook pages, we won't demand that Mubarak step down. But it's too late for that. We won't give up," Hassan says.

"I hope to God my parents aren't watching the news," I say.

"My mother's probably already called the American consulate," Deanna replies.

"Thousands are out there protesting. I never thought I'd see this day." Hassan's smiling so wide, his dimple looks like a crater.

"You can't believe it?" Ahmed stops pacing. "I'm triple your age, and I can't believe Egyptians are finally saying they've had enough. This is going to be bigger than the protests in the seventies. Down! Down with Mubarak!" Ahmed starts chanting and marching around the couch.

"Down! Down with Mubarak!" Hassan joins Ahmed.

"Down! Down with Mubarak!" Deanna joins in too.

I hesitate; just as I'm about to join them, a nurse rushes in. "Please, patients are resting. This is a hospital!"

"How's my grandmother?" I ask.

"The doctor's still with her. Now, please, keep your voices down." She gives us one last frown before leaving the room.

"That's one tough nurse," Hassan says.

"Not as tough as Sittu," I say.

"Ain't that the truth?" Ahmed takes a seat on the couch again.

I sit next to him and look into his eyes. "What are we going to do with her?"

"I don't know," Ahmed says, taking my hand. "I really don't know."

Across the room, Hassan takes a step toward Deanna. "Hey," he says to her, touching her arm.

"Yes," she says. Her posture reminds me of a puppy waiting for a treat. God, I hope I don't look that pitiful when I'm with Muhammad.

"I just wanted to say…" Hassan pauses.

"You just wanted to say what?"

"I have no right to tell you what you should or shouldn't do."

"Thank you. I shouldn't have reacted—"

"For God's sake"—Ahmed shakes his head at them—"what's the problem with you two?"

"I don't have a problem," Deanna says.

"Neither do I," Hassan adds.

"So why all the dramatics?"

"She thought he dissed her," I tell Ahmed.

"Mariam!" Deanna says long and loud like a whine. Ahmed looks confused. I start to explain the meaning of *diss*.

"I know what *diss* means," he says. "What I want to know is why she thinks this."

"She saw Hassan with another girl, and she thought she was his girlfriend, so she got jealous."

"Mariam! Will you shut up?"

"No, I'm not going to shut up," I say, walking over to Hassan and Deanna. "You're both being ridiculous."

"What do you mean?" Deanna says.

"It's clear you're both totally into each other. Deanna, you got jealous—"

"You were jealous? That was my sister," Hassan explains.

"I know that now."

"Hassan, tell us straight out: do you like Deanna?"

Deanna gives me her "you're dead" glare, which she only uses on Beth and Karen.

"I like her very much." He smiles.

"Really?" Now there's nothing but love in her eyes as she gazes at him.

"Ahmed and I'll give you a minute to yourselves. Is that okay, Ahmed?"

"Anything you say, boss." Ahmed gets off the couch and steps into the hallway.

"Okay, you have one minute to set things straight between you. Then we have more urgent things to take care of." I follow Ahmed into the hallway.

We both lean against the wall, and in my head, I begin to count: one Mississippi, two Mississippi... I've counted, like, fifty Mississippis when Ahmed begins to sing quietly, but off-key, some love song about cheating.

I elbow him.

"What? You don't like how I sing the Beatles? It's been at least two minutes," Ahmed whispers to me.

"Right," I say, and when I walk back into the waiting room, I can tell that Deanna's faith in romance and happy endings has been restored. She and Hassan are kissing like they're the only two people in Cairo.

I do that pretend-cough thing, but neither of them looks up. Then I say, "Excuse me, guys." Nothing. It's like I'm back at school—invisible.

"Time to break it up!"

Deanna and Hassan finally break away. They both look at me, but their eyes tell me I'm the last thing on their minds.

"Come on, I need your help now," I tell them.

"What do you need us to do?" Deanna sounds like she's with me now.

"You have to help me convince Sittu to take those tests. And, Hassan…"

He waits for me to say something, but before I can get the nerve to ask, Deanna jumps in, "Go find your friend Muhammad. Can't you see this girl is totally worried about him?!"

"Okay, I'll start calling around," Hassan says.

"Hey, boss." Ahmed walks in the room. "What do you need me to do?"

"Anything but sing," Deanna and I say in unison. We all laugh, and for one brief moment, life is just that simple.

chapter
TWENTY–FOUR

Deanna and I find Sittu out of bed with the heart monitor thingy off of her finger and the IV out of her arm.

"Sittu! What are you doing?" Deanna and I shout in unison.

"I'm going home," she says. "Where are my clothes?"

The nurse comes bustling into the room, shouting in Arabic over the loud beeping of the heart monitor. Sittu shouts back at her. The nurse looks at me and says, "Please. It's dangerous for her. Please."

"If I must, I'll leave wearing only this." Sittu pulls at her hospital gown. "I'll just expose my backside to the entire world." Sittu tries to walk past me, but I block her path and point to the bed.

"Now!" I order, surprising myself and everyone else. Instead of yelling at me again, Sittu actually gets back into her bed.

"Could we have a minute, please?" I ask the nurse.

"One minute," the nurse says as she turns off the heart monitor and then leaves the room.

Deanna and I walk over to Sittu's bedside. We stand opposite each other, in exactly the same places we'd stood in earlier, though so much has changed. Sittu's eyes are closed.

"Sittu, I'm sorry I yelled. I'm just so worried about you." She still won't open her eyes.

"We just want you to be okay," Deanna says.

"Please, I beg you. Talk to me, Sittu."

She opens her eyes and grabs my wrist. "This is how it started with Giddu. This is how it always starts. And where it ends is the same too." She shakes her head.

The fear in her eyes makes me wrap myself around her, and I whisper promises I have no right to make. "It's all going to be okay. It will."

When I let go, Sittu holds me so tight it's like I'm the only thing between her and the edge of a cliff.

"Baba," I say. "I'll call him. He'll come."

Sittu releases me. "NO!"

I can see from the look in Deanna's eyes she's as confused as I am.

"Please tell me you didn't call him!" She no longer sounds afraid, just seriously pissed off. "Mariam, tell me you didn't."

"Don't worry," Deanna says. "She couldn't call him. The phone lines are all busy."

"Thank God," Sittu says, taking a deep breath.

I'm so relieved Deanna's here with me. She always knows what to say.

"The last thing I need is my son coming to Cairo now. He's been through enough. You promise me, Mariam, you won't call your father."

Before I have a chance to answer, Deanna says, "Mariam won't call him if you let the doctor run the tests."

As soon as I hear these words, every muscle in my body goes into fight-or-flight mode. Sittu's not someone you give an ultimatum.

Sittu's head snaps toward Deanna so fast, it startles us.

"Did you just threaten me?" she asks.

"Of course not," Deanna says. She sounds as if she wishes she could take it back when she adds, "I just wanted to help Mariam convince you—"

"That's it. Get out." Sittu points to the door. "Both of you."

"I'm sorry," Deanna says, her eyes suddenly teary.

"Out!" Sittu repeats. "Now!" Deanna leaves. I grab the bed rail to stop myself from following her.

"What are you still doing here?" Sittu asks.

"I love you," I say.

"Love? That's the American in you talking. Everything is about love, all the problems and all the solutions."

"No, not everything. But I spent my whole life not knowing you. And being afraid of you." I smile at her. "You still scare me—but now that I have you, I don't want to lose you."

"Oh, *habibti*." She sighs. "You are so much like me but so much smarter. Tell the doctor I'll do her tests but not tomorrow. Tomorrow, we have a birthday to celebrate."

The first thing that comes to mind is Egypt and the rebirth of the country. But then I remember. Tomorrow I'll be sixteen.

"You know what would be the best present you could give me?"

"Fine. I'll take the tests in the morning." Sittu closes her eyes, and this time, I know it's for real. She's fallen asleep.

*   *   *

Dr. Nassif doesn't wait until morning. She gets Sittu in for testing immediately.

Later that night, while Deanna, Ahmed, and I are waiting in the lounge, she comes to tell us that the test results are positive, which isn't good. Doctors use the word *positive* for things that are really bad; it's like they're messing with our heads on purpose.

The doctor schedules Sittu for quadruple bypass surgery in the morning, and Ahmed translates for me, explaining that Sittu's heart is really messed up.

I finally get through to Baba. After he freaks out about what he's seeing on the news and finishes telling me he's trying to get us on the next possible flight home, I tell him about Sittu's open-heart surgery in the morning.

Baba doesn't ask me any questions. He's quiet for a long time. And if I didn't hear him breathing, I'd think he'd hung up. Still, there's something in his silence that makes me think he's expected this call, that he's been waiting for it for a very long time. Only I don't think he ever imagined I'd be the one making the call any more than the people of Egypt expected a young woman on Facebook to inspire a revolution.

When he finally speaks, all Baba says is, "I'll be on the next flight to Cairo, *insh'allah*."

Then he hangs up without saying good-bye.

chapter
TWENTY–FIVE

T he next morning, the *adhan*—the call to prayer—wakes me
up. I look over at Sittu, and she's still asleep. She was awake
for hours last night until the nurse finally gave her a sedative. Sittu
didn't even fight her. I never could've imagined anyone or anything
breaking Sittu's will, but when the doctor told her she'd need
surgery right away, she looked so defeated that a part of me wished
she still had the fight to get out of bed and walk out of the hospital.

She looks happy now though, and I hope she's dreaming of
something wonderful. I hope, when she wakes up, the feeling will
stay with her until after the surgery is over and she's well again.
Maybe, by then, Mubarak will have stepped down and we'll have
more reasons to celebrate.

I raise my arms over my head and stretch. My neck's stiff. Sleeping
in a chair all night totally sucks.

I hear the call to prayer again, and it sounds even more beautiful
than it did yesterday morning. Wow, was that only yesterday? It
feels like weeks ago already.

I don't think there's ever been a time in my life when I wanted to pray. My mom always made me think that, as Muslims, we should. But when I got to high school and stopped caring about what Mom thought, I stopped praying altogether. Yet today—right now—I really want to pray.

Sittu's prayer rug is in the corner, along with the other stuff she asked Hassan to bring her last night. And even though I'm focused on Sittu, I have to admit I'm anxious that he came back with no news of Muhammad.

I pick up Sittu's prayer rug, then remember I have to do my ablutions before I pray. I put the rug on the chair and walk into the cramped bathroom. The nurse hasn't picked up the urine container yet; they must have checked it a dozen times last night, and they took so much blood from Sittu, I began to wonder what they were doing with it.

As I look into the small bathroom mirror, I try to remember all the steps to do the cleansings. I close my eyes, and I can see myself with Mom, standing at the sink in her bathroom, while Baba snores in the other room. What was it Mom always said before we started? Oh, right: we cleanse ourselves to get our hearts and minds pure before we stand in front of God.

I open my eyes and turn on the water. I wash my right hand up to my wrist and between my fingers three times. Then I do the same for my left hand. Next, I rinse my mouth with water and spit three times, then rub my fingers across my teeth three times.

What comes next? I look into the mirror again. The nose. I pinch my left nostril shut, sniffing the water in and blowing it out of my right nostril. I do this three times, then switch nostrils. I splash water on my face, wash my right arm to my elbow, and then do the same for my left—all three times. It's all coming back to me now as I go through the steps.

I rub my wet hand over my hair, and with my right index finger and thumb, I reach over and rub around, in, and behind my left ear, then do the same for the other side. I do these things three times, and when I'm done, I realize I only had to do them once. But that's okay. I cup my hands under the faucet, and I pour water over my right foot and ankle then switch to washing my left foot. I think I'm done, but then recall I have to say something else, but Mom always says it in Arabic. *Why can't I remember?* I hit my forehead three times, hoping to shake the line loose from my brain.

"Mariam? Is that you?" Sittu calls out.

I shut off the water and rush to her side. "You okay?"

"Are you okay, *habibti*? Why the tears?"

"No tears." I wipe my face. "Just water from doing ablutions." I don't tell her that I do feel like crying.

"Not even one tear?" she asks.

"It's—I just can't remember what you say at the end." I lean over to hug her, and now, I am crying, harder than I ever have before.

"What is it?" Sittu asks, stroking my hair.

"I totally suck at being Muslim."

"Oh, *habibti*. I've made a lot of mistakes with my son. I know this, but I thought I raised him strong enough to raise a daughter who believes in herself."

"It's not Baba's fault. I'm the one who—" I stop myself from finishing.

"You're the one who what?"

"You'll hate me."

Sittu reaches up and holds my cheek. "I never believed I could love someone more than my own child until you. Now, you tell me whatever it is you need to say."

"Sittu, I'm the one who stopped being Muslim. I was ashamed of it."

"*Habibti*, you never stopped being Muslim. Maybe you stopped praying and doing the rituals, but you're a woman who shows compassion and love for others. I see how much you care for Deanna. That is what it means to be Muslim."

"I just didn't want to be like my parents. And it's not just because they're Muslim or Egyptian or because a bunch of psychopaths attacked New York City, like, forever ago. I don't know what it is, Sittu, but we're a family of freaks. We just don't fit in."

Sittu pats my cheek gently and shakes her head. "Everyone is different." She smiles. "So don't you forget to add me to that family freak tree." She says this and drops her hand.

"That sounds like something Deanna would say," I tell her.

"*Banat ghareeba, ageeba wa gameela begad*," Sittu replies.

"*Banat* what?"

"Weirdo girls," Sittu says. "Weirdo girls, you and Deanna."

"Weirdo girls?" I arch my eyebrow.

"Your face tells me I upset you," Sittu says.

"The Arabic sounds nicer. I mean, when people insult you in English…"

"Insult you? *Habibti*, I'm not insulting you. I'm giving you and

Deanna a great compliment. Maybe it is lost in translation, but it means that you both are unique and beautiful, and your weirdness is honest, true, real, and must never be lost."

"So weird is good?"

"It's not good or bad; it's just what is. God didn't make us perfect—*alhamdulillah*, thanks be to God. That's why humans do some very bad things. But it's also why we do some amazing and wondrous things. In perfection, there is no brilliance; nothing shines or stands out, and there's nothing left to discover. It's through our differences, our weirdness, our strangeness, that we show the world why we're so special."

"What if you just want to blend in?"

"That's your choice, *habibti*, but look at a rainbow. When all the colors stand side by side, they make magic. It's breathtaking. But what do you get if you blend them all together?"

"Yuck," I say. "It's ugly."

"That's right; it's a dull, muddy mess. You can be a part of that if you want. For some, it's where they are most comfortable. But just remember this: If you are ever going to find peace in this world—and I don't mean happiness, because that will come and go; I mean tranquility—you don't go around asking, 'Why am I a freak?' Instead, you raise your freak flag and ask, 'How high can I wave this baby?'"

"'Freak flag'?" I ask. "Where are you getting this stuff? From the Internet?"

"Hand me that," Sittu says, pointing to the prayer rug.

I give it to her. She waves it in the air and hands it back to me. "Now, if you still want to pray, go pray."

"Sittu, I can't."

"If you don't want to, you don't have to," she says.

"I want to," I say. "But I can't remember how you say the ending in Arabic."

This makes Sittu laugh harder than I've ever heard her laugh before. "If you were in the middle of the desert with little or no water, you would use sand to cleanse yourself. Let me say it another way. *Habibti*, ritual is to help us get closer to God, who is in here," she says, pointing to her heart.

That's exactly what Mom told me. "That's what's so funny?" I ask her.

"What's funny is you think God doesn't understand English."

"Okay, I get it." I wave the prayer rug over my head, thinking of all those people in Tahrir Square, waving Egyptian flags and risking their lives for their freedom. I walk to the foot of Sittu's bed. Then, looking at her, I point to what I think is the direction of Mecca. She smiles and points the other way. I lay the prayer rug on the ground, and for the first time in as long as I can remember, it feels natural to pray like this. And I do—for Sittu, for Muhammad, Ahmed, Deanna, and Hassan, and for Egypt— for all of our weirdo selves.

chapter
TWENTY—SIX

A nurse comes into the room as I'm folding Sittu's prayer rug. Her name tag says "Karima," with Arabic writing underneath it. She's pushing a cart with a lot of medical equipment on it. For a second, I wonder whether they're going to do the surgery right here in Sittu's room.

"It's time to get you ready," Nurse Karima tells Sittu, and I know the English is for my benefit. "How are we feeling this morning?" she asks. Her tone is serious and she doesn't smile, but there's something about her that makes me feel like she likes her job and does it well.

"*Alhamdulillah*—thanks to God—I'm good," Sittu responds, but she looks weaker than she did just a few minutes ago.

"Do you want me to stay, Sittu?"

"Go check on the rest of the group, *habibti*. Make sure they eat."

"I will call you when we're done here," Nurse Karima says.

"*Shukran.*"

"*Afwan.*"

"Isn't my granddaughter beautiful?" I hear Sittu say as I walk out of the room. She's using English for my benefit too.

In the waiting area, Deanna and Hassan are sound asleep on the couch. She's resting her head against his chest, and he has his arms around her. From the way Hassan's head is angled, his neck is definitely going to hurt, but somehow, I don't think he'll mind. I want to wake him and ask if he's gotten a text or a voice mail from Muhammad, but I don't. He and Deanna look too peaceful to disturb. Right now, I have to believe that no news is good news.

I don't see Ahmed. He's probably gone home, which makes me sad. It's been so helpful having him around, but he's already done so much. The poor man's only had, like, half a date with Sittu, but it's clear how much he cares for her. I guess for some guys, one date is enough to know that someone's special. I guess Deanna's right: love happens when you least expect it.

Muhammad and I haven't even had half a date yet, but I feel like we've known each other forever. I think Baba and Mom would like him—well, as much as they'd like any boy dating their daughter.

Last night, despite my promise to Sittu, I made a lot of calls to New York. My mother is trying to find a flight for her and Baba, but so far, no luck; many flights have been canceled and the others are overbooked. I can't believe she's actually willing to fly. Maybe it's a good thing they're not going to be here until Sittu's in recovery. It's hard enough holding it together right now. If Baba and Mom—the king and queen of worrying—were here, I'd totally lose it.

I take a seat facing Deanna and Hassan. I press my head against the back of the chair and find it's a lot more comfortable than the one in Sittu's room. I listen to Hassan and Deanna breathing in sync, which makes me yawn. *I'll rest my eyes, only for a minute...*

✳   ✳   ✳

"*Sabah an-nur*," Hassan says.

"The morning light," Deanna chimes in. They are both standing over me.

"I fell asleep?"

"Sittu wants to see you," Deanna says.

I startle and jump up. "Is it time?"

"Almost," Hassan says.

I hurry to Sittu's room. Suddenly, Ahmed shouts, "HAPPY BIRTHDAY!" He's holding a large chocolate-frosted cake covered with candles. Once again, I'd forgotten all about my birthday.

"I hope you still like chocolate as much as you did when you were a child," Sittu says with a smile. She's lying on a gurney, not her bed, and she looks so tired.

"There's, like, a hundred candles on that cake," Deanna chuckles, walking in behind me.

"Did you use the whole box?" Hassan asks Ahmed.

"Of course! Sixteen for the birthday and the rest for good fortune," Ahmed says. "So make a wish before we burn down Cairo."

Hassan and Deanna give him a slightly shocked look.

"Well, you know what I mean." Ahmed kisses me on the cheek. I look over at Sittu, and I know exactly what to wish for.

"You all need to help me," I say. "You too, Nurse Karima." This makes her smile. "On the count of three: *waahid, itnein, talaata*." Together, we blow out the candles on our very first try.

"So, someone has been learning more Arabic behind my back," Sittu says, reaching out to touch my hand.

"I'm very sorry," Karima says, waving the smoke away. "We have to take her to surgery now."

Ahmed hands the cake to Hassan. "Why don't you and Deanna take this into the waiting area?"

Deanna kisses Sittu on the cheek.

"Deanna, I am sorry I was so angry yesterday."

"Family never has to apologize," Deanna says, her eyes filling with tears.

"Ah, none of that," Sittu says. "I'll be back before you have time to miss me. Save your tears for this heartbreaker." She nods toward Hassan.

"You're still trying to ruin my reputation," he says.

"I'm still trying to give you one," Sittu says.

"Oh, my grandfather said to tell you that you can use the elevator free of charge when you get home, but only for a month." Hassan says this with a smile, though his eyes are tearing too.

"If he thinks I'll ever pay even one pound, you just tell your *giddu* to be ready for a fight." Sittu smiles, and for a moment, she looks as strong as she did when we met at the airport. Then she says to Hassan, "Now, you go and take the cake out to the waiting area and share some with the nurses. Deanna, you help him."

Sittu's about to be wheeled off to have her chest cut open, but she's still directing traffic. I think she's going to be just fine.

"I love you," Deanna says as she leaves the room. Hassan follows her with the cake.

"Mariam, when are your parents coming?" Sittu asks as Nurse Karima wheels her out of the room. Ahmed and I are walking on each side of her gurney as she rolls down the hall.

"You told me not to call them—"

"Mariam," she says, and gives me a you've-got-to-be-kidding look.

"They're trying to get a flight right now," I tell her.

"You must promise me something," she says.

"Anything," I tell her.

"Don't let them make a fuss over me. Those two will drive me crazy."

"Okay, I'll tell them I've fallen in love with Ahmed. That should divert their attention."

Sittu laughs, and so does Karima.

Ahmed looks at me and shakes his head. "You're as crazy as your *sittu*."

Karima hits the button when we reach the elevators. "Only one of you may come along," she says. "Hospital policy."

Ahmed starts to back away, but Sittu grabs his hand. "You come. Mariam, I need you to do something for me right now." The elevator door opens, and Ahmed holds it.

"Of course, Sittu—anything."

"Go eat two pieces of cake—one for you and one for me."

"I'll eat one piece, and the other I'll save for you," I say, swallowing hard.

"Even better idea," she says, pulling me to her and kissing me

hard on both cheeks, the same way she did when I first arrived—
only now I understand this means she loves me.

"*Yalla.*" She looks up at Nurse Karima. "I think the pill the
anesthesiologist gave me is starting to make me hallucinate."

"Hallucinate?" Nurse Karima sounds concerned.

"Yes. My granddaughter is beginning to look like a very mature
and confident woman." Sittu winks at me, and I feel grateful that
I've been blessed with such an awesome grandmother. I can't wait
for her to get better so we can hang out more.

"That's no hallucination," Nurse Karima says, pushing the gurney
into the elevator. Ahmed joins them.

"*Ana bahibbik,*" I say as the doors close. "I love you, Sittu."

C ake?" Hassan asks when I join him and Deanna in the waiting area. He's acting way too casual. Something's wrong. I can feel it in my stomach. And I don't think it has anything to do with Sittu's surgery.

"It's bad luck not to eat your own birthday cake," he says, handing me a plate with a slice of chocolate cake.

"I'm not very hungry," I say, putting the plate down on a small table by the TV.

The table wobbles, and Hassan grabs the plate just before it falls. He places the cake on top of the television. He says, "Here in Egypt, if it isn't broken, you keep it; and if it is broken, you still keep it. Well, maybe that's changing now." Hassan forces a smile. I assume he's talking about the revolution, but I can't bring myself to smile back. For once, I'm grateful Deanna can't smile, although I know she wouldn't even if she could. I know she's hurting as much as I am, and will be until the surgery is over and they tell us Sittu is going to be okay.

"We're going to be here a while," Hassan says. "It was close to eight hours with my grandfather's bypass, so you really should eat some cake."

"Oh my God, Hassan," Deanna says, "stop it with the cake and just tell her already."

Hassan gives Deanna one of those obvious "not now" looks.

"I knew it," I say. "What happened? What's wrong?"

"It's probably nothing to worry about," Hassan says.

"Then just tell me."

Hassan looks at Deanna.

"Tell her," she says.

"Let's sit down." I don't want to sit down, but I do. Hassan takes the seat next to me on the couch, and Deanna hovers beside me.

"Mariam." He looks at the floor, then back up at Deanna, who makes circles in the air with her hand, signaling he should keep going.

"No one's heard from Muhammad since yesterday."

"You called his house?" I ask.

"Yes, but I didn't expect him to be there."

"What did you expect?" I'm surprised at how calm I sound.

"He hasn't checked in with anyone."

"What do you mean?"

Hassan hesitates again.

"Let me tell her." Deanna kneels down in front of me and rests her hands on my knees. "Listen, you have to swear, on our friendship, that what I'm about to tell you never leaves this room—or even this couch."

"You know you can trust me."

"Swear."

"Okay, I swear."

"On our friendship," she repeats.

I'm starting to lose patience, but I pledge my oath. "I swear on our friendship."

Then Hassan says, "Muhammad and I were part of the April Sixth group—"

"They were the organizers," Deanna interrupts. "Yesterday too."

"We were a few of the organizers," Hassan explains.

I can't believe that they were involved at all. "You just seem like such regular guys."

"We are regular guys and girls. We don't really know each other too well. We don't make calls; we just text using SIM cards we buy for that purpose. We don't even use our real names, so if the police pick any of us up—"

"In case they torture you, they won't learn the real names of anyone else involved," I finish for him.

Hassan nods.

I think of Baba and wonder how different his life would have been if he'd never been arrested and tortured. Strange to think I might never have been born—or how different my life would have been if my parents had met here in Egypt.

"We never expected it to become such a huge protest," Hassan tells me. "The last I heard from Muhammad was when he texted all of us, asking to help him find an American girl. I knew it was him, of course. We texted back and forth a little, and I was having no luck finding her anywhere either."

"Oh my God, if something happened to him, it's all my fault," I say, realizing I was the one who sent him out to look for Deanna.

"No, Mariam," Deanna says. "I'm the one who's to blame."

"Stop it, both of you," Hassan says, looking first at me and then at Deanna. "You both need to get over yourselves. Feeling responsible for any of this is, well, egotistical. Muhammad makes his own choices."

"Okay," Deanna and I say in unison.

"Good," Hassan says.

"But we have to do something to help him," I say.

"Everything that we can do for Muhammad is being done," Hassan says. "People are out looking for him, and if—and this is only if—he's been hurt or arrested, we'll find out soon enough. Right now, all we can do is wait and eat the cake."

Hassan picks up my plate from the top of the television set, sits down on the couch, and begins to eat. Deanna and I sit too, and we wait.

A little while later, Ahmed comes into the room waving his phone. "Mariam, it's your mother. She sounds upset."

Deanna mutters to Hassan, "She always sounds upset."

Before I can tell her not to diss my mother, Ahmed shoves his ancient phone at me.

"Thanks," I say. "Mom?"

"Mariam, I'm so glad to hear your voice. I tried Sittu's cell phone, but I couldn't get through."

"Mom—"

"We still can't find a flight. You're staying in the hospital like you promised? Right? No going out. The TV is showing the police attacking people on the streets." Her voice gets louder and louder, and I can feel her fear right through the phone.

"I promise, Mom. Where's Baba?"

"We have to get you home right now," she says.

"Mom, it's okay. I'm okay. We're safe. Please, Mom. It'll be okay. Where's Baba?"

"He said he was going to speak with a friend of a friend who does travel bookings for businesses. I don't really know where he is right now." I hear my mother take a shaky breath. "I'm so sorry you're alone with all that's happening there and your grandmother in surgery."

"It's okay. I'm not alone. Deanna's with me."

"She's just a kid, Mariam."

"Mom, she's not just a kid. And I'm not a kid either. I'll call when Sittu gets out of surgery. Please give Baba a kiss for me." I end the call. I don't think I've ever hung up on my mother before.

"Thanks," I say, handing Ahmed his phone.

"Are you okay?" he asks me. I must look as sick as I feel.

"I've never heard my mother sound so worried before," I tell him.

"Parents are always going to worry," he says.

"I know." But this time, I'm probably just as worried as my mom—maybe even more. My mom's worried about me, but I'm worrying about Sittu and Muhammad. And when I look over at Hassan, who's pulling back the drapes to look out the window, I know he's worrying for all of Egypt.

"Ahmed, may I use your phone too?" Deanna asks. "I really should call my mother."

"Of course," he says.

Deanna takes his phone. "How old is this thing?" she asks.

"If it's not broke..." Ahmed says with a smile, but Deanna's already stepped into the hallway.

Hassan turns to me. "You okay?"

"I'll be fine," I say, walking over to join him. We both look out the window, and it's eerie how few cars there are on the road.

Then Hassan says, "I haven't known him very long, but he seems like someone who can take care of himself. He'll be okay."

"Thanks," I say, and my stomach hurts a little less until I see a tank rolling up the street.

"You have to see this." Hassan waves Ahmed over to the window.

"A tank!" Ahmed says, peering over Hassan's shoulder. "I've never seen tanks in the streets of Cairo before, not even during the sixty-seven war."

"It must be so hard living in a place like this," I say.

"A place like what?" Hassan asks, with an edge in his voice that I've never heard before.

"You know—"

"Oh, you mean a place where the government oppresses people and accuses them of crimes they didn't commit, then throws them in jail without trials?"

I stare at him. I can't tell whether he's angry or sad—or maybe a little of both.

"I think Hassan's talking about the U.S.," Ahmed says, watching what's happening below like Sittu and I watched the traffic from her balcony.

"I know things aren't perfect in America, but at least people have rights."

"Not all people," Hassan says. "Do you know how many people in the States have been put into prisons without ever going on trial?"

"That's against our constitution," I say.

"Mariam, Homeland Security doesn't have to follow the constitution," Ahmed tells me. "As long as the president declares something a national security risk, our laws get thrown right out the window." Ahmed is still focused on the street.

"My brother in New Jersey lost his job after 9/11," Hassan says, making a fist, but he keeps his arm at his side, "because Homeland Security officers came around, asking questions about him."

"What did he do wrong?"

"Wrong? He did nothing wrong. His name came up on some list because he donated money to a charity that gives medical relief to Palestine. There were no charges, but my brother's boss didn't want any problems. It took him almost a year to find another job, and he had to take a big cut in pay too."

"Okay, so a lot of bad stuff happened before, but at least now we have Obama."

"You mean your president who promised to close the detention camp at Guantanamo Bay?" says Hassan, sounding sarcastic. "Even your courts demanded that it be shut down, but your military continues to hold untried prisoners."

"Sounds like what happens here," I say.

"It's nothing like what happens here!" Ahmed sounds defensive.

"Well, he made a good speech," Hassan interjects. "Still, the tear gas dropped on us yesterday was made in America."

"This is true," Ahmed says, walking over to the couch and plopping down.

I lean against the wall, looking down at the chocolate birthday cake and the melted candles. I wrap my arms around myself, wishing I were at home. I miss my mother and father and the dorky birthday celebration they would've thrown for me.

Hassan's phone beeps and he pulls it from his pocket. As he reads the text, I watch the expression on his face, but there's nothing I can interpret.

Then Deanna practically dances into the room, she's so excited. "My mom says back home, people are organizing marches in Manhattan and Queens and in Jersey too, in support of the Egyptian people! Isn't that great, Mar?" She looks at me for approval. I manage a little smile, and she asks, "Hassan, did you hear me?"

He looks up from his phone. "They think Muhammad was arrested," he says quietly.

My head starts to spin. I reach out to steady myself, but the only thing within reach is the TV. It comes crashing down with me—along with the cake and any hope I still had that Muhammad was safe.

chapter TWENTY—EIGHT

A hmed helps me to my feet. "Ok?"

"I'm fine," I say, as Hassan dumps cake into a wastebasket.

Ahmed lifts the TV back onto its stand. "If it isn't broken," he says, almost to himself.

"Oh God—Deanna." I point down to her now frosted feet.

"They're just shoes," she says, and kicks them off to the side.

"Mar, take a seat on the couch," she says to me.

"Do you want some water?" Ahmed asks, looking over my head toward the doorway, like he's expecting Sittu to walk through at any moment.

"Not thirsty, thank you," I say.

Ahmed stands there for a minute, like he doesn't know what to do next. Finally he says, "You know, I think I'm going to go find a mop. Or maybe see if there's any news about your *sittu*."

"That sounds good," I say, even though I know it's way too soon for the surgery to be over. Sometimes you need to just keep moving, keep occupied.

When Ahmed leaves, Deanna takes a seat on the couch and pats the space next to her. I feel like we've spent a lot of time on this plastic-covered monstrosity.

Deanna puts her arm around me, and I rest my head on her shoulder.

"I know," Deanna says. This is one of the reasons why I love her so much. She never tries to pretend things are better than they are. "But let's try not to worry too much."

"I never told you how afraid I was when we were in jail together."

"So was I, but then I remembered I wasn't alone." She pulls me closer to her.

"Do you think they're torturing him?"

"Let's hope not," Deanna says, and we both look down at her socks, which are covered in tiny hearts.

"Maybe we should clean up your shoes."

"Where are my shoes?" Deanna asks, looking to where she kicked them off.

"Where's Hassan?"

"He must have snuck out and taken my shoes with him."

"Wow, if a guy will wash cake off your shoes without even being asked, he really must be in love," I tell her.

"Yeah, he's pretty great," Deanna says, giving me a squeeze.

I lift my head. "Your mother—maybe she can contact that group she is always raising money for."

"Amnesty International?" Deanna says. "I'm sure they're here already, but I can see whether my mom can do anything."

I know she's trying to be positive, but I remember what Ahmed said at the airport on the day we first arrived: "American lawyers are not what these people need right now. Prayers are what they need."

I close my eyes and pray until I run out of words. Then I rest my head on Deanna's shoulder until I fall asleep.

✳   ✳   ✳

"Maybe we should all get some air and some food," Hassan says.

"I don't want to eat," I say.

"Mar, come on. We'll get that stuff you love, with the pita and the vinegar at the bottom."

"You two go. I'll wait here. You can bring something back for me, okay?"

"How about *ful*?" Deanna teases, and she almost looks like she's smiling.

"Yes, *ful* is good," Hassan says, not understanding our joke. "It's the national food."

"She's allergic," Deanna explains.

"You sure you're Egyptian?" Hassan smiles.

"You know, Hassan, I'm sure. Very sure."

Deanna squeezes my hand.

"I'm Egyptian, but I'm no Cleopatra. And I'm obviously not putting my life on the line to change the world. I'm just Mariam: one hundred percent Egyptian and one hundred percent American."

"And one hundred percent crazy!" Deanna says. She hugs me so tight I can't breathe.

Hassan pulls Deanna away from me. "You're suffocating the woman."

Woman. That's the second time today someone has called me a woman—first Sittu, now Hassan. Strange that for so long, all I wanted was for my parents to stop seeing me as their little girl and start treating me as an adult. But right now, I'd give anything to be in Mom's arms while Baba makes me his special mint tea.

"Go ahead, you two. Get us some food."

"I don't want to leave you alone," Deanna says.

"I'll be fine. I'll probably just take a little nap. I didn't sleep much last night."

"You sure?" Deanna asks.

"Very sure," I say.

Deanna and Hassan leave. This is the first time I've been alone since... I can't remember. I don't think I've ever really been alone. The closest I get is when I'm in my room, asleep, but my parents are always right there in the next room. I think about putting my feet up on the coffee table, but I don't want to look like a rude American.

I stare at a painting on the wall. It's a picture of a sailboat, but the colors are so faded it's hard to tell where the water starts and the bottom of the boat ends. I don't know why, but looking at it reminds me of the pyramids. I was so dreading that trip, and it turned out to be such a wonderful day. Maybe today will turn out to be a good day too. I hope so.

"Mariam?" a nurse asks from the doorway.

"Sittu?"

"She's still in surgery. But you have a call at the nurses' station."

Maybe it's news about Muhammad, or maybe it's my parents. I race to the phone faster than I've ever gone anywhere in my life.

"The nurse said I have a call!" I practically shout at the woman behind the desk, who doesn't look much older than me. She nods and hands me the phone.

"*Habibti?*"

"Baba!"

"You okay?" Baba asks.

"How are you?" I ask.

"I'm fine. Just fine." I'm not going to add to his worries. It's so good to hear his voice.

"*Alhamdulillah!*"

"Someone's learned some Arabic!"

"*Shway shway.*"

"*Habibti!* This is like music to my ears."

"How's Mom? She was pretty upset."

"She's doing better now, but we still can't get a flight out," Baba says. "Any news yet about Sittu?"

"Not yet," I say. "It's okay, Baba. Don't worry."

"I love you, Mariam."

"Baba, I'm sorry about the way I treated you."

"I'm the one who's sorry. Sometimes loving too much can cause a person to be overprotective."

"Well, I know that loving someone can make even the sanest person act a little nuts."

Baba laughs. "You sound like your grandmother."

"Baba, can I ask you a question?"

"You just did," he replies, and I know he's smiling like he always does when he says something he thinks is funny.

I look up and make eye contact with the nurse. I turn away

for some privacy, cupping my hand over the phone so she can't hear me.

"*Habibti*, are you still there?" my father asks.

"Baba, I hope you know how sorry I am for what I put you and Mom through that night I got arrested."

"I know."

"Baba, when you were arrested by the police, was it really bad?" They have Muhammad and I have to know. "Baba?"

There's a long silence, and I can't even hear Baba breathing, but I know he hasn't hung up.

"Why are you asking me this?" he finally asks.

"Well, a friend I made here was picked up by the police."

"'A friend'?" Baba asks.

"A guy who was a big help to me yesterday."

"*Habibti*." He pauses.

"Yes, Baba?"

"I'm sure Sittu told you that she and my father made me leave Egypt because of what I experienced. They were fearful for my safety. But I was glad they made me go. I wanted to get away from Egypt, and when I left, I never wanted to go back.

"Mariam, what happened to me happened a long time ago. Maybe things will be different for him."

We both know that things are not different now, maybe worse. I love him for still trying to protect me.

The nurse is giving me some sort of hand signal, which I'm sure means she needs me to get off the phone.

"I should go now. I love you, Baba."

"I'm so very proud of you, Mariam," Baba says. I start to hand the phone back to the woman behind the desk when I hear Baba say, "*Habibti?*"

I put the phone back to my ear. "Yes?"

"Happy birthday." Then the line goes dead.

"*Shukran,*" I whisper, then hand the receiver back to the nurse.

"I'm sorry to rush you, but we only have one line and many families calling."

"I understand," I say.

"You're from America?"

"New York."

"I have a cousin in Queens," she says.

"I've never been to Queens," I say.

"Is it a big trip for you?"

"An hour maybe," I say.

"You should go visit. Little Cairo has very good food."

"There's a Little Cairo in Queens?"

"Yes, there's a very big Egyptian community there."

"I'll have to go there sometime."

She smiles at me, and I smile back at her.

"*Shukran,*" I say as I leave.

"*Afwan,*" she replies.

I'm not ready to go back to the waiting room. I decide to go outside for a while. On my way to the elevator, I pass a room with the door wide open. I can't help but look in. A very pregnant woman holds her back and paces as her husband walks beside her. She looks like she's handling the situation fine, and when our eyes meet, she flashes me a smile. Then she says something in Arabic to her husband, and he closes the door.

I press the elevator button, and I pray for Sittu, Muhammad, my parents, and the baby who will share my birthday.

chapter
TWENTY—NINE

T he elevator opens, and I go to step on, bumping into someone getting off. "Excuse me," I apologize.

"Mariam! Are you okay?"

It's Muhammad.

"Muhammad! You're here." I wrap my arms around him, afraid he'll disappear if I let go. "I was so scared something had happened to you."

When I step back, he looks startled. I can't blame him. I just met him yesterday, and I'm hugging him like he's been my boyfriend for years. Could I be any more of a dork?

"I'm sorry. Forgive me," I say. "I didn't mean to, you know, hug you like that. I'm just glad you're okay."

"Forgive? There's nothing to forgive. I was just taken by surprise. It's the first time I've ever been greeted at an elevator by a beautiful woman." He smiles as he says this, and takes a step closer to me.

Beautiful woman. I step closer to him too. I scan his face for bruises and cuts, but he looks the same as he did the last time I saw him. I'm relieved until I remember that police will do things to parts of your body that aren't usually exposed, that are private. I look down at his pants and I can feel my face get hot. *Oh my God, I'm looking at the front of his pants!* I quickly raise my gaze to meet his.

"It was never my intention to worry you," he says, as he leans in. I know this is it: he's going to kiss me—my first kiss.

I close my eyes, and his peppermint breath feels warm on my nose. I take a deep breath, and *ding!* The elevator doors slide open with a woosh. When I open my eyes, Muhammad has already moved away from me. Two men in white lab coats step off the second elevator. The hospital is only nine stories tall. Why couldn't they take the stairs? Don't they know it's better for their health? I watch their backs as they walk down the hall.

We're alone again, but the moment's gone, and my first kiss a no-show.

Muhammad stares at the numbers above the elevator doors, watching the lights shift as the elevators move from floor to floor. He hasn't pressed the up or down button, so I'm assuming he's not planning to go anywhere. But I wish he'd say something—anything.

I want to ask him, *Did they hurt you?* But I don't want to come off as too nosy or pushy. It's bad enough I jumped him the second he got off the elevator—not that he seemed to mind.

"How is your *sittu* doing?" he finally asks.

"She's in surgery now."

"Surgery?" He sounds concerned.

"On her heart."

"May God's blessing be upon her. I didn't realize."

"It all happened so fast." I turn to him. "After I got back yesterday—"

"Mariam." He turns to me. "I'm so sorry I lost you in the square. I tried to find you."

"I know. Hassan said you went to look for me."

"I tried to call Hassan, but my mobile battery went dead, and then so much happened, so fast, as you said."

"Your battery died?" Now I'm no longer embarrassed or shy—I'm pissed. "We thought you got arrested, that you were being tortured—and you're telling me the reason you didn't call was because your battery died?"

"You sound disappointed I wasn't tortured," he says.

Now I don't want to kiss him. I want to punch him in the stomach.

I feel like the biggest fool in all of Egypt. How could I have ever thought he liked me? Sure, he called me beautiful, but isn't that what they do here? Compliments are just this culture's way of being polite.

"I don't want to keep you," I say, pressing the down button for him.

"Of course not," he says. "I didn't mean to take up your time." Suddenly he's acting very formal.

"Thanks for coming to check on my *sittu*." The elevator door nearest me opens. Inside are an older woman and a man. Muhammad stands there until the man says something to us in Arabic. Then Muhammad walks past me and onto the elevator.

"It was good to see you," he says, and instead of walking away like I know I should, I watch the door slowly close. It's all I can do to keep from crying.

Muhammad's hand shoots between the doors and they open wide again.

"Yes?" I ask. The old man standing behind him grumbles something, but Muhammad doesn't respond.

"Do you want to tell me something?"

In an almost whisper, he says, "I hope all goes well with your *sittu*."

"Thank you," I say, pretending like my heart's not breaking.

Muhammad pulls his hand back inside, and this time, the elevator door seals shut. As I watch the numbers go down—9, 8, 7—my heart feels like it's plummeting. Before I even have a second to myself, the other elevator door opens. It's Deanna.

"Mariam! I have great news. But first, any word about Sittu?"

I shake my head, not believing that Deanna could have any good news for me right now.

"Guess who we saw downstairs on our way to get food?"

"Muhammad," I say.

"You told her," Deanna says to Hassan.

"When? I've been with you the whole time."

"Oh, right."

"He was just here," I tell them. "He stopped by to check on Sittu."

"Really?!" She sounds so excited, you'd think I told her I'd seen Zac Efron.

"He left already?" Hassan asks.

"Yes, he left," I say, not even trying to hide my anger.

Deanna and Hassan give each other confused, sideways glances.

"Mariam," Hassan says, "Muhammad didn't come here to see Sittu."

"He came here to see you," Deanna says with that why-are-you-so-clueless tone.

"It was nice of him," I say.

"Mariam, don't you get it?"

"Get what?"

"He's really into you," Deanna says.

"Sure he is," I say, rolling my eyes.

Hassan says, "She's right. With all the turmoil out there, do you think he'd come back here if he didn't really want to see you?"

"Mar, I know about these things," Deanna says. I look down at her shoes, which have been cleaned to look like new.

"Deanna, just stop it! Life is not a romance novel," I tell her.

"Well, at least my life isn't."

"What's up your butt?" she asks.

I turn to Hassan. "Will you please tell your girlfriend that I'm not interested in any guy who worries me out of my mind and then tells me he didn't call because his phone battery died? What, he couldn't borrow someone else's to call?"

"Mar," Deanna says. "Muhammad was in jail."

"For real?" I look to Hassan for confirmation.

"For real," he says. "The only reason he's even out is because one of his uncles is rich and, let's say, he knows where to make donations."

I think about what Ahmed said at the airport about knowing the right people.

"Why didn't he tell me he was in jail?" I demand.

He takes a step closer to me. "What is it you want to hear, Mariam?" Hassan's voice is cold now. "You want to hear how the police hit people so hard, they vomit on themselves? Or do you want to hear how, when they arrest you, they take turns beating on you while you listen to the screams coming from the next room, and the police tell you how lucky you and your friend are that you're not the man in the next room, who is slowly being fried from his insides out, with volts of electricity surging through his body? Do you want to hear that as they bashed his back with a baton, he prayed his spine would just break so the pain would stop? And when he tried to block the stick from pounding on his friend, the bones in three of his fingers cracked?" Hassan is in my face, and I can see tears in his eyes.

I look away from him. Deanna reaches out and tries to take his hand, but he snaps it away. That's when I see the scars across his knuckles, and I realize that he's talking about himself.

"Mariam," he says, backing away from me, "you don't want to know."

My chest aches. *What was I thinking? I am just a stupid American girl who couldn't get over herself long enough to see Muhammad's truth, which is also Hassan's truth, and Baba's truth. I don't deserve to call myself Egyptian.*

I open my mouth to tell Hassan I'm sorry, but I can see he knows what's going through my mind. "It's not your fault," he tells me. Then he reaches out and takes Deanna's hand, and her whole body relaxes.

"Mar," she says, "Muhammad will be back. I'm sure he will."

"I hope you're right, Deanna, but I doubt it. I messed up." I sigh. "I'll see you guys back in the waiting room."

"We're coming with you," Deanna says.

I don't bother telling her I'd rather be alone, because we'd both know it was a lie. As we begin to walk, Muhammad comes running up from behind.

"Muhammad?" the three of us say in unison.

"Where did you come from?" Hassan asks.

Muhammad's too out of breath to answer. Instead, he grabs Hassan's arm and leans over, gasping.

"Did you run up nine flights of stairs?" Deanna asks.

Muhammad nods.

"You okay, man?" Hassan asks, patting his friend on the back. "Is something wrong? Somebody hurt?"

Muhammad shakes his head, and Hassan's face relaxes with relief.

"Why'd you take the stairs?" Deanna asks.

"The elevator," he manages to get out before he huffs and puffs a bit more.

"Do you need a wheelchair?" Hassan says, and I can see now he's trying not to laugh.

Muhammad straightens. "I'm okay," he says. His breathing is still heavy, but at least he doesn't look like he's going to pass out. "The elevators were taking too long."

"Too long for what?" Deanna asks.

Muhammad says, "Could I have a minute alone with Mariam?"

Hassan says, "Of course, we'll meet you in the waiting area."

Deanna winks at me as they leave.

When it's just Muhammad and me, he says, "Mariam, I know you don't know me very well, but I hope to have the chance to show you that I'm a good person. We live worlds apart, but I really like—"

Before he says another word, I kiss him. And he kisses me back. I don't know what I expected my first kiss to feel like, but I can't imagine anyone in Cairo or New York or anywhere else having a more perfect first kiss.

But suddenly, Muhammad breaks away, grabs my hand, and, standing up straight, says, "Ahmed."

I'm confused, until I hear someone clearing her throat behind me. Dr. Nassif is standing there with Ahmed, Deanna, and Hassan right behind her.

My heart leaps. *Sittu must be out of surgery!* "Can I see my *sittu* now?" I ask.

Dr. Nassif is silent for a moment, then says, "There were complications."

chapter
THIRTY

D r. Nassif is speaking, but I don't register the words that she is saying.

"There were complications," Dr. Nassif repeats.

"What does that mean?" Hassan asks.

"It's something doctors say when they've screwed up." Deanna's choking back her tears.

"Believe me, the surgeons did everything they could." Dr. Nassif sounds like she's also holding back some anger. She turns to me. "I'm so very sorry. I know how hard this must be for you."

I don't feel anything—not sadness or anger or pain. None of this feels real to me. I'm standing in the hospital hallway, in a circle with these people, but it's like everyone is talking through a wall. I can only vaguely hear them, and I have to struggle to make out the individual words.

Dr. Nassif's pager goes off, and she looks down at it. "I have to go," she says. "Do you know who will prepare the body for burial?"

I think she is speaking to me, but my head and heart and mouth won't connect. Ahmed responds instead. "I don't know," he says.

He's clutching his prayer beads so tight, his knuckles have turned white.

"Prepare the body?" Deanna says. "Is there a funeral place we should call?"

"Deanna, in Islam, it's the family or members of the community who prepare the body," Muhammad explains.

"Sittu doesn't have any other family here. Just me," I say. "My father is trying to get a flight."

"It should be a woman," Hassan says.

"My mother will be coming too," I tell him.

"Do you know when your parents are due to arrive?" Dr. Nassif asks.

"They still hadn't found a flight when I spoke to them an hour ago," I tell her.

"With everything that's going on, that may be a while," Muhammad says. He gives my hand a squeeze, and I squeeze back, grateful to have him close.

"There's no embalming. We must bury her straight away," Ahmed says.

"No embalming?" I ask. "I thought the Egyptians, like, invented—"

"Ancient Egyptians," Hassan says. "Muslims don't want to disturb the body, so we do as little to it as possible. We try to bury the dead within a day."

"A day?" I repeat, barely able to comprehend it.

"Is there a close friend of the family you could call?" Dr. Nassif asks.

"I'm not feeling so good," Deanna says.

"You're very pale. Let me look at you," Dr. Nassif says.

"Don't touch me," Deanna says through her tears as she steps away.

The doctor's beeper goes off again. The sound makes me want to scream.

"Don't you have somewhere to be?" I say to Dr. Nassif. I know I shouldn't be so mean. She could've let the surgeons share the bad news. It was kind that she came to tell us herself.

"Please let the nurse at the desk know what you decide. And may Allah's blessing be upon your grandmother," Dr. Nassif says. She nods at me before heading to the elevator.

"What does it mean to prepare the body?" I ask Ahmed.

"There's washing."

"You have to wash the body?" Deanna holds her stomach. I'm afraid she's going to be sick. "With what?" Deanna asks.

"Like the way we do ablutions before praying?" I ask.

"Something like that," Ahmed says.

"Shouldn't that be done by some official religious person, like a priest or imam or even someone who's, like, very religious and prays all the time?" Deanna asks.

"No, it's not necessary. It's not like in the States. There's no certificate of any kind that you need. But someone who knows the steps usually does the preparation. Maybe my sister will be able to come," Ahmed says.

"Ahmed, you know what's happening in the streets in Giza right now," Hassan says. "It's just like what is happening here. I don't think your sister will even be able to get here."

Until now, I hadn't even given Ahmed's family a thought. He's been at the hospital the whole time with Sittu and the rest of us, and I've never even considered that he might be worried about his family.

"I'm really not feeling good. I need some air," Deanna says again.

"Can you make it to the water closet?" Hassan asks, but Deanna pushes him away and heads for the stairs.

Hassan starts to go after her, but I let go of Muhammad's hand and pull Hassan back.

"Let me," I tell him.

I find Deanna pacing on the sidewalk outside the hospital. It's already dark. I walk along beside her until I'm too tired to take another step.

"Deanna, please talk to me," I finally say.

"I had to get out of there. I just couldn't breathe," Deanna says. "How are you so calm?"

"I don't know. None of this makes any sense to me."

Deanna stops and turns to me. The streetlight is out, so it's too dark for me to see her face when she says, "She can't be dead. She just can't be. How is someone alive one minute and then dead? Gone!" I know when Deanna says this, she's not just talking about Sittu, but also the boy she saw killed yesterday. And as much as I wish I could have been there for her, I'm glad I didn't have to see that.

"She is dead," I say, wrapping my arms around Deanna. "Sittu's dead." And as I say this, every inch of my skin feels like it's been lit on fire. I don't remember anything ever hurting as much as this.

"Sittu wouldn't want us to cry," I tell Deanna, tears streaming down my cheeks and soaking Deanna's shirt. She's crying too. Her entire body shakes in my arms, and for a long time, we just stand there, holding on to each other. And then, just like that, I know what I have to do.

"I'm going to prepare Sittu's body," I say.

"Are you crazy?" Deanna pulls away, and although her eyes are still filled with tears, she sounds more like her old self. "You're not even all that religious."

"I'm the only family Sittu has here, and I think she'd want me to do this for her."

"Have you ever even seen a dead body?" Deanna says.

"No," I say, trying to sound like it's no big deal.

"Well, I have. My mom took me to a funeral when a woman at her work died. The casket was open—apparently that's a Catholic thing—and it was totally creepy. I had a hard time looking at it, and I didn't even know her."

I shrug and walk toward the hospital entrance. I know Deanna thinks she's helping. Like I don't already know how hard this is going to be? Sittu was my grandmother.

"Where are you going?" Deanna asks, catching up to me at the elevator.

"You always say it's the things you don't do that you regret, right?"

Deanna nods.

"I don't really want to do this. And I don't know whether I even can do this. But I have to at least try." I press the up button. "I can't run away from this." I swallow back more tears. "I promised her it'd be okay."

"That wasn't your promise to make," Deanna says. Her words sting, but I'm glad she doesn't try to make excuses for me.

We both watch the numbers descend until the elevator doors open. A woman with two small children gets out. I walk in, then hold the doors open for Deanna to follow. "You coming?"

"On one condition," she says.

"And that is?"

"You let me help."

"Deanna, you don't have to."

"Listen, I'm family too. Sittu said so."

I smile at her.

We ride the elevator in silence until Deanna says, "Ahmed said the body has to be prepared by someone who knows what they're doing."

"We can get him to write down the instructions."

"What if we make a mistake?" Deanna asks.

"If we don't do it perfectly, I think God'll forgive us. I know Sittu will."

chapter
THIRTY—ONE

The room smells like bleach, and the overhead light is so bright, I feel like we're on one of those CSI shows, trying to find clues to determine the cause of death. But despite my fears, it turns out there's nothing weird or gross or scary or creepy about Sittu's dead body.

"*Bismillah*—in the name of Allah," I say before we start, just as Ahmed instructed me. I don't think he was crazy about the idea of Deanna and me doing this, but I know he understood. Besides, when I called Baba, he sounded relieved that I'd be the one to take care of Sittu's body. He said Sittu would be happy it was me, someone who was family, and not some stranger.

"Her hair is so beautiful, but I wonder why she never colored it," Deanna says as she combs Sittu's long gray hair. "She would have looked so much younger." Deanna seems like she's going to be okay, and I've never been more grateful to have her with me.

Sittu always wore her hair pinned up to the back of her head, so I never realized it reached all the way down to her waist.

It's time to start the bathing. I squeeze excess water from a white washcloth that's been soaking in a basin of warm water and jasmine oil. I wipe Sittu's cheeks, her forehead, her chin, and along the sides of her nose (which really is exactly like mine, only it looks prettier on Sittu). Maybe as I get older, my nose will fit me better. Mom has always said it would.

"Ahmed said you don't have to clean the insides of her nostrils, like one does during ablutions," Deanna says, braiding Sittu's hair in three plaits, exactly as Ahmed had written in his instructions.

"I'm not," I say. "Can you help me turn her on her side?"

"You did her back twice already," she says.

"I'm supposed to do it three times." I tap the white notebook paper, torn from Deanna's vision book.

"Be careful, Mar. You're getting the paper wet," Deanna warns.

"I'm not getting it wet!" I can hear the snap in my tone, and I regret it.

Deanna doesn't say a word. She just puts down the hairbrush and walks over to my side of the table. Together, we move Sittu onto her side. Deanna holds her steady while I clean her back for the third time, starting from the nape of her neck to in between the crevices of her toes. When I'm done, we carefully guide Sittu onto her back again. Deanna goes back to Sittu's hair, the two of us working in silence until I move the white cloth carefully over the Frankenstein stitches holding Sittu's heart inside her body.

I reach out and touch Deanna's hand as she braids Sittu's hair. "I'm sorry."

"Like my mother always says, 'A good friend is allowed five cranky moments a year—a best friend, ten.' This is only your first offense, and it's early in the year." Deanna lifts Sittu's neck, clips the braids to the back of her head, and says, "Okay. Done."

With her hair styled, Sittu looks like she's just sleeping—a deep sleep—and she'll wake up soon.

"Thanks for doing this with me," I say.

"You don't thank family," Deanna says. "Besides, we're in this together, remember?"

I drop the washcloth back into the bowl of scented water, and with another clean white cloth, I dry Sittu's entire body. When I'm done, I cross Sittu's arms, right over left, like she's praying.

Deanna puts drops of jasmine oil on Sittu's head, forehead, nose, armpits, hands, and knees, also according to Ahmed's notes.

After sprinkling drops of the oil over a white cotton sheet, which Ahmed called a *kafan*, Deanna and I wrap Sittu the way Ahmed says mothers swaddle their babies, though I don't think it's exactly the same way.

Deanna ties the end of the *kafan* at the bottom of Sittu's feet, and using a piece of cloth cut from the same *kafan*, we wrap Sittu's head and make a knot at the top. Deanna walks back to my side of the table and takes my hand as we look at Sittu's covered body. We don't cry now, because Ahmed said we shouldn't cry for Sittu; she's going to a better place. We don't cry for ourselves, because as Deanna says, some things are way too sad for tears.

"She died on my birthday," I whisper.

"Wasn't it past midnight?" Deanna says.

"Not in New York," I say.

"Sittu would want you to celebrate her life. And like Ahmed

said, it's a better life she's moving on to, so in a way, it's kind of her birthday too." When Deanna says this, I feel lighter for a moment.

"Should I tell the hospital people we're done?" Deanna asks me.

"Sure," I say, and Deanna steps out of the room.

I untie the top of Sittu's *kafan* and uncover her just enough to sneak a kiss on both eyelids.

It hurts to say good-bye.

chapter
THIRTY—TWO

We have to go now," Ahmed says as Deanna and I return to Sittu's hospital room. There, at the foot of her now-empty bed, are Deanna's and my suitcases.

"What's going on?" I ask Hassan and Muhammad, who are each sitting on one arm of the chair I'd slept in. It's feels like so much has happened in the last few hours that I can't remember if it was last night or the night before. I notice neither of them will make eye contact with me.

"If we're going to make your flight, we have to go, and we have to go now," Ahmed says, picking up my bright red suitcase.

"*Yalla*," he says, turning to the guys.

Both of them jump up so fast, the chair almost turns over. They each pick up one of Deanna's yellow suitcases.

"Stop." I put out my hand. "I'm not going anywhere."

"There's no time to argue," Ahmed says.

"He's right," Muhammad tells me, and this time, he makes eye contact. It looks like he's been crying.

"What is going on?" I ask.

Deanna's gone totally silent. Not a question? No protest? Did we somehow enter a parallel universe or something?

"Deanna?"

"We're going home, Mariam," she says, staring at Hassan like this is the last time she'll ever see him.

"New York? There's no way I'm going back right now," I tell them.

Ahmed drops my suitcase. "Mariam, I called your parents and—"

"You did what?"

"It's not safe for you girls to be here right now," he explains.

"We're not girls!" I shout. "We're women. And we're not going anywhere." I turn to Deanna for backup, but she's still staring at Hassan.

"There's a car waiting downstairs. We have to go now," Ahmed says, picking up the suitcase again.

"Muhammad?" I ask as Ahmed walks past me.

"He's right, Mariam. I wish to God he wasn't, but things may get worse before they get better. Mubarak's desperate, and there's no telling what will happen."

"*Yalla*," Ahmed calls from the doorway. "Now—we have to go now."

Muhammad, Hassan, and even Deanna follow him out of the room. I can't believe this is happening. There's no way we're leaving like this. Not now. Not right after I cleaned my grandmother's body. Not before we bury her. If Sittu were alive, what would she say about her granddaughters abandoning Egypt in the middle of a crisis?

I sink to the floor and fold my arms across my chest. It's not long before the four of them are back.

"What is she doing?" Ahmed shouts. "We have to go! There may not be another flight—"

"I think she's staging a sit-in," Hassan says.

"Are you joking?" Ahmed walks over to me, reaches down, and tries to pull me up by an arm, but I go limp, like I've seen antiwar protesters do in movies.

"Her head is as hard as her grandmother's," he says, dropping my arm.

"Harder," I say.

"Mariam." Ahmed's voice is softer now. "*Habibti*, please…"

"Don't you dare call me *habibti*," I say, looking up at him. "I'm not your *habibti*. You called my parents, you traitor. What would Sittu say if she were here?"

"Mariam," Hassan says, kneeling down so he's face-to-face with me.

"What?" I say, knowing I sound like a two-year-old.

"Sittu…" He takes in a breath. "She told Ahmed if she didn't, well, make it, he was to contact your parents and get you home."

"I don't believe you," I say, but I know he's telling the truth.

"Mariam, she was worried about you and Deanna, and she wanted you safe."

"I don't care what Sittu wanted!" I shout. "She's trying to do to me exactly what she did to my father!"

"Mariam! Don't you dare talk about your grandmother like that." Ahmed sounds like Baba. But he's not my father.

"I love Sittu, but no one is going to tell me to leave Egypt. This is my country too. Deanna and I want to stay."

"No, Mar. I want to go home." I've never heard her sound so defeated. "Mariam," she says, sitting down next to me. "I'm so sorry, but I really want to go home now. Please."

I look at her. She's been through a lot during the last few days, and when I look at Hassan, who's still kneeling in front of me, and then up at Ahmed and Muhammad, I realize we all have.

"Fine," I say, "let's go home."

Muhammad takes my hand, and I don't let go until we're outside the hospital. We head to a big black car that looks like the ones you see driven by CIA agents or mafia guys in movies, tinted windows and all. The driver puts our suitcases in the trunk, then walks over to the back passenger door and holds it open for us, just like Salam did that first day when we arrived. Only this driver doesn't smile, and his name doesn't mean *peace*.

Hassan hugs me first. "When you come back, I'll take you all the way to the top of the pyramid."

"Okay, but when you come to New York, you have to come with me to the top of the Empire State Building. And we're taking the stairs. Well, at least a few flights, anyway."

"Deal," he says, and hugs me again, and then we kiss on both cheeks.

He moves over to Deanna, and although they should be close enough for me to hear what they're saying, I'm too distracted by Muhammad to care.

"Life can be pretty unfair," he says.

"But it can also be pretty awesome," I say as he reaches out to shake my hand.

I don't get it. A handshake? I want a kiss, and not a cheek-to-cheek kiss like Hassan just gave me, a real kiss. But then I remember something Baba once told me: "If a boy really likes you, he shows respect; and this means he never kisses you in public." This thought makes me smile. I take his hand, and I shake it firmly, like good Americans do, and when he laughs, I hear, *I love you.*

Now it's Ahmed's turn. He hesitates, and I open my arms. We hug as if I've known him my whole life.

"You don't really hate me," he whispers in my ear.

"I could never hate you," I whisper into his chest. "Besides, when Sittu speaks, we listen."

"Yes, we all listen," Deanna says as she wraps herself around us both.

"The time, sir," the driver says, and the three of us let go of one another.

"I need to take care of your *sittu*'s affairs, or I'd come with you to the airport."

"I'm glad you can be here for her," I say.

"When are you going home?" Deanna asks.

"I think I'll make Egypt my home again for a little while. My sister is on her own now, and she can use my help. Besides, the only family I have left in America is my son, but he lives in Los Angeles, and I don't get to see him all that much."

"You also have us," I say.

"That's right." Deanna nods. "We're your family now too." She sounds a little like Sittu did when she was insisting on something.

Ahmed takes both of our hands in his and says, "Please take care of each other. And call me as soon as you get home, okay?" Ahmed kisses Deanna on both cheeks. Then he turns to me. "Mariam, your grandmother and I didn't have much time together, but in the time we had, I saw a beauty and strength in her that's so rare in this world." He swallows hard, barely holding himself together.

"It's okay." I squeeze his hand. "You don't have to say anything more. I know how much you loved her."

"*Love*, present, not past tense, *habibti*."

"Thank you," I say. I don't know if Sittu was in love with Ahmed too, but I bet she would have been, in time.

"*Habibti*." He steps back and looks at me. "It is I who must thank you." He turns to Deanna. "And you. If it weren't for you two kooky girls adopting me at the airport, I would never have believed an old man like me could find love."

"But it was for such a short time. It's not fair," Deanna says.

"Maybe, maybe not…but it is better to have loved and lost than never to have loved at all."

I smile. "Hannah Montana said that, right?"

"You are a very funny girl—woman, Mariam. You are so very much her granddaughter." Ahmed kisses my forehead, drops both of our hands, turns to Hassan and Muhammad, and takes them both into his arms like they're his family too. "*Yalla*," he says.

Deanna quickly kisses Ahmed, Muhammad, and Hassan on one cheek (well, she lingers a little on Hassan's cheek) and gets into the car. I've just barely gotten in when the driver shuts the door behind me.

As the driver starts the car, there's a knock on the window, but

the window won't roll down. After all I've been through, the driver
has the childproof locks on!

"Please, the window." Deanna taps the driver on his shoulder,
and the window rolls down.

"I almost forgot," Ahmed says, pulling a packet from the inside
of his suit pocket. "She asked me to give this to you." He puts
several folded sheets of blue stationery into my hand, then raps on
the car door. The window goes up, and the driver pulls away from
the curb.

"What is it?" Deanna asks.

"I think it's a letter," I say.

Deanna doesn't push. She nods and looks out the window, and
now there are a few more cars on the road. After a few minutes,
I unfold the letter. I can smell Sittu's perfume—or maybe I just
imagine I do. In any case, it feels like she's still here with us.

My dearest Mariam,

*The doctor says the heart is a very fixable organ. But you can't
fix what isn't broken. It will soon be my time to leave this earth.
Allah knows best, and I'm blessed to be with Allah now.*

*I asked Ahmed to give you this letter after all was said and
done. He's a good man, and I thank you and Deanna for
bringing him into my life. Sometimes our greatest experiences
are only moments long. I'm sure he told you not to cry for me,
but if he didn't, he should have. I am in a glorious place. If
you need to cry for yourselves, you should, but not for too long.*

There's too much you need to do and enjoy. There will be other things for you to cry over in your life, so don't waste all of those tears on me.

Mariam, you are the light of my heart. To see what a strong and courageous woman you have become is the greatest blessing I could have hoped to receive. Please tell Deanna it is more than I could have prayed for to have been blessed with another granddaughter—particularly one as bold and beautiful as she is.

I nudge Deanna and share the letter so she can read it too. When she gets to the part that Sittu wrote about her, Deanna says, "'Bold and beautiful.' Wasn't that some soap opera?"

I point to the next line.

Oh, and no reference to that TV show intended here.

"Wow, she's reading our minds from the beyond," Deanna says.

"Just read," I say.

I don't have to tell Deanna to speak up for herself or to believe in herself, because she already does. But, Mariam, you tell her Sittu says she should never let anyone tell her she can't smile. Her eyes smile and laugh as loud as a thousand children. She doesn't believe this yet, but you can help her to see it is true. My advices to her are simple: Deanna, keep your heart as open to the world as it is today, and when it breaks—and I'm so sorry, habibti, it will, because that's just the way life works—believe me when I tell you the pain will end. Nothing on this earth lasts forever. Except maybe plastic.

Please tell Hassan he's a good man and he should stay that way, especially if he doesn't want me haunting him from the grave.

And, Mariam, my habibti, I have only one advice for you. Okay, actually, I have a few. Our flaws shine when we become parents. It's only when we become grandparents that we get it right most of the time. You will see this one day if you decide to have your own children, insh'allah. For now, give your parents a break.

Remember to be true to yourself. You are who you are, and that is all you have to be. Don't be afraid to speak up. Trust in yourself, and life will be yours to experience. I want you to have anything I've left behind, but please, if you decide to take the true mirror, just remember, it's not the real you and—well, I think you know why.

"Why?" Deanna says, but I ignore her and try to keep reading. "Tell me why," she repeats, poking me in my side.

"Quit it."

"Then tell me."

"She means because it shouldn't matter how others see me. It should only matter what I see," I say.

"Sittu was very wise," Deanna says with admiration, and I continue reading.

One day you will look into any mirror and see the real you—the Mariam that is the beautiful and brilliant ghareeba wa gameela.

"Deanna, what does that mean?" I ask.

Now Deanna taps on the blue paper. "True weirdo."

So wave your freak flag high, and know that even if you try, you will never be able to forget Misr. She's forever a part of you.

Oh, and I'm sorry I didn't have more time to get to know Muhammad, but I can tell you one thing for sure—he's a real cutie.

Love,
Sittu

P.S. And one last advices, Mariam. You are sixteen now, so go and get yourself on Facebook already!

"True weirdo," Deanna says. "We should start a fan page for True Weirdos everywhere."

I fold the letter, and through the tinted glass window, I see two cars have just had a fender bender. I wonder whether our driver will stop and give advices, but he just keeps driving and doesn't stop until we reach the airport.

I miss Sittu already.

chapter
THIRTY—THREE

On the flight home, I read in one of Deanna's travel guides that more than five hundred thousand living people actually live in the City of the Dead—a cemetery in Cairo. There are mothers, fathers, daughters, sons, *sittus*, and *giddus*—all alive—but there's no statistic for the number of people buried there.

Now Sittu is one of them. She's in a family mausoleum next to Giddu and his parents, his brother, his brother's wife, and their two children. There's space left for three more people. It will be up to Baba to decide what to do with those places now. He says it's the custom to visit a grave a year after a person is buried, so next year, our whole family—and that of course includes Deanna—will go to pay a visit to Sittu's place of rest.

It's been two weeks since we left Cairo. In some ways, it feels like two years, and in other ways, it feels like we never left.

The curtains are drawn, and my room is so dark I have to feel around for my cell phone on the nightstand to see what time it is. Almost eleven in the morning. It's Friday, a school day. But when I got up earlier this morning to pray with my mom, she said the bags under my eyes were large enough to pack for a family of six. She insisted Deanna and I needed to rest, so we were to sleep in. Mom's never kept me home from school unless I have a fever, but since Deanna and I have been back, Mom has kept me home now and then. I've said very little about our time in Egypt, yet somehow my mom seems to know how falling in love and fleeing from a country in revolt take a lot out of a person.

But instead of going back to sleep, I've been lying here, wide-awake, listening to Deanna roar. She's snoring in the twin bed next to me. She's even louder than she was in Egypt. Her mom's had to work late the last few nights, so Deanna's slept over. She doesn't like to be alone all that much anymore. The therapist her mom took her to said she's suffering from PTSD, post-traumatic stress disorder. She's seen this shrink a few times now. She saw some bad things on the streets in Cairo, and while she's acting normal, I'm glad she has another adult to talk to, too.

And I like having her around, so I don't even mind the snoring. At least she stopped screaming in her sleep, which she did the whole first week after we got home.

The truth is, it's not really the snoring that keeps me from sleeping. There's just a lot of stuff swimming around in my head. The school psychologist called me into her office yesterday and asked if I wanted to talk.

I told the counselor I didn't feel the need just yet but maybe some other time. I mean, it's only been two weeks since everything happened. If I were totally feeling normal, it'd actually mean I was Deanna's kind of FINE: freaked out, insecure, neurotic, and emotional.

It's all over school that Deanna and I were just in Egypt, and rumors have been going around about the two of us punching out cops and saving babies from the hands of progovernment forces. I guess it's easier to imagine Deanna and me as action heroes than it is to see us as real people. Ironically, my being Egyptian and Deanna being my best friend have suddenly made us popular. Karen and Beth have each asked me to hang out. I told them thanks but no thanks. Funny how having Karen and Beth not hate me was all I've wanted since elementary school, and now that they want to be my BFFs, I couldn't care less what they think of me.

The day Deanna and I traveled back to New York was the most violent in Egypt. When we got home, Baba showed us YouTube videos of the police firing water cannons at crowds. Those people were peacefully saying their Friday prayers on a bridge that crosses the Nile. Some kept praying, but others pushed back until the whole line of police retreated with their water cannons.

Baba and I must have watched the video a dozen times, and with each viewing, a part of me wished I were still there. But to be honest, a bigger part of me was glad to be home and safe with Baba and Mom.

Deanna and I didn't believe Baba when he told us CNN had shown men riding camels through Tahrir Square, swinging swords and terrorizing protestors. Camels and swords? I mean, how much more cliché can you get? All I could picture was the stupid cover of Deanna's romance novel, minus the couple. But when we watched the videos on YouTube, there they were—men on camels and horseback, riding through the square with swords.

It was crazy. Deanna and I spent hours watching every video we could find to see whether any of the camel guys were Hakim or George from our day of touring in Giza. But we couldn't make out any of the riders' faces, and we both wanted to believe Hakim and George would never be a part of something like this. Baba said they were probably disgruntled men who were losing a lot of money because there are no tourists. Mubarak's people paid them to attack the protestors. Baba says people do desperate things when they're feeling desperate.

Mubarak's government shut down the Internet and most cell service, so it was days after we arrived home before we heard from Hassan, Muhammad, and Ahmed. For some reason, this time I wasn't worried. Something told me they were okay, and they were. Now Hassan and Muhammad text or Facebook message us almost every day.

And believe it or not, my parents got me my own cell phone for my birthday—and not one of those cheap who-cares-if-you-lose-it phones. It's not an iPhone, but I have unlimited texting and the phone has a camera, so Muhammad and I can exchange pictures and video clips whenever we want. Mine usually show me making funny faces or trying to look sexy. He always texts back "LOL" or "hot."

I've only sent Muhammad one video. For some reason he wanted to see the inside of my school cafeteria. He said the video clip made him hungry, but I told him the smell there would take care of that.

Muhammad's photos are usually of other people. He sent me all these pictures of people giving flowers to the Egyptian military or kissing them when they came into Tahrir Square to help them stand up to Mubarak's police. He sent some great shots of people camped out in Tahrir Square too.

The police eventually left the city and released all the jailed protesters. Baba was afraid there'd be looting and all this other horrible stuff, but video clips popped up everywhere of ordinary people working in neighborhood safety committees. They not only protected each other and their homes, but they also distributed food and medicine, and were "taking care of business." That's how Muhammad described it. He uses that as the title for all of his pictures.

Right after he sent me a clip of kids and older people sweeping the streets and picking up garbage, he used the last minutes on his SIM card to call me. He said never in his life did he imagine he'd see Egyptians voluntarily cleaning the streets of Cairo. He sounded so happy and excited. I could totally imagine how adorable he must have looked as he told me about it. He doesn't send me images of the bad stuff we see on the news. I think he's trying to protect me. Or maybe he's just trying to focus on all the good stuff.

We also hear a lot from Ahmed, but he prefers to call. He says, in that way, he's old school. He tells us about what's happening in Giza, but mostly he asks questions about what we're doing—and the weather. I think he misses the States.

Still, everyone in Egypt is waiting for Mubarak to step down. Here too. Eighteen days of turmoil and protests, and the guy still won't give it up. It's hard to believe it's only been eighteen days since the revolution started, and it's almost impossible that Deanna and I were in Egypt for fewer than five days. It felt like a lifetime.

I want to get out of bed now, but the longer Mom thinks I'm asleep, the better she'll feel. She's been trying to treat me more like an adult, but she's still got that crazy overprotective-parent gene working.

Yesterday at breakfast, while Baba made coffee, Mom held the Benadryl, waiting for me to break out in hives because I ate the *ful* Deanna made for us. Mom just couldn't believe I could outgrow my allergy.

Without thinking, I said, "Can your whole life change in less than five days?"

I didn't expect an answer, but Baba looked at Mom and said, "Well, if a person can fall in love in five seconds, why couldn't a life or a country change in five days? Or even five hours?"

Mom put the Benadryl down to kiss him. The coffee spilled over, and Baba didn't even care.

I'm thinking again about getting up when the door opens and Baba announces, "Time to get up!"

"Deanna, wake up," I echo.

Baba gives me a big smile, and goes over to Deanna, nudging her arm. "She snores like my father did," he says.

"What time is it?" Deanna asks, sitting straight up.

"Time to celebrate!" Baba shouts. "Mubarak stepped down! Thirty years of tyranny—over. Egypt is free."

I get out of bed and hug my father, and then I hug Deanna, who is still half-asleep.

"I hope Sittu's looking down on us and seeing this day she thought would never come," I say.

"I'm sure she is," Baba says.

"You know, Baba, Sittu had great advices. But she was wrong about one thing."

"What's that?" Deanna asks.

"In the hospital, when I told her that I love her, she said that it was the American in me talking, because in America, 'Everything is about love, all the problems and all the solutions.' But I know now it was the Egyptian in me talking."

Deanna yawns and says, "Or maybe it's a little bit of both."

"Maybe," I say.

Baba laughs. "*Habibti*, you get to choose what we do today," he says. "After all, we never did celebrate your birthday."

"Dinner at Applebee's?" Deanna suggests.

"No—I want to go to Queens today," I say.

"Queens?" Deanna asks.

I say, "Yes, to Little Cairo," and Baba nods.

"Where better to celebrate than with our New York community of Egyptian Americans?" Baba says.

"I know exactly what I'm going to wear too," I tell them.

"Sittu's dress!" Deanna shouts.

Hassan or Ahmed had packed it into my suitcase. I decided to leave the trim unfinished, just like Sittu left it—a little bit imperfect.

"Of course, *habibti*," Baba says, kissing me on the forehead. Then he kisses Deanna too, and I know from her eyes that, just like me, she's smiling right down to her toes.

Acknowledgments

To Asmaa Mahfouz, a young woman who showed the world that one person can make all the difference, and to the people of Egypt, who proved that the people united will never be defeated.

If it takes a village to raise a child, then it takes a village and a half to write a novel. There are so many people who have helped me make this book possible. I'm grateful to them all. There are some whom I must thank personally because they have also enriched my life in ways that have made it possible for me to write. To my agent, Cynthia Manson, for her talent, expertise, and for believing in this book. She's proven to me that miracles can and do happen. To my editor, Annette Pollert-Morgan, whose hard work and exceptional eye for detail helped me to make every word count.

To Alexandra Soiseth: there aren't enough superlatives to thank you for all you have done for this book and me. I am prepared to spend a lifetime showing you how grateful I am.

To Allan Tepper, for bringing music back into my life, for always supporting my writing, no matter how late into the night, and for being the best grammarian a person can marry.

To Ahmed Nassef, for his faith in this book. To Evelyn Fazio, whose genius helped make *Rebels by Accident* possible and whose mother's prayer group prayed for my son when we needed prayers the most. To Leila Rand, my great friend and Web designer, who, with passion, compassion, and patience, brings our vision to life.

To my writer's group, the fabulous five (Alexandra Soiseth, Jimin Han, Kate Brandt, Deborah Zoe Laufer, Gloria Hatrick), who meet week after week to discuss our writing, lives, loves, and hates. Without your love and commitment, I would not be writing today.

To Adrienne Dunn Petilli, my mother: thank you for always pushing. Ma, you have taught me three of the greatest lessons a writer needs to learn: never, ever give up; never take no for an answer; and when all else fails, ask to speak to the manager. To John J. Dunn, my father: you made it possible for me to dream, and encouraged me to take risks and never be afraid to fail.

To Eugene Petilli, my stepfather, whose red gravy has nourished both my son and me so I could spend time writing instead of burning dinner. To Safi Nassef, my son's grandmother and a great inspiration to me. It's her strength and her lineage of strong Egyptian women on whom I based Mariam's history. To the late Fikry Nassef, my son's grandfather, a great legal mind and brilliant poet, who was a constant reminder to me that only God creates; we are just the vehicle. To Trina Lynn Dunn, my sister, an artist whose honesty and eye for detail has made this book richer. To John E. Dunn, my brother: you have shown me over and over again why it's important to make people laugh, and when one door closes, you build another. To Alix Dunn, my sister-in-law, who helped me get my book out into this world when I was ready to stick it in the drawer for good. To Robin Chance, my aunt, who has spent many hours caring for my son so that I could write. To Angela Fekete, my godmother, whose prayers for me have been answered over and over again. To all of my nieces and nephews—Alex, Jack, Katie, Julia, Kai, and Zavia—you are my constant reminders why I need to keep trying to make a difference in this world. To my family at Sarah Lawrence College: you make my day gig a place that feeds my creativity.

To the many who have read various revisions of this book: without your feedback, this novel would never have found its place in this world. I give you a million trillion thanks, Fatma B., Maria Maldonado, Lyde Sizer, Jamal Dillman-Hasso, Mary Knight, Raymond Lai, Leora Tannenbaum, Maureen Fallon, and Muriel Harris Weinstein. A very special thanks to Sean McNeil and Amina and Ash Rand-McNeil for spending part of their vacation at my kitchen table, helping me to find the right title for the book.

To Jimin Han, friend and co-teacher, who has taught me more about writing, teaching, and raising children than almost anyone I know, who always listens and says, "If we don't defend our stories, then who will?" To Kathleen Hill, my mentor, who told me this book was important and needed to be read. To Cassandra Medley, whose writing exercises helped me channel Mariam's voice. To Myra Goldberg, who told me if I really wanted to know what to do with my story, I needed to get up from the computer and go look at a painting. To Linsey Abrams, for the best writing advice ever: keep your expenses low. To Melissa Shaw, friend, astrologer, and free spirit, whose caretaking of my son, Butterscotch, and myself made it possible for me to finish this book. To Stevie Gonzales, who, under the Costa Rican moon, lit candles with me for this novel to find its right home. To Grace O'Toole, for holding the faith when I couldn't. To Alia Yunis, who shares in the struggle.

To Sam Aboelea, Jawad Ali, Mohja Kahf, El-Farouk Khaki, Daisy Khan, Ayesha Mattu, Nura Maznavi, Kristin Sands, Pamela Taylor, Amina Wadud, and Ani Zonneveld, who are just some of the courageous American and Canadian Muslims I've known whose work for justice and equality, coupled with their love of humanity, has inspired me to write characters who are Muslim, real, and flawed and human.

To my students, who give so much to their classmates and to me. You show me that no matter what life throws at you, keep writing.

Thanks to Doctors Linda Granowetter and Timothy Rapp and everyone at the Stephen Hassenfeld Children's Center for Cancer and Blood Disorders for helping my son to heal and giving me the peace of mind to finish this work.

Finally, to Ali Ahmed Dunn Nassef, my son, who always tells it like it is (whether I want to hear it or not). He gave me no choice but to write this book.

About the Author

Patricia Dunn's writing has appeared in Salon.com, *Christian Science Monitor*, *Village Voice*, *The Nation*, *LA Weekly*, and others. With an MFA in creative writing from Sarah Lawrence College, where she also teaches, the Bronx-raised rebel and former resident of Cairo is now settled in Connecticut, with her husband, teenage son, and toddler dog.